THE STAND-IN

THE
STAND-IN

STEVE BLOOM

carolrhoda LAB
MINNEAPOLIS

Carolrhoda Lab™
An imprint of Carolrhoda Books
A division of Lerner Publishing Group, Inc.
241 First Avenue North
Minneapolis, MN 55401 USA

For reading levels and more information, look up this title at www.lernerbooks.com.

Library of Congress Cataloging-in-Publication Data

Names: Bloom, Steven L. (Steven Lawrence), 1956– author.
Title: The stand-in / by Steve Bloom.
Description: Minneapolis : Carolrhoda Lab, [2017] | Summary: After seventeen-year-old Brooks Rattigan agrees to be a stand-in Homecoming date for a friend's geeky but wealthy cousin, he realizes becoming a (completely platonic) rent-a-date for the socially awkward could help him earn college money.
Identifiers: LCCN 2015043912 (print) | LCCN 2016006286 (ebook) | ISBN 9781512410235 (th : alk. paper) | ISBN 9781512411218 (eb pdf)
Subjects: | CYAC: Dating (Social customs)—Fiction. | College choice—Fiction. | Moneymaking projects—Fiction. | High schools—Fiction. | Schools—Fiction.
Classification: LCC PZ7.1.B64 St 2017 (print) | LCC PZ7.1.B64 (ebook) | DDC [Fic]—dc23

LC record available at http://lccn.loc.gov/2015043912

Manufactured in the United States of America
1-39571-21270-4/13/2016

To the women in my life—
Ruth, Jennifer, Nora, and Liza

MAY

I know what you're thinking.

What the hell am I, Brooks Rattigan, doing in Hackensack?

At the Holiday Inn on a precious Saturday night?

Twerking the hours away with Gabby Dombrowski?

Now, don't get me wrong. There's nothing wrong with Gabby Dombrowski. Just like there was nothing wrong with Burdette's cousin or Sylvie Frohnapfel or Alana What's-her-name or any of the rest of them. Even Celia Lieberman, when you get right down to it. Fine, upstanding members of the fairer sex. Attractive, intelligent, accomplished. Engaging conversationalists, convivial dining companions. Student government presidents, science fair winners, champion figure skaters. Each and every one a total knockout in her own special way. May the Force be with them all.

Nice girls. Nice girls with nice homes in nice neighborhoods with nice things. Nice moms and dads, nice brothers, nice sisters. The well-meaning faces blur before me. Each so different, yet all so the same. Infected with the same raging, incurable disease. FOMO. Fear of Missing Out.

FOMO, you might say, is the Rattigan bread and butter.

Homecoming. Winter Formal. Spring Fling. Prom. I mean, when you think about it, which I'm sure you don't, it's amazing how many once-in-a-lifetime events there are during the course of a single high school year. And when you multiply that by an equal number of momentous events at every high school in the greater tri-state area, well, let's just say, it can get a bit overwhelming. Actually, sometimes it can get to be a real drag.

Sorry. Where were we again? Oh yeah. Gabby Dombrowski.

No, there's nothing wrong with Gabby Dombrowski. She speaks three languages and plays four instruments. Nothing, that is, except for the slight fact that Gabby's also president of the Spirit Club and six one without heels, six five with them on, can kick my ass, and is about to dislocate both my arms from their sockets. For those non-Hackensackians among you, Gabby Dombrowski, in addition to all of the above, just made All-Conference as the star center of her basketball team, which went all the way to the semis, which, in north central Jersey, is really saying something.

Around us, colored lights strobe and flash as babes, super made-up, in sexy, low-cut gowns, and slicked-back dudes in lumpy rented threads, get down to the bangin' beats. A wide cross section of the chaos that is high school, perfectly paired off. Jock with jock. Dork with dork. Stoner with stoner. Dweeb with dweeb. You know, the cool with the cool, the uncool with the uncool. But in sets of twos. It's surreal how it all kind of evens out.

Only one couple's disproportional. Me and said Dombrowski. We're a mismatch in every way. For one thing, although I enjoy shooting a hoop or two, I basically pretty much suck at b-ball. For another, I have no spirit. But the main thing is—I don't like Gabby Dombrowski. I mean, I like Gabby Dombrowski fine, just not in the way to be with her this way. How could I? I don't know Gabby Dombrowksi, and for that matter, Gabby Dombrowksi doesn't know me. Although we are together, we just met three hours ago.

Another stab of pain shoots through my battered body as Gabby enthusiastically twirls me, which I'm supposed to do to her. Dips me, which I couldn't do to her. Finally, mercifully, the song ends. Woozy, I smile gamely, trained professional that I am.

"Thanks, Gabby," I gasp. "That was, uh, invigorating."

My stepped-on feet ache for the band to take five. Instead, the lights dim and I get a smooth segue to a soft, romantic number. Oh God, no. "Stairway to Heaven." An oldie but goodie. And the world's longest slow song ever.

Gabby beams down at me. I cringe inwardly. Shit. Slow songs, especially superlong ones, are the bane of the trade. And "Stairway To Heaven" is the mother of them all.

"Gabby, what do you say we sit this one out?" I suggest, rapidly inching away.

But Gabby's All-Conference reflexes are way too quick for me. I am nabbed and yanked by the lapels of my just-paid-off tux jacket.

"Careful!" I yelp. "That's expensive material!"

All goes dark as I am buried deep into the vast canyon between Gabby's well-toned breasts. Lifted and clutched like a rag doll as the time-tested music weaves its spell.

How did it happen? Where did I career so far off the rails? All I wanted was to earn a little extra for college. To get something more out of life, better my meager circumstances while at the same time filling an urgent niche in the marketplace. Is that such a crime? I mean, getting ahead, isn't that what we're taught we should do? And all for naught. Because, let's face it, I'm not going anywhere.

Gabby's lacquered fingers creep like attacking spiders down my butt. I slap them away.

"Hey, watch the hands!"

Yes, I know what you're thinking. Brooks Rattigan, despised by Shelby Pace, not to mention by most of suburban New York and substantial portions of lower Connecticut. Shunned, cast out by respectable high school society. Scorned by The Murf, my oldest, bestest pal, a great guy who never did me or anyone else a bad turn. Repudiated

4

by my family, what there is of it. Hey, I can't even stand myself, but there's not much I can do about me at this point. So here I wallow in Hackensack. Brooks Rattigan, slimeball, scum of the universe. Brooks Rattigan, tragic figure, a man all alone in the world, doing the bump and grind with Gabby Dombrowski to warmed-over Zeppelin.

Yes, my friends, I know what you're thinking. How did you sink to this, Brooks Rattigan?

Funny. I'm asking myself the very same question.

I think way back to the beginning. Was it really just months ago? Back to those last, forever-lost days of blissful ignorance. Back before I ventured Beyond the Great Divide, out into Uncharted Waters. Back to September.

DAY ONE

"HEY HO, LET'S GO! HEY HO, LET'S GO!"

The Ramones thrash. It's my ringtone. "Blitzkrieg Bop," my personal mantra for senior year.

I don't have to crack a bleary lid at the display on my iPhone. I know what time it is, having caused my own misery by setting the alarm. It's 5:45 in the a.m. I groan. Like any red-blooded teenager, I'm not exactly a morning person. Especially after staying up 'til one desperately trying to find meaning in *The Waste Land* for my already overdue AP English paper. The friggin' thing's written in some kind of top-secret code and, for the life of me, I can't figure out the key. Poets. I just don't get them. If they've got something all so important to say, why don't they just come out and say it?

But the coffee's preset and brewing and the grains in the hourglass are dwindling. Of the many things I lack, time has become the most precious commodity of all.

October 13. Lucky 13. I only get one more shot at this, and October 13's a mere three weeks off, coming up way too quickly. So, exercising superhuman self-discipline, I grab a cup and halve a stale doughnut from the kitchen and then drag my sorry behind through the cluttered maze that is my room to my even more cluttered desk, dig out the latest, dog-eared prep book, and begin the daily regimen.

Math review. Data analysis, probabilities, statistics. I drink them in for thirty minutes at the crack of each dawn like my orange juice. Complex equations, figures, graphs that would tax a PhD student besiege my dazed adolescent mind. But it's cool. Math's a relative strength, and my most current Nonverbal score inched up last time just within target range. Even so, I can't be complacent, can't let the ol' guard down.

Because there's Verbal. It's Verbal that haunts my long, restless nights. Reading comprehension. Error identification. Sentence completions. Vocabulary. These are the torments of my existence, the peaks I must conquer, or perish in the attempt.

The SATs. Ten sections. Three hours and fifty minutes. A speck of time that can determine the course of an entire life. A pivot point in aspiring to upper-middle-class existence. Not too much pressure. And don't hand me that "it doesn't matter" shit again. Because we all know it does. I mean, ever notice that all the big experts who say it doesn't matter where you go all have Ivy League degrees? I mean, if it doesn't matter, why does it matter to so many people who matter? It matters. Plenty.

And the SATs are key. The so-called Great Leveler between the haves and have-nots. Yeah, I know. Yeah, right. As if you can't buy a good score like you can everything else. No private tutors, personal trainers, or high-priced SAT boot camps for Rattigan. I'm going to have to do it on my own. Thing is, a good score doesn't cut it these days, and a great one barely passes muster. No, these days, you pretty much have to be perfect. And the stakes are higher than ever before. Let's get real: the way the planet is going down the drain, there are only so many Bright Futures out there, and there are more of us competing for fewer spots than at any time in recorded history. I mean, let's not kid ourselves, these days the Brand is everything. And there's no Brand like a first-tier school.

Problem is, getting into second-tier schools is like what getting into first-tier schools used to be, third tier like second. And those old dependable state universities that used to be there, waiting to save the day? Well, think again. You only go around once in the Admissions Game. Screw it up and you're screwed for good.

Shuddering, I decide to refortify myself before the next go-round. I pad back to the kitchen. As usual, Charlie's dishes and crap are piled high in the sink. Even though I'm pressed for time, I scrape, rinse, and load them like I always do. I can't help myself. I admit it, I'm anal-compulsive. But it bugs me. Big time.

"Asshole," I mutter.

The next hour and fifteen minutes pass in another typical frenzy of panic. I flip pages. I fill in bubbles. I comprehend nothing. I identify squat. My completions are incomplete, my vocabulary's for shit. I'm doomed. I have no Bright Future.

It is 7:15. I am already exhausted, and homeroom's in forty-five minutes.

As usual, there's no hot water in the shower. I drip and shiver like a stray dog. But I grit my teeth, willing myself on.

Ameliorate. Verb. To make better, to improve.

Example sentence: I will *ameliorate* my SAT scores or I will kill myself.

— — —

Now, believe it or not, comes the really hard part of the morning.

Charlie.

Usually I make it a point to leave him alone when I split for school. Entire seasons go by without a word between us during daylight hours. And I'm down with it. In fact, I like it. It makes life so much easier. But today I have no choice. Today I have to do what I most *loathe*—verb, to detest or abhor—doing. I have to bug him.

His room is even more of a disgusting pit since the last time I was compelled to enter. Although it's right next to mine, I never go in. It's not that I'm forbidden or he keeps it locked or anything weird like that. It's just that I get really bummed out whenever I do go in.

I switch on the lights and sweep open the curtains. Moldy socks, musty books, and mildewing takeout litter the cheap, stained carpet like carnage on a battlefield. I gingerly step through the darkness to a ratty mattress piled high with dirty underwear, old newspapers, and crinkled wrappers. I recoil. Besides demonstrating astounding sloth and a complete lack of standards and self-control, Charlie's room is seriously unsanitary. And, with my SATs impending, I have been exercising, eating right, living clean, zealously safeguarding my health. Now all is at risk. I don't want to complain, but the last thing I need at this critical juncture is to get really sick. I try not to breathe.

I jab the prongs of the large serving fork I've brought with me into the moldering mound.

"Okay, Charlie," I say. "Up and at 'em."

Nothing. I poke again—much harder.

Beneath the layers of debris, I discern the slightest of movements.

"It's seven twenty!" I bark like a drill sergeant. "You're going to be late for work."

"So what?" Charlie's voice growls. "I'm always late for work. No one gives a shit."

His submerged figure stirs, lifts up, then flops over like a beached whale on its other side to keep sleeping.

I stand there, fuming but determined.

"Not today, Charlie. Today I need you up, shaved, and semi-focused."

"What's so great about today?" his muffled voice questions.

"It's Friday. You're meeting Strack at noon."

"Never heard of him."

"Edith Strack. *She's* my college advisor," I explain patiently, but erupting internally. "This is my first and only appointment with her."

A shaggy head emerges. I am startled. Like I said, it's been a long time since I've seen Charlie in natural light. He looks awful. Gaunt, salt-and-pepper stubble, long hair oily and stringy. I mean, the guy looks like a serial killer in a good limited series. My heart stops. My hopes, slim as they are, do a nosedive.

Groaning, Charlie creaks a droopy lid open.

"What's that got to do with me again?" he says.

"Parents have to be there. I've only told you about it like fifty million times."

Yes, boys and girls, this is what technically constitutes my father. This wreck of a human being, my sole support. Although we are flesh and blood, we couldn't be more different. In a way, you could say Charlie's my greatest inspiration in that I refuse to be like Charlie. He's what I most fear becoming. But I won't let it happen. Unlike him, I will give a shit.

Suddenly he breaks into a coughing fit, chokes, and turns all red like he's going to keel over, but just manages to survive by hocking up a massive loogie that, not wanting to be rude, he forces back down. Although I should be used to it, I still gag. And Charlie, he just yawns and scratches like it's all normal, which it is for him.

"That coffee?" he asks, sniffing.

It is indeed. Along with the fork, I have brought a steaming mug. Charlie gropes for it like the caffeine addict he is. But I withhold his chemicals, haggling.

"It's really important to me, Charlie."

He props himself up higher and opens the other blood-shot eye. I see he's slept in his clothes. One more item in a long list of what deeply repels me about him.

"I suppose this means I have to take a shower," grouses Charlie, not joking.

I give him the coffee. He gulps it down greedily with both paws. I turn heel and then stop in the doorway.

"Twelve sharp, Charlie. Don't be late. I just get ten minutes."

Downtown Pritchard's a ghost town. No Starbucks or Jamba Juice or Banana Republics here. Even at its heyday, Pritchard was never pretty. But once upon a time, at the dawn of another century, my not-so-great hometown had a Sears and a Penney's and a cool art-deco movie theater. Now they're rotting away, like ancient tombs. Then GM restructured and the plants closed and the money vanished with them and the rest of the planet moved on. And what was left behind is a hollow, empty place with nowhere to go but further down. Which is why I have to get the hell out.

As again I weigh the sheer magnitude of my quest, The Murf happily sucks on a fatty the size of a small cigar. The Murf and me go back to preschool and have been in so many mutually compromising situations and shared humiliations that we could blackmail each other for eternity. But bottom line: The Murf's got my back and I've got his. I pick up The Murf for class every morning. Anything for a pal. Besides, he's right on the way and chips in for gas. And with the Beast—my 1990 Electra, eleven miles to the gallon; they don't make 'em like that anymore—every little bit helps, believe you me.

Bopping, exhaling a ginormous cloud, The Murf cranks up the Stones—we are classicists—and offers the aromatic blunt to me.

I'm sorely tempted. My gut's churning, and a quick toke would certainly take the edge off. But with my impending interview with Edith Strack, I have to be on my toes and keep my wits about me. So instead I sternly say: "You better lay off that shit or you'll end up like my old man."

"Oh, c'mon, we're seniors," The Murf responds. "It's our sacred duty to get wasted."

He takes another giant hit. I hurriedly roll down my window, brushing out the potent fumes. Can't chance Strack smelling anything on me.

"Hey, that a new shirt?" The Murf inquires.

It *is* a new shirt and I am pleased that The Murf—that anybody, in fact—notices. This morning I'm impeccably groomed. Hair neatly parted and combed, wearing shoes that shine. I'm looking sharp.

"Old Navy?" He tilts his seat way back.

"Only the best. The Gap," I say. "First impressions are essential."

The Gap. Fancy-schmancy. The Murf, attired in a tie-dyed Brian Jonestown Massacre T-shirt and torn sweatpants that hang loosely on his gangly frame, is suitably impressed. He reaches to experience the upscale fabric. I shoot up a warning hand.

"No touching the material."

The Murf leans back and closes his eyes to enjoy the buzz. "You're in an outstanding mood this morning," he observes, sarcastically.

It's true. I am a jerk this morning. Since senior year started, I'm a jerk too many mornings. I feel bad. It's not The Murf's fault that I'm totally losing it.

"Sorry, just bracing myself for The Cold Dose of Reality."

"The what?"

"The Cold Dose of Reality," I explain, grateful for any chance to *expostulate*—verb, to discuss, to examine at length. "When Strack tells you where you're going, and more importantly, where you're *not* going, to college."

The Murf's untroubled countenance clouds over, and he looks at me like he's about to have a small seizure. Between you and me, lately I've begun to notice that whenever I bring up my admission process with him, he gets that way. Even so, I plunge on.

"Every aspect of your application's assigned a numerical value. Strack adds them up and then breaks down your list of colleges into three categories. At the top there's your Reaches, which in turn are divided into three subcategories: Far Reaches, Near Reaches, and your basic Hail Mary. Getting into any of them is the equivalent of winning the lotto."

"That's the great thing about CC, man," The Murf says contentedly. "It's open admissions. Long as I'm eighteen and breathing, they gotta take me!"

CC. As in community college. I give him a pitying look. The Murf's complete lack of ambition's a running, sore topic between us. Despite my unrelenting advice, The Murf refuses to take all guidance.

"Which leaves your Fifty-Fifties," I continue. "Odds are you should get into at least one or two of these suckers. You'd think that'd provide a *scintilla*—noun, iota, trace amount—of security but it doesn't. Why not, you wonder?"

Actually I know The Murf doesn't wonder, not remotely. But I can't stop the self-punishment.

"Because there's no guarantee you're getting into a single one of them either," I wail. "What if nothing pans out? Suddenly, you're in free fall, being sucked down a black hole into nameless oblivion. You frantically latch on to a nondescript safety school and pretend to grin and bear it, but it's slit-your-wrists time."

Settling for a safety school. The dreaded worst-case scenario. I'm beside myself. In dire need of solace.

But The Murf's staring out his window at the football field, where the Poms are rehearsing for tomorrow's big game, as we turn into the parking lot. A super-endowed one leads the others in cheers, shaking and thrusting in a tight sweat suit.

"DO IT AGAIN!! HARDER! HARDER!!" she exhorts.

The Murf's glazed eyes are black dots, transfixed.

"I'll do it again, baby," he murmurs. "Just give me a chance."

I coast into a space and cut the engine, regarding him in exasperated disapproval.

"Murf, our entire futures are at stake. How can you think about sex with Julie Hickey at a time like this?"

"Are you kidding?" he answers. "It's all I think about."

See what I mean? The dude's hopeless.

We cross the vast lot, joining the exodus of kids heading to serve out their time at Pritchard High. I trudge like a Sherpa, hauling about fifty pounds of textbooks in my pack. The Murf flits about, free as a bird, carrying nothing.

"Whoa, check it out!" he says.

The red Beamer shines like a beacon in a sea of used economy cars and beat-up clunkers. I approach it reverently.

"Wonder whose it is?" asks The Murf.

"Burdette's," I answer. "His old man ordered the new Mercedes CLA250. Guess it finally arrived."

Burdette's old man is a professional, an orthodontist, and a bit of car nut. When he moves up a notch in automotive class, so does Burdette. I tell ya, there's no justice in the world.

"You mean this belongs to that dick?"

"*This*, as you so indelicately refer to it, is a BMW 335i," I say disdainfully. "Twin 3.0 turbos, four-wheel ventilated disc brakes, and a nine-speaker sound system. A new peak of precision German engineering. Do you have any inkling what these suckers start out at?"

The Murf shakes his head. It's beyond his grasp, almost beyond mine too.

"Try fifty large. And that's starting, without all the essential extras." I caress the hood like a lover, caught up in the perfection that only major money can buy. The Ultimate Driving Machine. Someday, I vow. But who I am fooling? Right now I'd do backflips and bark like a seal for a car that starts reliably and has a working CD player.

"Hey, Brooks," says a girl's voice, penetrating my fine automotive reverie.

It's Gina Agostini. She smiles shyly my way, every voluptuous inch of her, more enticing than ever.

"Hey, Gina."

Gina and me, we've been circling each other since late middle school, when our respective hormones kicked in. And recently, the circles have been getting tighter and tighter, if you catch my drift. Another few close encounters of the kind we've been having and we could become an unofficial official couple, a condition that doesn't displease me in the slightest.

"It was fun the other night," she smiles again—meaningfully.

I quiver, reliving the sublime sensations. I'm not one to talk out of school, but it *was* at that.

"Fun?" I stupidly grin back at her. "Try life-altering."

She laughs. And bats liquid-brown eyes, which I'm adrift in. "You going to Fluke's kickback Saturday?"

"Yeah, I hear his granny bit it so his 'rents are out of town," The Murf chimes.

"Maybe I'll see you there," Gina says invitingly.

I soak in every voluptuous inch of her. But then I spot Burdette's new hand-me-down Beamer, and it evokes an even more pressing mission. Somehow I summon inner strength.

"Sounds amazing, Gina, but unfortunately I already have other plans."

"Too bad. Should get pretty sick."

She slowly sashays away to rejoin her girlfriends at the edge of the lot. I admire the softly swaying, hip-hugging view. So does The Murf. I shake my head. Man, that was *close*. The Murf turns to me, incredulous.

"Have you lost it?" he demands. "What other plans?"

"I'm hooking up with a hot SAT practice book."

"Gina Agostino! Oh, c'mon, Rattigan! You can't let that get away!"

He makes a valid point, which doesn't help my resolve.

"Nope, from now on, I'm in training. Until 11:31 on October 13, yours truly is going monk-mode. No diversions, no temptations, no getting sidetracked. Which means no kickbacks, no parties, no social gatherings of any persuasion. This body's a temple. Which means no alcohol, no illegal substances, and absolutely positively no babes. Until 11:31 on October 13, we're talking concentrated concentration. Total focus."

The Murf rolls his eyes. He knows me too well.

"You'll never make it."

HIGH NOON

We're packed tight, lambs to the slaughter. No, that's too good for us, we're even lower on the devolutionary scale. We are paramecia, we are pond scum. For there's nothing more pathetic than a first-semester senior, except for a first-semester senior with his or her parents about to have their collective illusions shattered. And there are at least twenty of the aforementioned sweating it out in one cramped institutional space. You can cut the desperation with an X-Acto knife.

The door to Strack's office gapes open. Tricia Prindle staggers out, sobbing. Tears flowing, snot running—I mean, just wailing. We hastily clear a path to avoid her bad karma.

Ten minutes with Strack has rendered Tricia Prindle into quivering cafeteria Jell-O. Tricia Prindle. The name may not register with you, but boy, it sure does with me. Tricia Prindle's Little Miss Perfect, first-class brownnose, all-around suck-up. You know, straight-A student, signs up for every activity there is to pad the resume. Of course, she's not taking any AP or honors courses, nothing too challenging that might actually threaten the precious GPA. But still, all things considered, I must concede, an extremely solid candidate for higher learning.

Tricia's parents straggle after her, trying to keep it together. Mom's all limp and needs to be physically supported, Dad's biting on his hand so hard he's drawing blood. I gulp. This does not bode well.

"Next!" snarls Regina Severance, Strack's evil secretary. Severance could be Ilsa, She Wolf of the SS's twin, that is, if you add forty pounds and thirty years to the mix. "Have your questionnaire ready, and your answers had better be legible!"

I happen to know my head's next on the chopping block, but I look around along with the others, playing innocent, stalling for time.

You see, it's ten after twelve and Asshole's not here.

Severance squints through her scary-thick bifocals at my name pulsating on her computer screen.

"RATTIGAN!"

Miserably I grip my many painfully completed sheets, documenting in mind-numbing detail seventeen years of modest achievement. Although I try to be invisible, I'm like a flashing neon sign in the shape of an arrow pointing down at me, the only kid without a parent. Plus, I'm squirming. Severance, sensing weakness, zooms right in.

"Well?" she glowers. "Where is your parent? Why are you parentless?"

"Have a heart," I plead. "He'll be here. Just give me another minute . . ."

"Going once!" she crows.

There are over six hundred kids in my class and only two guidance counselors, and the other one's been on maternity leave for like five years. I have to see Strack. I have to make an Indelible Impression on her. I must get her to give me a Glowing Recommendation. It's Now or Never.

"Another minute, please. I have to get my Glowing Recommendation!"

"Going twice!"

I sink to my knees, groveling. "For the love of all that is good and holy, I beseech you! *Beseech*, verb, to beg, to demean oneself completely!"

"Going, going . . . ," she says, eyes gleaming, index finger poised above the chopping block.

"No, don't delete me from the System!" I yelp, "I'll never get back in!"

And then, just as I'm about to become history, Asshole strolls in, mellow as can be. He notes the heavy silence, the somber kids, the angst-ridden parents.

"Jesus, who died? This place is like a funeral parlor."

Leaping to my feet, I grab Charlie by the collar and drag him bodily back to Severance's desk.

"One bona fide parent!" I proclaim in quivering triumph. I'm heaving, sweating, soaking through my new button-down Gap shirt, an utter embarrassment to myself. But I do have the small consolation of ruining Severance's day. Her bloodlust has gone unsated, her kill denied. Scowling, she allows us passage. But I know and she knows this will not be forgotten. From now on, I am on Severance's permanent shit list. Thanks, Charlie.

He smiles at me, most likely already baked. "Guess I just made it, huh?"

I want to strangle him, but gathering what's left of my dignity, I merely propel him through the inner door to Stack's lair. Suddenly we are plunged into darkness. My flesh goes clammy in the rank, stagnant air. It's like entering a crypt.

"Sorry, Brooks, traffic sucked," Charlie whispers.

"This is Jersey. Traffic always sucks!" I hiss back at him. "The one time I ask you to do something for me."

In the gloom, yellowed files are piled high on the floors, on shelves, everywhere. Each folder a hopeful future, with big plans and unrealistic aspirations. The numbers are staggering. If the waiting room wasn't traumatic enough, I am now crushed under the true immensity of my insignificance.

"Mrs. Strack?" I venture.

Dwarfed by rusty, overstuffed file cabinets, a small figure hunches behind a large drab government-issue desk, stacked high with more folders. She slowly looks up from a bulky computer that should have been junked decades ago. Her eyes are sunken, her skin waxen and pale. We're talking Crypt Keeper. Again, not a promising sign. I tremulously deposit my file on her desk. Up close, she looks way too shrink-wrapped for someone I happen to know is in her mid-thirties.

"It's Ms. Strack, not Missus. *Ms.* Strack." The pencil she's gripping snaps in half in her hand. "I've never been married. I have no personal life."

She giggles. Not knowing what else to do, I chortle along with her. Charlie, giving me the wary eye, chuckles nervously.

"It's all such crap!" she laughs uproariously. "Jimmy's potential is unlimited, Janie's surface is barely scratched, Bobby would be a tremendous asset to any institution. I know it's crap, and the colleges know it's crap. Nobody reads what I write, but I have to write it anyway. Do you have any comprehension what it's like to crank out six hundred student recommendations by myself on antiquated equipment for peanuts, year after year after year?"

"Crap?" Charlie ventures.

"Such crap!" Strack howls, obviously not a well woman. "Sit!" she grunts, pointing.

There's a small clear space between teetering stacks of files on the couch. Charlie and I wedge ourselves into it. I give him the once-over for the first time. He's marginally presentable, clean-shaven for once, hair tied back in a ponytail, and in a relatively clean uniform. And not *uniform* in the metaphorical sense. An actual bona fide blue postal one. Yes, I'm the son of a mailman.

Strack gravely peruses my vitals with a jaundiced eye as she unscrews a gigantic thermos of what has to be, by the way her hands are vibrating, her tenth cup of coffee.

"There's no Mrs. Rattigan?"

"My mom's kind of out of the picture."

Strack's expression actually flickers with interest, appraising Charlie. Then he speaks.

"He means my old lady split on us nine years ago. Not a word since. Not even a stinkin' Christmas card . . ."

Way to pour on the charm, Asshole. Charlie's suitability as a mate is instantly rejected and dismissed, as well it should be. Pouring into a truck-sized mug, Strack spills coffee all over my pristine, hand-printed questionnaire. She blots it dry with some other student files.

"Only two schools?" she notes, as I knew she would. Two schools, while not unheard of, is a little off the beaten path.

It's either Columbia Early Decision or Rutgers. My choices couldn't be more stark or extreme—am I to be one of the rarefied few or one of the common rabble? Those, I've decided, are my only two real options. So I'm going for it. Columbia Early Decision means I can hear in December and have to commit to go if I'm accepted, which statistically is supposed to improve the odds a few decimals. But Columbia Early Decision's a dangerous roll of dice, because Columbia can also turn you down flat, which means then I'm out of the derby for good. There's no Late March, when in the Greater Applicant Pool I might possibly shine. I'm done, over. The strategy's Do or Die.

"The Ivy League," Strack continues. "Aiming rather high, don't you think, Brad?"

"Brooks," I correct meekly.

Aiming high? I'm shooting for the stratosphere. Last year, Columbia received 33,531 applications and accepted 2,311. That's a 6.89 percent acceptance rate. Seven out of a hundred. That's way, way up there, just after Stanford, Harvard, Princeton, and Yale. Daunting as they are, the numbers only tell a small part of the story. Because these aren't 33,531 anybodies applying, these are 33,531 super-high achievers. The valedictorians, class presidents, all-everythings; the offspring of zillionaires, of celebrities; the legacies, the kids who invented some huge new app in their bedrooms. But, like I said, at least if I go down in flames, I'll go in style.

"Columbia," Strack sighs.

Yes, Columbia. Because it's close by, in the City that I love. But mostly because, unlike the Big Four, Columbia might actually, possibly, really be doable for me.

"There are many other excellent institutions besides those in the Ivy League," Strack says, which is what I expect her to say.

"That's what I keep telling him," Charlie interjects. "Who needs a degree from some fancy bullshit school? You can get a great education anywhere."

I glare. Charlie shifts sheepishly. "Besides, I don't have the bread."

"Columbia is very expensive, Brad," Strack says, as if I

need her or anyone else to remind me. Tuition runs almost forty-seven grand. That's one year, not four, without room and board.

"I figure if I live at home and keep working part-time, I can swing it. I already have almost three thousand dollars saved up. I mean, I know it's not much, but I should qualify for some kind of financial aid . . ."

"With your grades and scores," Strack says, telling me what I already know, "you're a cinch for a full ride at Rutgers."

"Exactly. That's what I said," Charlie jumps in again. "Rutgers. A perfectly fine institution of higher learning!"

I know where he's going with this. Where he always ends up going. I shoot him a warning look.

"I mean, I went to Harvard," Asshole proclaims. "Lotta good it did me!"

"You went to Harvard?" Strack's aghast at the senseless waste of it all, as any normal person would be.

Harvard. A day doesn't go by when he doesn't mention it at least fifty times.

"Ms. Strack," I persist, desperate to stay on subject. "All I want to know is if I have a chance at Columbia. And if I do, will you go to bat for me?"

"Your GPA's right up there, Brad," Strack says, re-scrutinizing my sheet. "Your extracurriculars are a little exotic and more than slightly suspect, but abundant."

"Brooks," I correct again, shifting in my seat uneasily. Here comes the stretch of the profile I've especially been dreading.

"Co-captain of the Pritchard High School fencing team?" she asks rhetorically. "In the twenty-three years I've been here, I wasn't aware we even had a fencing team."

The Pritchard High School fencing team consists of me and The Murf. Our foils are wire hangers. No wimpy pads or helmets or officials for us. It's balls-out, anything goes, no holds barred. A great after-school activity. I highly recommend it. Mostly 'cause, since I outweigh him by a good forty pounds, I flail The Murf's ass raw every time.

"It's new," I say weakly.

"President of the Pritchard High School Greco-Roman Association?"

The Pritchard High School Greco-Roman Association also consists of just The Murf and me. Another of my many innovations, a nifty excuse for us to imbibe while wearing bedsheets as togas. So far, it's convened once.

"Also new," I maintain.

"Secretary-General of the Pritchard High School Ethno-Percussion Society?"

Charlie bursts out laughing, confirming to me he's most definitely baked. I elbow him in the side.

"Secretary-General?" she repeats.

I wince guiltily at the vision of me and The Murf by the Reservoir, both of us totally fried, hair flying, joyfully thumping in savage jungle cadence on industrial-sized overturned plastic buckets that we liberated one night from a Dumpster. Probably pushing the envelope, but I'd figured it was worth a shot.

"I suggest you try again with something a tad less creative," Strack says wryly, though not unkindly.

"Hey, I've got one," Charlie cracks. "Grand Poobah of the Fellowship of Flatulence."

He guffaws, thoroughly entertained by himself. Neither Strack nor I is amused. Giving him another look, she resumes her summation of my paltry life.

"Unfortunately, your SATs, excellent as they are in the larger scheme of things, are at the low end of the range for Columbia. Especially your Verbal."

Verbal. I flinch at the dreaded mention of my nemesis. My heart pounds. I get that familiar churning pit in my stomach.

"I'm retaking them again!" I squeak.

"Again?" she repines, registering my multiple columns.

"Again-again."

"Again-again?" She raises a skeptical brow.

"Well, again-again-again," I admit, reduced to a puddle.

Meanwhile, Charlie, he just keeps snickering at his lame joke, which he thinks nobody gets but him because he went to Harvard.

I have made an Indelible Impression, just not the one I intended. Strack looks at Charlie, sizes up my pitiful situation. I can tell she feels sorry for me having a burnout pothead like Charlie as a parent. Degrading and depressing as that is, hey, I'll take what I can get. I look at her abjectly.

"Columbia, Brad?" she sighs once more, closing my file, my interview, as far as she's concerned, over. "I don't think you fully comprehend what you're up against. Last year, the University of California, Santa Cruz rejected sixty-three applicants with scores of twenty-two hundred or above. This for a school, Brad, whose mascot is Sammy the Banana Slug!"

I swallow hard. This is truly disturbing news.

"It's Brooks," I say firmly. "If you're just going to blow me off, at least get my name right."

She gives me a long look, then reopens my file and clicks her pen to jot notes. "Any minorities in the family tree? Aleutian, American Samoan, Creole . . ."

I shrug, glance inquiringly at Charlie, who just continues to snigger.

"None that I can think of," I reluctantly, but honestly, answer.

"Foreign travels? Rich relatives? Triumphs over adversity?"

"Only defeats," I glumly conclude.

"Physical handicaps? Learning disabilities? Congenital defects?"

"My second toe's longer than my big one!" I declare, brightening.

Strack clicks her pen again, puts it down, and rubs her temples. "Why does it always have to be the Ivy League?" she asks the ceiling. "Why?"

Then, suddenly, she bolts into action. Assigning a

numerical value to every aspect of my application, she punches the keys of an ancient adding machine with the skill and dexterity of a crazed accountant during the height of tax season. Nobody knows her formula, only that it's an algorithm of such complexity and top secrecy it would do a hedge-fund manager proud. And she's never wrong. If she says you're out, you're out. Strack's like Pritchard High's very own Oracle of Delphi.

Finally, she rips off my sum worth from the spool of paper. A long beat. I brace myself for The Cold Dose of Reality.

"Bring your Verbal up seventy-five points and write a killer personal essay, and maybe, just maybe, you might be in the hunt," she concedes at last. "But I wouldn't get your hopes up."

SIDETRACKED

I'm on cloud nine. I'm high-fiving. I'm slam-dunking. For I totter on the cusp of Greatness. Usually at this point after school, sleep deprivation has kicked in and I'm stumbling around in a semi-coma. But, after my minimally encouraging parley with Strack, the synapses are firing on all cylinders. I am revitalized, refortified, coursing with renewed energy and purpose.

I might be in the hunt! Okay, only if I somehow miraculously raise my Verbal seventy-five points and come up with a killer essay. But, for the moment, I choose to ignore those minor details. However remote from shore, I am still within the realm of possibility. Yeah, I know Strack said maybe, just maybe. I know I shouldn't get my hopes up, but I can't help it. They're sky-high.

My thoughts turn to the task nearest at hand. The Personal Essay. Let's face it, at Columbia's *august*—adjective, inspiring awe and reverence—level, everybody and their kid sister has the grades, the boards, the extracurricks. Which leaves the connections, of which I'm most lacking. Which makes the Personal Essay all that much more crucial to nail.

"Seven hundred fifty words or less of pure profundity," I extol to The Murf, who, of course, since he's settling for CC, doesn't have to write a single syllable. "Seven hundred fifty words or less to separate myself from the herd. To express incredible depth and extra-fine sensitivity, but without getting all gushy. The Personal Essay must be imbued with youthful optimism, yet be light on self-importance. Unique without being too out-there. Don't want to freak them out or make them think I'm some nut job. I'm telling you, Murf, it's a fine line I'm treading."

"Pickles, onions, olives," The Murf says, not listening.

I plummet back to orbit. I'm at work. Wearing asinine oversized fedoras and suspenders, The Murf and I comprise a two-person assembly line behind the counter at The Submachine Gun. The conceit of the joint, if you can call it that, is gangsters and molls. Submachine guns, submarine sandwiches. Get it? Real original, right? Apparently the owner, whom no one has ever actually met, is a major *Godfather* freak. Like, who isn't? Anyway, The Gun's supposed to be the first in a budding franchise, but in reality, it's a lone outpost not much longer for this world. But, for the time being at least, it's the only place besides the pool hall open downtown after six so it does some business.

"Mustard? Mayonnaise?" growls The Murf.

"I said lots of everything, moron!" snarls our customer, a ten-year-old skate punk, who, adding insult to injury, pops his gum right in our faces.

The Murf starts to climb over the counter to throttle the little bastard, but I restrain him.

"I can't believe I let you rope me into working at this dive, just like you rope me into everything!" he seethes.

"I never roped you into anything," I mildly protest, even though I did, always have, and do.

Our beloved night manager, Pat Wilson, the owner's morally challenged nephew, just out of jail for the third time, leans back on his swivel chair from his cubbyhole. Nobody knows what he does in there, just that he's always in it. Nobody wants to know.

"Hey, cut the chin music!" His Lordship commands. "You're ruining the mood!"

"Blow me, Pat!" The Murf answers by way of clever riposte.

Pat disappears from view again, his executive duties done for the day.

"Oh yeah, what do you call the fencing team?" The Murf says as we heap on lots of everything.

"Just trying to broaden your horizons."

"Yeah, well, I still have the welts."

Through the front window, I spot Burdette's brand-new old Beamer pulling up at the curb. Practice must be over. Burdette and the rest of the offensive line pile out in their letter jackets, whooping and body slamming each other.

"It's Friday night," The Murf says, not seeing them. "We should be broadening our horizons by getting laid, or at least trashed in the pursuit thereof. But no, not you. You've gone monk!"

Burdette and his three fellow lunkheads barrel one after the other through the door, each successively larger and beefier than the last. Only in our national pastime is gluttony so esteemed.

"Hey, you sack of shit, double meatball all round!" bellows the massive mound of lard known as Cartelli as he deposits himself with the others at a table. The chair literally buckles under his weight.

"Meatballs, I'll give them meatballs!" The Murf says, grabbing a mushy fistful to bombard them. He and I have a long, humiliating history with the offensive line.

"HEY, HOW ABOUT SOME NAPKINS HERE!" booms Burdette.

"Use your sleeve, asshole," The Murf glowers back at him.

"And wipe the table while you're at it, Murphy. This place is a pigsty!"

Point of fact, the place is a pigsty. It's filthy. Every table needs to be bussed, the floor needs to be swept, the trashcans need to be emptied. Under Pat's inspiring non-supervision, The Murf and I make it a point of pride to do as little actual work as possible.

As I shove The Murf out of the way to get the napkins and grab a rag and tray, I can't help but overhear what passes for conversation.

"The chick gets stood up and suddenly I've got to find her a stand-in," Burdette says, tossing cans of soda from the cooler to his buddies.

"Give it up, Burdette," cracks Cartelli. "Nobody's taking your loser cousin in Havendale Hills to Homecoming tomorrow."

Cartelli's a fine one to talk about losers. Besides being freakishly rotund, the guy's already been held back two years. At the rate he's going, he's going to be the first high school senior in the state of New Jersey to legally drink.

"At least check out her Facebook page," Burdette appeals to Flanagan, another behemoth. "Maybe you could score with a hot friend at the after-party."

They raise their arms like lords of the manor as I clear and wipe down their table like a *vassal*—noun, slave, servant. As a non-varsity athlete, I have little, if any, status. As someone who actually has to punch a clock to keep gas in the car and maintain a halfway decent phone plan, I have less than none. Me and my kind are nonexistent to them.

"No way," Flanagan says, shaking his Coke and then opening it. "I've got a rep to maintain."

Coke sprays everywhere. Real class. Fuming, I go to grab a mop.

"Well, somebody's gotta do it," Burdette moans. "She won't go with me, and my old man's all over my ass."

I return with the bucket on wheels. They lift their feet as I swab around them.

"My aunt's made it into this huge tragedy. Dana's a senior and she bought a dress and it's already been altered or some shit." Burdette makes a grotesque whiny face. "*Wah. Wah. Wah.* And she's never gone before—"

"And she never will!" Cartelli snorts, farting loudly in emphasis.

They laugh uproariously. I don't know why, but they're really getting under my skin. Hey, I'm not asking for any medals or someone to erect a statue of me or anything, but meanness, especially deliberate meanness, always gets me going. Especially meanness against someone who's not around to defend themselves. Especially a girl someone. Especially by a bunch of supersized dumbasses. It's like all my buttons are being pushed at the same time.

"One friggin' night." Burdette turns to the last of the gruesome foursome. "C'mon, Butnik, I'll pay you fifty bucks."

"I wouldn't do it for fifty thousand," declares Butnik, starting center, three hundred pounds of slobbering blubber, pretty much subhuman. The idea that even Butnik wouldn't take Burdette's cousin to Homecoming is the height of hilarity to the others. They jiggle with cruel merriment. For some reason, I am short-circuiting; I am reaching boiling point.

"I'll do it," I blurt out before I realize what I'm saying.

Suddenly the laughter stops. Suddenly I have the rapt

attention of over half a ton of suet. Burdette acknowledges my existence for the first time.

"What did you say, Rattigan?" he asks in disbelief.

"I said I'll take your cousin to Homecoming tomorrow, Burdette." Again, swear to God, it comes out before I know it.

Cartelli finds this a crack-up and doubles over. Flanagan and Butnik join in the hilarity.

"Shut the fuck up!" Burdette slugs Cartelli, who bitch slaps Flanagan, who smothers Butnik in a headlock. Burdette readjusts his girth to face me.

"You will?" He breaks into this big grin. He'll take anybody. Even me, which kind of ticks me off. "No shit?"

"And it won't cost you a cent," I announce grandly. I mean, I wouldn't take Burdette's money if he put a howitzer to my head.

"Done!" Burdette all-too-swiftly seals the deal by crunching the bones in my hand in his iron grip, impressing on me the dire physical consequences if I fail to honor said commitment. It all happens in almost a blink of an eye. The Murf, finally showing up with the napkins, just when I don't need him, watches my pact with the devil, stunned.

"Have you flipped?" he says in horror. "You can't take Burdette's cousin to Homecoming! Look at Burdette!"

I look at Burdette. Then I shut my eyes and fight to suppress the mental picture of a female version of him.

"Yeah, Rattigan," Burdette beams. "She's a real grenade."

— — —

Later, as we turn off the lights and close up, The Murf's still in a state of shock. I am too, but I'll be damned if I'll let him know it. I repeat again what has been an almost nonstop three-hour litany of rationalizations.

"So what if I do someone a good turn?" I philosophize. "Maybe I'll get a decent meal out of it. I could use one."

The Murf, sucking down a cold Guinness from Pat's private reserve, remains extremely dubious.

"Yeah, Brooks, but Burdette's cousin."

If he says it one more time, I'm going to throttle him. I know it's friggin' Burdette's friggin' cousin. So what if she's Burdette's cousin? That doesn't necessarily mean she has to look like Burdette, even though they both come from the same gene pool. Somehow I maintain the noble facade.

"Anyway, I felt kind of bad for her," I say, pulling down the grate across the storefront and padlocking the entrance.

"True. She is Burdette's cousin." The Murf inhales on the last embers of a roach. The weed has made him contemplative. "That can't be easy."

The Beast's parked down the block. We trudge through the dark chill toward it.

"What happened to being in training?" asks The Murf, polishing off the can. "Clean living? Total focus?"

"One night's not going to throw me off my game," I say dismissively, although I would kill for a belt or a hit of anything, preferably both now that the possible repercussions of my rashness are finally registering.

I climb behind the wheel, lean over, and unlock and jar open the dented, aging passenger door. The Murf slides in, pulling out another purloined stout from a jacket pocket.

"Plus, I've always been meaning to scope out Havendale Hills," I add. "Be nice to get out of Pritchard for a change."

"What's wrong with Pritchard?" he says, taking a gulp.

It's ten o'clock and we're the only two people in downtown Pritchard getting into the only car on the street. The Murf's hopeless. I don't even know where to start. So I don't.

UNKNOWN QUANTITY

The weather's unseasonably warm, a big orange sun's setting over central Jersey, and the northbound Garden State Parkway's miraculously clear as I embark on the trek to Havendale Hills. I've got a full tank of gas and I'm speeding, unencumbered, from Pritchard and, I must say, it feels mighty fine. I should have Bruce cranked to the max and be grooving to Clarence's tasty licks to orchestrate the moment. Instead, I'm listening to yet another SAT practice tape.

That's right, *tape*, as in *cassette*. The Beast, cherished and pampered as she is, predates the advent of the CD, let alone the MP3 player. So make do I must. I scored these tapes for a pittance on eBay. They're from the seventies. But I figure obscure, polysyllabic vocabulary words with simple meanings never go out of fashion with those ETS jokers over in Princeton.

"*Lugubrious*," the somber voice enunciates. "*Adjective, looking or sounding sad and gloomy.*"

The guy on the tape couldn't be more lugubrious. He sounds like he's officiating at somebody's funeral. Mine.

"*Example sentence*," Mr. Personality continues. "*Just because I am a bit down today doesn't mean I am in a lugubrious mood.*"

Then another voice joins the conversation. A perky voice. A hot chick's voice.

"*In fifty feet, turn right at the next exit.*" It's Google Maps on my iPhone.

"Jesus!" I curse. "How about a little warning!"

Dropping the hammer, I'm forced to cut sharply across three lanes of traffic, barely missing getting flattened by a big rig. But I take the exit. It's an exit I've never taken before.

Although Havendale Hills is all of thirty or so miles from Pritchard, I've never been there. But I know something about it. The 07078's one of the poshest—if not the poshest—zip codes in the entire state of Jersey. Its mall is the most humungous, with all the top chains. We're talking Saks, Neiman, Barneys. No piddley-ass mom-and-pop outfits in the 07078. Not with a median household income of upwards of two hundred g's.

I cruise along wide, clean boulevards. I am in a foreign land, a charmed place free of worry and woe. A land of thin, perfect-teethed, gluten-free people. I take in the block after block of manicured yards, the luxury craft gleaming in circular driveways, the glittering houses the size and scale of small hotels. They're like palaces to me.

As well they should be with an average asking price in the multi-millions.

"*Catastrophic*," the tape intones.

I gulp, overwhelmed by it all. What am I doing here? What have I gotten myself into?

"*Adjective. Of, or relating to, a terrible event or complete failure.*"

I switch off the tape before it can go on.

"*You have reached your destination*," pipes my iPhone.

I stop before what can only be described as a walled estate. This is wealth beyond my limited experience, beyond imagination.

"Example sentence," I murmur to myself. "Brooks has a bad feeling that the evening is going to be *catastrophic*."

But I've come too far to turn back now. I nose up to the solid titanium front gate built to withstand a siege from the justifiably outraged masses, roll down my window, and then lean out and press the intercom button on a high-tech security panel. An electronic orb swivels and rotates and gives me the stink eye.

"*Please identify yourself*," a mechanical voice commands.

"Uh, it's Brooks Rattigan," I stammer, "the stand-in."

Without another word, the gate magically swings open, revealing Versailles crammed onto a half-acre lot. Four stories high, with turrets and towers and all sorts of slanty things. It doesn't work, not in Jersey, but the monumental expense and excess of it all is still impressive. My humble Electra sputters up the grandiose, if short, drive as a middle-aged man in a suit races out, aiming an elaborate, professional-grade digital camera my way. Burdette's uncle.

"Thanks for coming!" he exults, fumbling for my name.

"Brooks," I say.

"Brooks!" he repeats, all hale and hearty. Gripping my hand like a steel lock, he practically lifts me from the car, taping through the eyepiece the whole time.

Burdette's aunt clatters behind on high heels across the imported flagstone. Attractive, although right on the verge of having too much plastic surgery and being grotesque, she throws herself at me, hugging me effusively.

"You're an angel!" she gushes. "An angel from heaven!"

She's followed by not one, but two sets of glowing grandparents. They stampede around me like there's no tomorrow, which I guess for them is kind of true.

To say I'm surprised by my reception is a major understatement. I don't know what I was expecting—mild disapproval, begrudging tolerance, maybe—but I sure wasn't expecting this. I am dumbstruck and strangely gratified. For not only am I acknowledged, accepted, and welcomed, I am embraced, pounded on the back, and pinched on the cheek—over and over again. I am appreciated, on the verge of being worshipped. It's as if I were a young *deity*—noun, supreme being—to them.

They practically carry me on their shoulders inside the castle—I mean, mini-mansion. The cavernous entryway's also way overdone and not to my taste, but awe-inducing nonetheless. What must be Burdette's cousin's kid sister, mouthful of braces pigtails flying, bounds up all excited.

"Dana, *he's* here! *He's* here!" she giggles.

Burdette's aunt thrusts a fancy corsage the size of a small shrub at me. "This is for her," she beams. One grandma whips out a brush and starts adjusting a few stray strands on my head. The other one gravely issues me instructions like the guy you never see on *Mission: Impossible.*

"We've made reservations at Dana's favorite restaurant. Giuseppe's promised to take extra-special care of you . . ."

"Nothing's too good for our princess!" the granddads proclaim in unison, then shoot each other dirty looks.

"Dana's got a boyfriend! Dana's got a boyfriend!" Burdette's cousin's kid sister screams, skipping around like she's spastic.

"Shut your face, Ariel!" bellow both parents and both sets of grandparents in chorus.

Meanwhile, I'm just standing there, not speaking, just grinning like the village idiot. That's when I get my first sighting of my date for the night. Shyly descending the curved stairway beneath a crystal chandelier, she makes an entrance out of some old Disney musical. All shiny, all done-up – nails, hair, face. She's her own work of art, the polished finished product of some very serious thought and salon time. Her gown—that's the only thing you can call it—is slinky, a little daring and obviously high fashion. Not girly stuff, very grown-up. Definitely not off the rack. Megabucks. I can see why Burdette's aunt was ready to blow a gasket when Burdette's cousin was stood up.

She stops before me so I can take in the whole picture. Burdette's cousin's not bad. A little bookish maybe. Okay, I'm not going to lie, not a knockout by any stretch, but more than acceptable. How's the song go? She's no beauty queen, but, hey, she's all right and that's all right with me. Or something like that.

Burdette's cousin bites her professionally red-lipsticked lips, nervous and uncertain.

"I look like a total dork, right?" she asks me.

Seven sets of eyes turn expectantly my way. The pressure's on. I feel like one wrong word and I could easily have my head lopped off and put on a spike.

"No, you look cool," I say, more than a little relieved. Because, best of all, thankfully, Burdette's cousin looks nothing like Burdette.

Apparently it's the perfect thing for me to say. Because Burdette's aunt breaks into tears. Both grandmas dab their eyes with hankies. The granddads shake hands, congratulating themselves. Burdette's uncle, digitally recording in one hand, slams me on my already bruised back with the other.

"What size are you, Brooks?" he asks, all jovial-like.

Suddenly, I'm too aware I'm the object of their collective scrutiny and found severely wanting. Although I'm wearing my best khakis, my only sports jacket and tie, my one pair of genuine leather shoes, I'm hardly Prince Charming to her precious majesty.

Next thing I know, I'm upstairs in the His of His and Hers closets, each bigger than my bedroom. Rows of expensive suits whir by on automated racks. The parade of abundance is dizzying. Burdette's uncle is about the same height as me. Admirably fit for his age. With my honors course load, SAT study regimen, job schedule, and resultant lack of regular exercise, I'm slightly out of shape for mine. Which makes us a match.

"Forty-two regular. I think I've got an old Armani around that size," he muses.

He can't find the Armani, but he does snag what must be a three-thousand-dollar Hugo Boss sailing by. As I change in the giant bathroom with more His and Hers everything, the fine material fits like a calf leather glove. Linking my French cuffs, I almost don't recognize myself in the full-length adjustable lighted mirror with wireless remote. I'm like James Bond, you know, all debonair and shit. So I'm feeling pretty dang dapper as I pose in the living room before a giant stone mantelpiece with Dana, who pins a boutonniere to my lapel.

"Okay, now present her with the corsage!" snaps Burdette's aunt like an Off-Off-Broadway director. "Dana, stand straight!

We both smile wide for posterity. We shift positions. More shots are taken. The immediate family. Just with mom and dad. One pair of grandfolks, then the other. Girls. Boys. The configurations seem endless. Then, for the big finale: the group shot with Burdette's uncle scrambling to get back in place before the shutter snaps. Again and again, the camera flashes.

As we move in a herd to the front door, Burdette's uncle pulls me aside and discretely tucks something into my palm. It's a thick—and I mean thick—wad of bills. No ones and fives, but twenties and fifties.

"Five hundred enough?" he whispers like we're partners in some top-secret conspiracy.

It's by far the most money I have ever seen in one place at one time in my entire life. And I'm holding it in my grubby Pritchard hands.

"More than ample, sir," I croak.

Outside, Burdette's cousin's kid sister is examining my patched-up, rusted-through Electra with real curiosity.

"Ariel, don't touch! It's dirty!" scolds Burdette's aunt, pulling her back.

"Actually I just had it washed," I murmur apologetically. I actually did. And hot-waxed, for that matter. From the Rattigan perspective, the Beast's in primo condition and has never looked finer.

Burdette's aunt looks pointedly at Burdette's uncle. He hems and haws and then, under her lacerating gaze, relents.

"Brooks, why don't you two kids take the Volvo?" he offers *munificently*—adverb, to be generous or bountiful.

Dana stomps a spiked heel, pouting. "Daddy, we are not going to Homecoming in Mom's station wagon!" Then she turns to me, smiling. "Are we, Brooks?"

I don't know, a Volvo sounds plenty cush to me, but Burdette's aunt gives Burdette's uncle another stern look. He staggers back as if struck. His expression registers total horror. You know, one of those "No, God no, anything but that" looks. Because, although I don't know it, that only leaves . . .

"Brooks." Burdette's aunt smiles at Dana with maternal triumph. "Why don't you two kids take the Lamborghini?"

– – –

The Aventador LP 700-4 Roadster rides like a thoroughbred, not that I would know what a thoroughbred rides like, but if I did it would be like this. The sleek aerodynamic design slices through the wind. The carbon fiber chassis hugs the pavement low to the ground, nimble yet possessing tremendous tensile strength. The dual hydraulic brakes and power-steering system are frisky and fun but responsive, sensitive to the lightest touch. I shift gears like a Formula One race car driver, putting all seven hundred horses to the test. We whip around curves, accelerate up inclines, chew up ground. The precision-tooled Italian engine handles everything I give it effortlessly. Plus I got Andrew W.K.'s "Party Till You Puke" thrashing on satellite radio from, count 'em, twelve Dolby surround speakers, and I'm detecting layers of subtleties and complexities to his work that I never imagined possible. My expectations are exceeded. This is style. This is class. This, my friends, is where it's at.

The deluxe GPS tracking system takes us within the exact millimeter of our destination and, I might add, with plenty of advanced warning. I stop on a dime before a plush red velvet awning. A valet in a commodore's uniform swings opens Dana's door. As I climb from the cockpit, I toss him the wireless key fob, grinning ear to ear.

– – –

Giuseppe's as good as his word and takes extra-special care of us. Candlelit corner table for two with minimal foot traffic and an unobstructed view of the gurgling fountain with little cupids and spouting fish-thingies. He serves us sparkling water. He recommends the specials. First, the *Insalata di Bietole*—beet salad. *Cozze alla Marchigiana* for the *antipasti*; the mussels, he confides in an appealing hint of an accent, are fresh off the boat. For the pasta course, he suggests *Pappardelle al Cinghiale*, some kind of flat noodle in a wild boar *ragù*, whatever that is. For our *carne e pesce*, the *Filetto di Manzo*, as in Filet Mignon, baby. We order them all. I mean, who am I to argue?

"So then Graham G-chats me in Calc that he suddenly has to go out of town . . ." Dana is saying, by way of back-story to how exactly I got to be here.

"What a tool," I sympathize. The mix of the red beets with walnuts and Gorgonzola is pungent, yet not unpleasing. I fork in some more.

"So I I-message the bastard that I've already told everybody and my mom's bought a dress and what the fuck's going on?" Her mascaraed eyes well up, remembering her disgrace. "But I know what happened. His friends said I wasn't hot enough, so Graham wimped out."

Now, I'm usually not a mussel man. Usually I find them gooey and stringy. But these, simmered in a delicate white wine and garlic sauce, I'm finding quite tender and flavorful. So this is what fresh is all about, I marvel.

Giuseppe hovers, alert to our slightest beck and whim.

"More breadsticks, sir?" he inquires.

"Absolutely, my good man! Absolutely!" I respond. What can I say? I have a jones for breadsticks. And these are the best I've ever had the privilege to crunch down.

"This guy Graham's a dumbshit. And you're way hot," I comfort Dana. "In fact, if I wasn't a gentleman and this wasn't our first and only date, I'd be hitting on you right now."

"Really?" she asks shyly. "You're not just saying that to be nice?"

"You are definite potential-girlfriend material," I assure her as I savor each delectable bite of my perfectly grilled steak. Filet of anything is not exactly a regular staple of the Rattigan family menu, let alone grass-fed. More like chemically injected ground round, and that's when I'm lucky.

Dana laughs, and when I look up the tears are gone and she's smiling. She's radiant. She's glowing.

"Anyway, thanks for doing this. It's a really big deal to my parents, especially my mom."

"No worries," I say. "My pleasure!"

Another basket of breadsticks arrives. I ask you, can it get any better?

The rest of the night goes down like the mussels. We cruise in the Lambo to Dana's school, where the actual dance is. It's got color-coordinated lockers. The gym, where the action is, is like an NBA stadium compared to Pritchard's. No bleachers that fold out, but real seats and high-tech video scoreboards. The floor's packed and the DJ's tight. We work off the calories, burning a groove with the best of them. She shows me a few steps, I reciprocate with a couple of mine. Afterwards, we zip to an all-night diner to grab some grub with her crowd. Her friends are nerdy but supersmart, interesting to talk to, and refreshingly non-judgmental for a bunch of rich kids. Before I know it, it's a quarter past one in the morning and I'm gallantly escorting Dana up her front walk.

"Anyone who tells you it doesn't matter what college you go to is a liar." I'm expounding on my new favorite subject. "They're either a success who went to a good school trying to make you feel better—"

"Or a loser who didn't," she finishes my thought. "Rationalizing a life of disappointment and mediocrity."

Precisely. Dana, it turns out, is applying Early Action to Yale, retaking her SATs again-again, although not again-again-again, and I have found her to be most agreeable company. Arriving at the front door, we pause and look at each other awkwardly, knowing our paths will forever part, never to cross again.

"That dumbshit Graham really missed out," I whisper.

Dana's eyes glisten. For her, it's the perfect end to what has turned out to be a perfect evening. I've made a dream come true. I've lived up to the fantasy. The power's intoxicating. Suddenly, the door opens from inside and Burdette's aunt's sticking her head out.

"So how was it?" she shrieks, giving us both heart attacks.

"Never mind that. How's the Lamborghini?" grunts Burdette's uncle right behind her.

They both loom anxiously in their bathrobes, shattering what could have been a beautiful moment.

"*Mom!*" Dana yowls in embarrassed protest.

"Don't *Mom* me! Who was there and what were they wearing? Tell me everything! Tell! Tell!"

Burdette's aunt pursues Dana up the stairs. It's the last I see of her. I'm left alone with Burdette's uncle. Not knowing what else to do, I turn to leave.

"Uh, Brooks . . ." he says.

"Yes sir?"

"The suit."

Upstairs, standing in my boxers, I carefully hang the Hugo Boss back on the rack in the immense warehouse of a closet. It's like I'm a character in Cinderella. Except I'm not the prince, I'm the girl.

Burdette's uncle's yawning by the front door, eager to get to bed, when I trot back down the curving stairway in my own diminished evening wear. I pull out a still-thick wad of cash from my hip pocket to return his change.

"Uh, dinner was $153 including tip, and then there was another eight for parking . . ."

"Keep it, Brooks," he says, too beat to deal with minutiae. "You've made my little girl's night. You've earned it."

— — —

I sit in my pumpkin in the driveway, staring at the $312 in my paws. No exaggeration, my heart's pounding like a Keith Moon solo, my hands shaking. It takes a good five minutes before I can pull it together to drive home.

A GROWING CONCERN

"Three hundred bucks? You gotta be shitting me!" The Murf says when I debrief him at work the next day.

"I shit you not," I state, still somewhat in shock. We're in the men's room, doing our usual *desultory*—adjective, superficial, perfunctory—job of mopping the grungy tile. We don't bother with the gunked-up sinks and the toilets; you don't want to know about them. Let's just say we consider them a no-go zone. In short, the men's room at The Gun's not a place you want to spend a lot of time in, hence our extreme haste.

"Three hundred non-tax dollars," I report, swiping like mad. "More than we take home in a whole month slaving in this dump."

"For one crummy night?" The Murf says. He's shielding his nose and mouth with a sleeve to protect his lungs from the industrial-strength disinfectant he's pouring indiscriminately. The stuff's pure poison but covers the stench.

"That's just it, it wasn't crummy. Dana was all right. I pretty much had an outstanding time," I muse. "Incredible food at a place I'll probably never be able to chow down at again. Awesome tunes by a really sick band . . ."

"And the Lamborghini!" The Murf wheezes, having inhaled some fumes despite his best precautions. "Don't forget the Lambo!"

Keeping all physical contact to a bare minimum, I kick open the swinging door for The Murf to make a quick retreat from the chamber of horrors. We abandon the bucket and mop. I scramble right behind him.

"I don't get it. What's the catch?" The Murf protests, breathing in and out, once we are safely outside.

There is no catch. My one brush with the one percent is history. Never to happen again. But the brief taste of it has left me hungry for more.

— — —

Why Columbia? The two simple words stump me. I've been staring at them on my laptop for going on an hour now.

The Gun's closed Sundays, another brilliant move by upper management. Because if The Gun was open on Sundays, it would be the only place open to chow down in town. Duh. But I'm glad. Because I use the Lord's Day to play catch-up. And every week, I have more and more to catch up on. I battle through two overdue mid-terms papers, one in AP English and the other in Honors

History, and endure hours of tedious reading in Honors Biochem, Spanish, and AP Calc. So it's not until almost midnight that I am finally ready to start tackling my application to Columbia. For my last meaningful semester, I've chosen a brutal academic schedule, but it can't be helped. I need the weighted points. With my marginal scores, the transcript's more vital than ever. Rubbing my bleary eyes, I refocus on my screen and the latest monumental task at hand.

Why Columbia? It's the topic for my all-important first short essay question. I have three hundred fifty words and, though I've racked my brain for weeks now, I can't come up with a single one. Not like my application to Rutgers, which took me all of an hour because Rutgers doesn't bother with profound, pointless questions. Why Columbia? The honest answer? For the Brand. For an Ivy League degree, the golden ticket, the magic pedigree that will open all the right doors that otherwise will never open for me. For the same self-serving reasons that everyone else has. Because I want to do something interesting and of consequence with my life, to be all I might be if I was only given a chance. But I can't write the honest answer. Because personal advancement's too crude and crass for the Admissions Committee's delicate sensibilities. Mere monetary gain's so beneath them, the gatekeepers to the Good Life. Of course, they're all loaded; the ones who get to do the asking always are. No, I have to act all lofty and high-minded. I have to profess to want to make the world a better place in some small, insignificant but symbolic way. In the immortal words of Strack, it's such crap.

Bursting with indignation, I furiously type:

Why Columbia? Why Filetto di Manzo? Why Lamborghini? Why Boss? Why, for that matter, Johansson? Why Columbia? Like it's not totally obvious. But no, they have to make you come out and say it, to make you get down on your knees and beg. Why not fucking Columbia, you sick sadistic assholes? Because it's the best. Duh. Why ask such a stupid bullshit question?

Then I stop typing and frantically backspace, taking hold of my senses.

That's it, Brooks, alienate the crap out of them in the first paragraph of your application. *Alienate*. Verb. To totally piss off . . .

"HEY HO, LET'S GO!"

I snatch up my cell before I can check the display, grateful for any interruption.

"Igor's House of Pain. Igor speaking."

A long pause with lots of background noise, and then a deep, muffled voice responds: "This Rattigan?"

It's a sinister voice. A voice that sends shivers shooting up and down my spine. A voice that sounds like it's in the concrete business and can either personally pound me into pulp or order someone else to do it. I gulp. The past has finally caught up with me. My mind reviews who I've recently offended. I get lost. It's a substantial list.

"And this is?" I ask cautiously.

"Brooks Rattigan?" the voice repeats ominously.

"Sorry, but I think you have the wrong number." I hurry to click off, when the voice yelps, "No, don't hang up! It's Lou Frohnapfel! I work with Todd Burdette! He said I should call!"

Todd Burdette? Todd Burdette is Burdette's uncle. I pause. Why would Burdette's uncle tell Lou Frohnapfel to contact me? Then I almost start to laugh as it dawns on me what has to be the answer. Because it can only mean . . .

"Let me guess," I say. "You have a daughter?"

"A lovely girl," Lou's tone warms considerably. "Honor Roll. Co-captain of the Passaic field hockey team. Homecoming Dance is this weekend . . ."

"Look, Mr. Frohnapfel, I'm really sorry . . ." I can't believe it's happening again.

"Sylvie's never been, and she has her heart set on going, and no one's asked her . . ."

"Love to help you out, but I just can't. I work weekend nights." Besides, I think to myself, unlike Havendale Hills, Passaic is hardly new territory to me. I've been to Passaic. And it's not that much different than Pritchard.

"I'll pay you fifty dollars."

Fifty whole dollars? My pride, which I didn't know I had, is actually hurt.

"I'm the Assistant Weekend Night Manager," I haughtily inform him. "I've already taken one Saturday off."

"Okay, seventy-five! My wife's all over me!"

Seventy-five. Frohnapfel's not even in the ballpark.

"If I ask for another, I'll be fired." I am finished with the conversation.

"One hundred!"

I roll my eyes. My hackles are up. I mean, I'm not going to do it, but I'm not going to do for a lot more than a lousy C-note. I feel compelled to set the record straight.

"For your information, Mr. Frohnapfel, last Saturday I netted over three hundred."

"Three!" Frohnapfel shouts. "Burdette told me two, you little rat!"

I am outraged. The son of a bitch is trying to lowball me.

"Two-fifty," I say, just to let him know who he's dealing with. "Take it or leave it."

"Okay, okay, I'll take it!" shrieks Frohnapfel.

Two-fifty. Two-fifty's real money. I glance at my laptop screen. At the words that have come to define my life: "Why?" And the resounding answer: "Columbia!" Another two-fifty lets me quit the mindless drudgery at The Gun and buys me the time and edge I so desperately need if I am to raise my Verbal those crucial seventy-five points. Another two-fifty's worth risking my job for. And, like The Murf noted, what's the catch?

I lean back in my chair and put up my feet. In an instant, our roles have reversed. I'm in the driver's seat, and he's the mule pulling the cart. I know I shouldn't, but I smile despite myself.

"I'll need to rent a suit. I don't own one," I say reluctantly, still on the fence.

"And the suit! We done now?" he snarls.

"And gas." I know I'm pushing the envelope, pressing my advantage unfairly, but the rush of having actual leverage for once in my life is so great I can't help myself.

"Gas? It's just forty minutes! We're in Passaic!"

Forty minutes without traffic, he means, which there always is. Try more like ninety minutes on a good day—and that's each way.

"I use high-test," I say. "Last time was murder. And tolls. They really add up."

"You're killing me, kid!"

"Nice chatting with you, Lou." I grin. I hold all the cards. I silently count to myself. Whatever will be, will be. Going once, going twice, going, going, go—

"All right! All right!" the once-mighty Frohnapfel squeals. "Two-fifty plus the suit and gas and gratuities! Satisfied, you bloodsucker?"

I am.

– – –

Well, folks, it all kind of snowballs from there. At work the next day, when Pat threatens to fire me if I take off another Saturday night, I experience the supreme satisfaction of telling him to buzz off and walking off the job. I am fine with it because the way I figure it, where there's one Frohnapfel, there's got to be more. Greener pastures beckon. Standing in, I decide, will become my new temporary vocation. The Murf, needless to say, is less than understanding.

"You do realize you've completely lost it?" he asks as he exhales a huge cloud, offering the bong to me. I beg off, pulling up my jacket in the crisp night air.

"So I make a few girlish dreams come true and rack in the ducats at the same time," I posit, for the sake of argument. "No harm, no foul."

We dangle side by side on the swings in the playground of the elementary school we once attended together. We go back that far. Since those *halcyon*—adjective, tranquil, happy—days, the swings have been our favorite place to kick back and *ruminate*—verb, to contemplate one's place in the world.

"But it's like being gigolo!" The Murf declares.

"Gigolos have sex, dude. I've given that up, remember?" I get a little huffy. "They're paying me to spend time with their little darlings, not make time with them. I do have some standards, you know."

"Since when?"

I smile. My friend knows me too well.

"I need this, Murf. If I don't have to spend one-third of my waking hours punching a clock anymore, I can keep up with my classes, which means I can work on my application and cram for my boards."

"You're a sick man, Rattigan. A very sick man." The Murf shakes his head woefully.

"And with the kind of money I make, I can afford Farkus."

"Farkus?" The very sound of the word repels him. "What is it, some kind of banned brain steroid?"

"Close. An SAT coach," I explain. "Farkus knows all the tricks, traps, shortcuts, ins and outs, dos and don'ts. Not only the dorks in Science Club but the dweebs on the Robotics Club swear by him. Plus, at two-fifty a crack plus expenses, I might actually bank some serious dime toward tuition."

"Dude," The Murf cautions. "Senior year only comes by once and it's going by fast and you're fucking wasting it."

"So I'll be missing a few parties," I admit grudgingly.

"A few parties?" The Murf jumps in. "Try one non-stop one!"

"I'm investing in my future," I say doggedly. "And if you ever got your shit together, you'd be buckling down too."

But, like always, The Murf's not hearing it. He just shakes his head.

"Gina Agostini, man," he says sorrowfully. "Gi-na A-gos-ti-niiii."

Gina Agostini. Of dark backseat and darker back room. For a second, the sweet tingling sensations sweep over me. The promise of late nights and early mornings of overheated passion, which I risk forfeiting. But in the end I don't waver. Because I'm hurtling at supersonic speed to a crossroads, maybe the biggest in my life. And, as the great Yogi Berra advises, I'm taking it.

The Murf and me look at each other. For the first time, a gulf is forming between us. We both feel it.

"So you're just going to desert me to fend for myself in that hellhole?" he grumbles. Unlike me, The Murf can't just up and quit. He needs the cash to make ends meet and The Gun, pitiful as it is, is one of the only places offering gainful employment around Pritchard.

"I'll visit whenever I can," I promise. I feel guilty. The Murf is going to be lost at The Gun without me, but desperate times require desperate measures. Somehow, I resolve, I'll make it up to him.

— — —

I'll spare you the blow-by-blow with Sylvie. Let's just say, for Lou Frohnapfel's daughter, she's astoundingly attractive. And if you'd ever met Lou, you'd appreciate what I mean. And the Frohnapfel abode. It has sort of a giant Egyptian temple thing going on, but in Passaic. Now there's a combination for you. Sylvie looks radiant in her new grown-up dress as I deftly pin on the corsage. I do my usual configurations for the camera with the extended, and I mean extended, Frohnapfel clan. Then it's off in Lou's Lexus LS 460. It lacks the oomph and acceleration of the Lambo, but I'm genuinely impressed by the ergonomics. Those Japanese designers pay such attention to detail.

My culinary horizons continue to broaden. I find both the Chateaubriand and the level of Sylvie's conversation enthralling. Her reach is Cornell. She goes to parochial school so the dance is over way early, at like ten. We stop for a burger with her crowd and, before I know it, the Lexus is back at the door by eleven. Sylvie's mom's weeping tears and Lou gets all misty-eyed and slips me an extra fifty. We actually hug. I ask Lou to spread the word. Lou says he'll see what he can do.

Monday morning I get two calls, one from Montclair, the other from Piscataway, for the same Saturday, and suddenly I have a couple of tycoons on call-waiting engaging in a bidding war in five-dollar increments for my services. To my credit, I feel honor-bound to accept my first offer. Mustn't be too greedy. Don't want to get a bad rep when the enterprise is just launching. Tuesday I get three more inquiries for the Saturday after that. Wednesday I'm turning down business left and right. I'm fitted for a suit at Bissell's Menswear, which is purchased on installment, which I figure I can double and add as a surcharge.

— — —

Alana Schmitz has a great smile and a slight acne problem but nothing that won't clear up with time and the right medication. Having met like just two minutes ago, we nonetheless pose arm in arm before an enormous carved mantelpiece like we've been together for years. She's applying Early Decision to Brown, wants to be an actress, and knows the lines to every movie every made. I know because I try to stump her but can't. Her dad owns a Jag F-Type. We're talking supercharged V8, top speed well over two hundred. This baby moves like a bullet. I find my allegiance to the Lambo is sorely tested. We sup on sushi. A first for me, but definitely not the last. I dig the brininess. We get down at the big dance and then afterwards hang with a bunch of her over-emotive, kind of dippy—but in a nice way—theater friends singing wacky folk songs around somebody's fire pit. At the stroke of twelve it's back to the castle, where I am fawned over by effusive parents. Strictly routine. *Ka-ching!* I net a cool two-eighty.

By my fourth Saturday, all mantelpieces look the same. Brianna Karp wears a beige halter number and braces that were supposed to come off last year. Mrs. Karp practically suffocates me in her bosomy embrace. She's divorced and there is no Mr. Karp, so I'm forced to make do with her Land Rover, which drives like a Sherman tank compared to my previous modes of luxury transport. Yeah, I know—oh, the sacrifices we make, right? We have yakitori. Another first-but-not-last for me. I love the whole skewer thing. Bri-Bri's a gas with a wicked sense of humor and a nastier moonwalk. She's hoping for Swarthmore. *Ka-ching!* Chalk up another two-seventy-five in the kitty.

When Charlie asks what's up with the suit, which I'm stunned he's even noticed, I tell him I found a new gig with a fancy caterer. He doesn't suspect a thing. In the meantime, my phone keeps buzzing. And why not? My testimonials are through the roof. Permit me just a small sampling:

"Thanks, Brooks, you've made this the happiest day of my life!" Sylvie Frohnapfel, Passaic.

"*God bless you, Brooks Rattigan!*" Marjorie Karp, West Orange.

"*Brooks Rattigan treats a girl the way she wants to be treated, even if it's just for one night.*" Alana Schmitz, Montclair.

"*So polite!*" Burdette's aunt, Havendale Hills.

"*Discrete.*" Burdette's uncle, Havendale Hills.

"*Responsible.*" Jack Schmitz, Montclair.

"*Respectful.*" Joanne Schmitz, Montclair.

"*A great listener!*" Dana Burdette, Havendale Hills.

"*A true humanitarian!*" Lou Frohnapfel, Passaic.

"*And he's a terrific dancer!*" Bri-Bri Karp, West Orange.

How's the song go? Got to keep the customer satisfied. Well, I do, and at the same time I'm living the high life. Everybody's happy. It's too easy. Then comes the fateful Lieberman call. But I'm getting way ahead of myself.

Because it's now almost October 13 and Zero Hour approaches . . .

FINAL SHOWDOWN

The SATs are less than a week away, and as the last precious minutes tick by, I am increasingly panicked and on edge. Despite my endless hours of mental toil, my practice Verbal's going not up but down, and all this abstinence from everything worth living for has me busting at my fraying seams. I'm chugging Red Bull like water and taking long cold showers to stay alert. But I know it's all going to come down to Farkus.

He's expensive. Like really, really expensive. Farkus commands an hourly rate a Wall Street lawyer would envy. Try $325 an hour. I've budgeted myself five hundred, which gives me just over ninety minutes. Lily Gunkel says that's more than plenty, and her scores shot up over two hundred. After just one session with Farkus, Phil Chen's went up almost three. The man, I'm assured by one and all, is a giant of the craft, a genius, a game changer. And you can't argue with results. Even so, I'm apprehensive because

I can never quite get the specifics about what exactly makes Farkus so fantastic.

I pace back and forth. It's three after the top of the hour, and when you're being charged by the minute, every minute matters. I peer outside through the blinds and spy this spanking-new cherry-red Porsche Boxster GTS—list price at least seventy large without the extras—whip up along the curb to my dingy garden apartment complex. A telephone pole's blocking my view so I can't see who gets out, but I can hear slow, ominous steps making their way across the courtyard and up the three flights of stairs. They seem to take forever. The suspense is killing me. I am in my own horror movie.

Finally, there's a knock on my portal. I spring to it, swing open, and stare out. I see nothing because Farkus is about two feet tall. Not two feet literally, but he's short. Five feet, maybe an inch or smidgeon more. Maybe.

"I am Farkus," he snarls in a sinister East European accent I can't quite place. The dude's in his early twenties, big clunky glasses, prematurely bald, and wearing major bling. Gold chains, pinky rings, multiple hoops in his lobes. And he's got on this dippy one-piece velour sweat-suit ensemble.

"What a dump." He swaggers past me inside, making a great display of disgust. A geek on a power trip. Only in the bizarro subterranean subculture of SAT preparation could a runt like him be a stud. In normal circumstances, I could wipe the floor with his smug ass. But these aren't normal circumstances, and I'm his bitch. He dusts the seat of a chair before he sits down. "Thought I was in the wrong place," he says patronizingly. "Farkus is used to a much more select clientele."

"My money's good as anybody's," I say a little hotly, sitting down.

"Then fork it over, chump," he instructs, crooking a tiny finger.

"Show me yours first," I say, bridling.

"Oh, you don't trust Farkus? You want to check out the Farkus bona fides?" Sneering, he unsnaps a briefcase and takes out a small rectangle of paper encased in a transparent sleeve, which he tosses casually on the coffee table. "Sure, no problemo."

I pick up the sheet. It's the official ETS printout of Farkus's very own, personal SAT scores. And I can't believe what I'm seeing. For I'm clutching the Holy Grail in my pitiful, trembling hands. Triple Eights. As in three eight hundreds. The fabled trifecta of perfection. I'm holding what I was previously convinced was only legend. Twenty-four hundred. For real. Farkus, diminutive and obnoxious as he is, knows the Game inside and out. It goes without saying I am convinced. I pay my wages of sin readily, even eagerly. I'm so blown away I would have paid him six times over. Only after Farkus takes a full minute thumbing back and forth through my hard-earned boodle like a bookie does he *deign*—verb, to condescend—to acknowledge my presence again.

We get right to it. First, he insists on a review of the basics. Four number-two pencils honed to a dagger point, battery-powered sharpener, smelling salts. Smelling salts? That's encouraging.

"Know your calculator," he lectures me, holding one up. "He can be your best friend or your worst enemy."

"Extra batteries," he proclaims. "Alkaline."

At $5.42 a minute, I'm more than a little underwhelmed by the level of the instruction, but for the time being keep it to myself. Next he moves on to coping with test anxiety. We murmur together:

"It's only a test! It's only a test! I can do it! I can do it!"

Then he demonstrates a series of relaxation exercises you can do while you're sitting.

"Squeeze those buttocks!" he orders from the seat next to me, swigging from, like, a gallon jug of Gatorade, offering me none. "Make 'em burn!"

Finally, after another four minutes or so of this, we move on to maintaining a competitive edge. He takes out a whiteboard. He scrawls the word "SEX" on it with a marker, then emphatically crosses it out.

"None! For at least seventy-two hours!"

It's been weeks since I've had any so I'm way ahead of Farkus, on this score anyway, but I raise my hand. Even though I'm in a classroom of one, he won't recognize me otherwise.

"Does that include—" I ask, curious.

"Especially that!" he thunders. "Chew gum! Go on long runs!"

At least a hundred bucks has gone by, and Napoleon Bonaparte here hasn't told me anything I don't already know. I can take no more.

"Hey, when do we get to the good stuff?"

He glowers at me. I haven't raised my hand. I raise it.

"Look, this is all great information, but could you speed it up a little?"

"Wise guy, huh?" he snaps back at me. "Thinks he knows everything?"

"Actually," I say, "I'm acutely aware of my limitations, which is why I'd like to move on to something more critical like Critical Reading, which I really suck at."

But Farkus won't be swayed. Farkus has got his method, and Farkus is going to stick to it no matter what, damn him.

"We've reached the question-and-answer period," Farkus says. "You're full of questions. Go ahead, smartass. Ask me anything."

I really think we should be doing Syllogisms but decide to humor him. I raise my hand again.

"What about the Christmas Tree Pattern?"

The Christmas Tree Pattern, for those of you not into shadowy conspiracy theories, is the ultimate high school urban myth. I know it's ridiculous, but there are these rumors floating around that the Educational Testing Service is some sort of diabolical, top-secret society like Google or the Shriners. Some people are all paranoid that standardized tests are just a nefarious plot to control the planet. Some people—not me, mind you—are convinced that the answers are in some sort of clandestine ETS code. A repeating pattern of letters that spell out some sick inside ETS joke or form some sort of esoteric ETS symbol. Totally implausible, right?

Farkus gives me a pained look.

"Last year, I heard it was the words to 'Thong Song' by Sisqo," I chuckle hollowly, a bit ashamed to have asked such an asinine question.

"Last year, it was the chord progression to 'In-A-Gadda-Da-Vida' by Iron Butterfly, schmuck," he tartly informs me. "You want to get down to business, let's get down to business."

The next seventy-three-and-a-half minutes are the longest in my life.

I will forever quake with fear and horror at the terrible memory of number twenty-two of Section Four. I am eyeball deep in Passage-Based Reading, my greatest adversary, confronted by eight questions based on five paragraphs taken from a book on sleep research. I know, I know. Sleep research? Who comes up with these topics? It's like the ETS designs them to induce a vegetative state.

Here was my question: *Which of the following, if true, would effectively undermine the "simple definition"?*

Well, first off, I have no friggin' clue what the question is asking. There is no "simple definition" or simple anything in the dense jungle of verbiage I've just endured,

plus I don't understand what they mean by "undermine."
My ass is grass.

For the record, here are my choices:

All people sleep.

Some people require long periods of sleep.

Some people don't require long periods of sleep.

Some people sleep only when they are tired.

Some people sleep even when they are not tired.

I couldn't make this shit up if I tried. I mean, this is a real-life question. I stare, I cogitate. My five alternatives blur together. I blink to stay awake. All these mentions of sleep have made me just want to roll over and take a super-long nap.

The seconds tick relentlessly on Farkus's upraised stopwatch.

"Not so smart now, are we, buddy boy?" he taunts.

"*E*?" I venture, going with what I know.

Farkus smiles. He has been waiting for this moment, waiting to pounce. He unsnaps his briefcase and takes out a thick eighteen-inch ruler, which he hefts in one hand. I regard it and him warily. There's a certain gleam in his eyes and practice to his grip that unsettles me.

"Think," he hisses. "It's an easy one."

Maybe it is for Mr. Twenty-Four Hundred, but not for mere mortals like Mr. Nineteen Eighty-Five and only if you add my best scores. I rescrutinize the text. After a period of deliberation, I make my choice.

"*C*," I announce with conviction.

Next thing I know, my ears are ringing and I'm seeing stars. Farkus has whacked me upside the head with the ruler.

"Hey, you hit me!" I squawk. "It really hurts!"

He whacks me again, careful to aim at a place that won't leave scars. The pain's sharp and excruciating. For a little guy, he sure packs a mean ruler. I leap to my feet and scramble to the other side of the table. He stalks me.

"These are the SATs, sonny. When those columns of fill-in bubbles are staring you in the face, Mommy and Daddy can't buy you out of this one!"

I don't know which is more traumatic—the fact that a deranged pipsqueak is pursuing me with an eighteen-inch ruler or the concept that I am paying for it.

"THINK!!" he screams, red-faced, veins bulging.

He slashes. Utilizing my fencing expertise, I duck. I am in fear for my life. I am beyond terrified. This, I abruptly realize, is the secret behind Farkus's success, the reason he rakes in the big bucks. Farkus is a paid assassin, hired to do what helicopter parents cannot bring themselves to do to their hothouse flower children. Namely, to knock some fucking sense into them.

"*B!*" I squeal like a stuck pig. "Some people require long periods of sleep!"

In an instant, calm is restored. Farkus sheathes his sword and sits back down.

"Always go for the paradox," he says.

A paradox. Of course. It's so obvious. I willingly, if tremulously, edge back to my seat. For suddenly, I have discovered logic in all things and am experiencing supreme clarity through the throbbing pain and stinging sensations. My focus, for the first time ever, is absolute and total.

For the rest of our short time together, the eighteen-incher remains within Farkus's easy reach. Under threat of bodily harm, I breeze through whatever he throws at me—Sentence Structure, Sentence Completions, Passage-Based Reading time trials—rattling off correct answers like a well-oiled machine.

"*Sweep is to broom as cut is to scissors.* An atlas has many maps. A book has many pages!" I bark like a trained seal. Farkus has harnessed me, ridden me, broken my soul, crushed my fragile ego, obliterated all trace of former personality. I'm in his box. And I love it. If he wanted me to, I would roll over, I would lick his hand.

"WHAT ARE YOU GOING TO DO ON SATURDAY?" my lord and master demands.

"KILL!" I scream. I am his. We are one.

"I'M NOT FEELING IT!" Farkus snarls.

"KILL! KILL! KILLLLLLLL!!!"

— — —

Like two seconds after Farkus departs, I drop like a hanged man, mentally, physically, and spiritually depleted. I beach like a whale, breathing in and out, waiting for the adrenaline, testosterone, and welts to subside. My hand flops limply down to the floor and I feel the corner of something poking out from beneath the couch. A book—a large one—of some kind. Curious, I lift it up. It's a photo album, one I know Charlie usually keeps in a moldering box under the bed in his slum of a room. Guess he must have been looking through it. Anyway, it's been years since I've seen it.

I crack open the worn cover that is barely attached to a tattered spine. I examine the fading pictures carefully mounted inside. I see a super-skinny Charlie with a full head of hair and long, ridiculous sideburns and his whole life ahead of him. I see him camping at the beach, skiing down slopes, hiking trails. A self-starter, a doer, a go-getter. I see him grinning ear to ear with a bunch of equally skinny, hairy pals in their graduation gowns in Harvard Yard, overflowing with supreme confidence and mountainous expectations. Harvard! Do you realize how fucking hard it is to get into Harvard? Try impossible, even back then. Maybe even harder back then, because back then they used to take a ton more legacies and the rich and connected from fancy boarding schools. The right sort of people, don't you know. To get into Harvard from public school from here in north central Jersey, you had to be flat-out brilliant, to be extraordinary, a certified superstar. And Charlie had done it, incredible as it is to believe. But there it is in living color before me. Proof.

Then another new, dazzling figure enters the pictures. My mother, dark hair and blue eyes, just like me, but petite and delicate. They'd met when he was a senior and she was a sophomore at Simmons College, a small, kind of arty women's school right next door to Harvard in Cambridge. She was a dancer of some sort, though obviously not too successful because whenever I look her up on the Web, nothing's ever there. When I was a kid and would ask where she went, all Charlie would say was that she went crazy or had problems, or he'd fall back on the regular standby that he didn't want to talk about it. So long ago, I pretty much stopped asking.

But here they are, mister and missus, together, radiantly happy. Tanned and fit, him in Bermuda shorts, her in a bikini, arm in arm, at the helm of a sailboat in the sunny tropics. In seedy Atlantic City, cheerfully brandishing their winnings—one thin dime. Bundled together, welcoming the New Year in Times Square, crushed together, kissing.

I conjure up a parallel existence for myself. One in which everything isn't so dire or, better yet, dire at all. Nothing too grand or elaborate. Two stable, well-adjusted parents with actual concern for my welfare. A somewhat spacious house in a well-tended 'burb, new cars to drive at my will, vacations overseas. As the Beach Boys once sang, "Wouldn't It Be Nice?"

Then I hear the rattle of a key in the lock. Charlie, home from what he calls a job. Hurriedly I shut the photo album, shove it back under the couch, click on the TV, and pretend to be chilling. He shuffles in, hunched over, shaking off the rain that must have just started. He's wearing his beat-up old parka patched with duct tape on both elbows. Why doesn't he get a new one? Even he can afford a new one.

He sees me looking at him. "What?" he asks. He's his usual unshaven, sloppy, disheveled self. Unkempt, but not in a making-a-statement, deliberately slovenly, slacker kind of way, but rather in a ratty, unsanitary way, almost like a street person.

How did it—he—come to this? He—they both—had so much going for them. Beauty, brains, talent, each other. It's the great mystery of my being. The Great Unaskable, the Probably Unanswerable.

"Crystal Palace," Charlie says, heavily depositing a bag of greasy takeout on the counter. "I got some of that Kung Pow Chicken you like so much."

"Kung Pao," I correct a bit too testily. "I said *Kung Pow* once when I like three and you'll never let me forget it."

"It was cute." He attempts a smile.

"Maybe to you, but not to me," I snap back, repudiating his familiarity. "And no thanks, I'm trying to stay off the MSG."

He doesn't ask why, because he doesn't care or doesn't want to know or both. He just commences eating while standing, chopsticking right from the carton. No plates, sitting down, or token pleasantries, thank-you-very-much-please.

I stand, disgusted, deflated, and still a little wobbly from my bout with Farkus.

"My SATs are on Saturday," I huffily inform him, although I don't know why I'm bothering.

He stops chewing for a second but doesn't look up.

"Huh," he grunts, then resumes feeding.

No *good luck* or *attaboy*, let alone *what can I do to help?* But what did I expect?

– – –

By Saturday morning, I'm pumped up again, in fighting trim. So pumped up, in fact, that I barely slept Friday night. So when my alarm finally sounds at 5:45, I'm already wide-awake and wired. I perform my calisthenics, shower, force down a healthy breakfast, lay out my instruments of battle, all the while softly chanting my mantra.

"KILL! KILL! KILL!!!"

I don't limber up with flashcards and I dispense with the practice tapes. At this point, it's too late. If I'm not ready now, I never will be. For better or worse, my die is cast. On the drive to school, as I vigorously chew my gum, I struggle to stay positive. Fourth time, baby, fourth time's the charm. I can do it, I can do it. It's only a test, it's only a test . . .

Bullshit it is. More like Rattigan's Last Stand.

When I arrive at Pritchard High, there's already a long straggly line of kids, all vigorously chewing gum in the early morning pre-registration air. The repressed energy's palpable. Over-caffeinated, sex- and sleep-deprived teenagers jostle into each other for no discernible reason.

"Stop shoving! Watch it! Quit breathing on me!"

We file, like the clones we are, past card tables manned by somber adults.

"License and registration! Let's go! Keep it moving!" they shout.

The girl in front of me is having a meltdown.

"You don't have a license?" a guy with a nametag that says "Menzer" asks her.

"I forgot it," she whimpers.

Rookie mistake, I think pityingly.

"No photo ID?" this Menzer dude asks, caring less.

"I have my dad's gym membership card," she brays, all weepy and shit. "That ought to count for something!"

"Next!" Menzer grunts.

She is firmly led away, first victim of the many pitfalls of inadequate test preparation. Quickly and efficiently, I display the proper documentation and am ushered into the inner sanctum. I try to ignore Tricia Prindle, who lingers nervously at the door, breathing in and out, being massaged and prepped like a heavyweight boxer by her overwrought parents.

"It's only your entire Future . . . ," Tricia's mom soothes her.

"Whatever you do, don't tense up!" her dad warns. "Because this is the last chance you're ever going to get!"

For the first time ever, I am actually grateful that I am essentially an orphan.

The school cafeteria, scene of so many food fights and flirtations, is now a gladiatorial arena of cerebral combat. Across the grim, cavernous chamber, warriors prep for battle at their respective desks. I too set out my equipment at my appointed position. Calculator, spare alkaline batteries, stopwatch, four freshly sharpened number-two pencils, and lucky rabbit's foot, which hasn't done shit so far for me but I'm still too superstitious to get rid of. The guy next to me rubs a crystal. This one girl crosses herself. Another has her hands together, praying. Behind me, a smug-looking guy who I want to smack on sight sharpens his pencils like a pool shark chalking a cue stick. Then suddenly the guy with the crystal panics.

"Oh my God, I don't have any pencils!" he cries, fumbling through his backpack and pockets. "I forgot my four number-two pencils!"

I, along with everyone else, ignore him. Then the poor bastard jumps to his feet, calling out plaintively, appealing to the entire room.

"Will no one lend me a number-two pencil?"

There are literally hundreds of us with four or more number-two pencils, and not a single one of us will part with a single one. Things are rough all over. Though I deeply sympathize with his plight, it's a cruel world, buddy. Survival of the Fittest, man.

"My kingdom for a number-two pencil!" the guy moans,

then starts sniveling like a baby, still refusing to go. It's really starting to get on my nerves. I thrust a pencil at him.

"Here!" I growl.

"Bless you, kind sir!" He snatches the proffered implement. "I won't forget this."

"For the love of God, would you please just shut up," I say. Out of the corner of my eye, I spot Smug Guy rotating his arms and legs, squeezing his butt cheeks, counting backwards. We haven't even started and I'm already falling behind! My relaxation exercises! Hurry!

Me and every other sucker in the room are squeezing our butt cheeks ragged. As our official numerically assigned packets are handed out, Strack, looking even more unhinged than usual since it's the height of application season and being a proctor is the last thing she needs, reads aloud from a prepared text.

"Welcome to the SAT," she drones. "The SAT is a standardized test for most college admissions in the United States and the rest of the planet."

Tell me something I don't know. I am impatient, champing at the bit, itching to get to it, to just get it over with.

"The SAT does not measure intelligence," Stack continues reciting. "It is not an IQ test." She snorts skeptically. "Yeah, right."

Somehow I don't find Strack's attitude encouraging.

"The SAT only measures how well you do on the SATs. It is not a predictor of future success." She snorts again, mumbling, "Who do they think they're kidding?"

Sighing, she raises her official stopwatch. Hundreds of young anxious eyes fixate on her finger, poised just above the trigger.

"Oh, the hell with it."

She clicks the tab. The race is on. We're on the clock.

"You have twenty-five minutes."

Yellow number-two pencils explode into action on computerized answer sheets. I crack open the seal of my booklet and flip to the first page of the first section to my first question. It's a math section, a relative strength. I quickly compute my first answer, but when I go to fill it in, nothing's happening in my first bubble because my pencil has no point. Around me, my competition vaults through problems like champion hurdlers. I cast the defective instrument to the floor and scoop up another pencil. Now I am down to only two spares. I'm rattled.

"Kill! Kill! Kill!" I hyperventilate to myself, in and out. "I can do this, damn it!"

I hear the pitter-patter of hundreds of fingers tapping calculator keys. The soft creak of graphite rubbing against paper. The relentless ticking of a veritable sea of individual watches.

I sprint to play catch-up, am at a full gallop and on my last question when Strack's voice cuts through the silence like an executioner's ax. "Time's up."

I push it to the brink, filling in my final circle a millisecond after she clicks her stopwatch. I've made it just under the wire. But before I can absorb my achievement, the Scholastic Aptitude Test marches on.

"Please turn to Section Two," Strack intones. She clicks. "You have twenty-five minutes."

Section Two is Verbal, Passage-Based Reading, my greatest nemesis. Even worse, the passage is a poem. And it's about fucking flowers. My heartbeat goes all loud and slow-motion. *THUMP-THUMP-THUMP*. The words are like hieroglyphics to me. On my stopwatch, the long hand sweeps around, the short one shifts an increment. A whole minute has passed, and I'm still on the first question. I sit paralyzed. It's desperation time. I summon up Farkus and his words of hard-paid wisdom.

"The obvious answer is usually the right one on easy questions . . ."

I decisively fill in the letter *B* for the first question. Then I hear Farkus again.

"On hard questions, the obvious answer is a trap."

I hurriedly erase *B* and fill in *D*, then erase that too and cast my fate with *E*.

The next three hours and twenty minutes pass in a blur. A blizzard of dense text, complex math diagrams, sentence completions, equations, word analogies, and graphs fly at me like attacking spaceships.

"There is no penalty for wrong answers on grid-ins," Farkus advises, Yoda-like. *"So when in doubt, guess, guess, guess!"*

I draw mental straws. I fill in *A*.

"Wrong answers can kill your score on sentence completions," I'm warned. *"Whatever you do, don't guess!"*

I erase *D*, refill in *C*, my original second answer. Around me, I hear a chorus of flipping pages. The others are surging ahead. I gulp bottled water to steady myself.

"Never read directions. It's a waste of time. Directions never change . . ."

I gladly skip ahead.

"Except in the experimental section."

I stop in place.

"Nobody knows which section the experimental section is."

I frantically backtrack. Panicked, I read the directions, I fill and re–fill in spaces. Faster and faster.

"Pencils down," Strack intones. "Time's up."

She clicks her stopwatch with a conclusive, concussive snap. I look around. Crystal Guy springs to his feet and is first to hand in his answer sheet, then struts off with my fucking pencil. Smug Guy's right behind, smiling. I could murder them both. Even the reliably gelatinous Tricia Prindle is looking spry and remarkably together. It's over. And I am nowhere close to being done. I shakily close my booklet. A hollowed-out husk.

"Answer sheet, if you please."

Strack pries my last hopes from my death grip.

– – –

As I stagger back outside into the glare of normality, a bunch of adult lowlifes are lounging by their cars, reading the sports page, rolling dice, smoking. Seeing me, they bolt into action, jockeying for position by the doors as other brain-weary seniors straggle into view behind me. We are swarmed with printed flyers.

"Post-SAT special at the Acme College Counseling Center!" one lowlife bellows. "Somewhere out there's a school you've never heard of just for you!"

"Karen Richardson, licensed psychologist!" another booms. "You could have a learning disability and not even know it!"

"Blowout tonight at McClellan's Bar and Grill!" yet another declares. "Kamikazes half-price!"

In a stupor, I wade through a virtual gauntlet of cottage industries that bottom-feed on the admissions process. There's even a Hare Krishna dancing in circles, pounding on a tambourine, spouting gibberish. I actually contemplate joining.

— — —

Six hours, five Buds, and four bong rips later, I'm still PTSD, numb, staring into space. I can now defile the bodily temple. But, though I'm no longer denied the meager compensations of late-adolescent existence, though I have tossed abstinence to the winds, though I can even consider the remote possibility of sex again, I'm without solace.

"I feel very positive about it," I inform The Murf for like the thousandth time since he got here. We're wedged against the refrigerator, shouting into each other's faces in the packed kitchen at some party of a girl neither of us knows, whose parents are away. The Murf, just off work, is still in full Gun regalia—fedora, striped vest, and shirt.

"I mean, I wish I had more time," I admit. "But everybody feels that way."

The Murf doesn't say anything, merely replenishes the bowl.

"So there were a couple of sections I didn't finish. Okay, more than a couple. But the answers I did answer, I definitely knew the answer. Except for the answers I guessed. Overall, I feel very positive."

"Well, you're bumming the shit out of me." The Murf thrusts the pipe and the lighter at me. "I'm going to scope out Julie Hickey. She's wearing a V-neck you wouldn't believe."

He abandons me to myself, leaving me alone in the happy crowd.

"*Bomb*. Verb," I croak, belting down another brew. "To achieve complete and utter ruin."

I could cancel my scores. I have before. Only this time I can't. Because the best aggregate of my old scores is still seventy-five points short of the Promised Land. I have to stick with the new ones, come what may. It's never easy for me. *Never*. Suddenly, I brandish a clenched fist at the ceiling.

"I did everything right! Everything!" I roar. "Ate my proper food groups! Slept with my calculator! Squeezed my buttocks 'til they were black and blue!"

I stop, realizing I am getting strange looks. Then, through the clamor, I feel the Ramones vibrating. My iPhone's ringing. I dig it out from my pocket and click on.

"Suicide Hotline. Charles Manson speaking."

"Brooks, Harvey Lieberman in Green Meadow again," says a voice so meek I can barely hear it.

Lieberman. The name's vaguely familiar. But there's been so many on the ol' voicemail lately. The voice mumbles something inaudible.

"Speak up, man!" I command, straining to hear.

I cover my ears to block out the noise. The voice on the other end barely increases in volume: "I hope I haven't caught you at an inopportune time . . ."

I light up and suck on the pipe The Murf's so considerately provided.

"What can I do you for, Mr. Lieberman?" I ask, like I don't know.

"Actually, it's Dr. Lieberman. And it's not for me. For my daughter, Celia."

"A wonderful girl," I say in a monotone, exhaling a humungous cloud of smoke.

"Secretary-treasurer of Chess Club," he recites by rote. "Captain of the Debate Team. National Merit Scholar . . ."

"But the Winter Formal's coming up and she's never been," I cut in. It's all so predictable.

Now that Homecoming season's finally winding to a close, Winter Formal season's just starting. I'm almost booked through November.

"Her mother believes—and I agree very strongly—that it's important for Celia's normal maturation process not to miss out."

"When?" I'm all business, not in the slightest interested in any theories of child development, particularly inane ones.

"This Saturday?" he says meekly. I can feel him cringing. "I know it's soon."

Lucky for Lieberman, I've had a sudden cancellation. I sigh. After my latest debacle with the SATs, it seems so pointless to soldier on, but soldier on I must.

"Green Meadow?" I say. "That's in New York."

"I know it's a little far . . ."

"Out of state will run you twenty-five extra."

ACROSS ESTATE LINES

If Havendale Hills is a tad crass, slightly tacky, and nouveau riche, the village of Green Meadow is refined, tasteful, and old money. Big old money. The kind so enormous it not only doesn't brag about it, but doesn't want word to get around. Touching up the sideburns with my trusty electric razor, I cruise in the Beast past the quaint little shops and boutiques, sprinkled here and there with super high-end jewelry stores. There's even a furrier, as in a place that sells furs. You know, like mink coats and dried-up chinchilla carcasses. I've always wondered who the hell actually wears those things.

I'd heard about Westchester County, of course, but even though it's less than an hour away from Pritchard, I've never before had reason to visit. I admire the glittering wares pyramided high like treasure behind shop windows and envy the charmed inhabitants of an almost fairy-tale land, free of drudgery and unfamiliar with want. This is a place of abundance, without thought of cost. When you don't have much of it, everything's about money. But not here in Green Meadow. Because here in Green Meadow, everyone already has everything.

I pass block after manicured block of stately houses on spacious wooded lots, monuments to the rewards of plunder, whether self-acquired or inherited. Glimmering fortresses, inaccessible behind wrought-iron gates, imposing and elegant, seemingly without end.

My iPhone directs me up a long, shaded driveway leading to what some would call a large architectural mélange, but I would call a large architectural mess. You know, all glass and corrugated steel and junk parts and weird angles, but jumbled together. I get out, check myself one last time in the side view mirror, and stroll up the walk to the front door. As I reach for the bell, I hear all this screaming and yelling from inside. I can't make out the words or what it's about, but it sounds bad, real bad, like a season finale of *Breaking Bad* bad.

Despite the potential loss of income and considerable distance already traversed, I'm instantly having serious second thoughts. If you could you hear what I'm hearing, you would too. Guttural animal noises, stuff breaking, footsteps stomping around all over the place. So, having no desire to be the star of my personal slasher flick, I do the logical thing and turn to bolt. Unfortunately, my survival instincts are a fraction too slow.

The door opens and a claw-like appendage shoots out

and latches onto the tail of my suit jacket, which I still owe seven payments on. I'm running in place. If I move away, the semi-fine wool blend will rip. So I stop mid-stride. Trapped.

"Thank God!" says Dr. Harvey Lieberman, staring at me through thick Coke-bottle glasses that magnify his microdot eyes. Harvey looks just the way I pictured he would on the phone. All jittery and twitchy, like a rabbit terrified that any second something bigger's going to squash him, which, in this psycho ward, could be a very real possibility. "We thought you'd never get here."

Harvey smiles weakly. I do too. Even though I go slack and become dead weight, he's able to kind of tilt me over inside. He closes and bolts the door behind us.

"Celia's very excited."

"Yes," I say. Somebody sure as shit is.

The house is just as whacky inside as it is out. Geometric furniture you can't sit on. Grotesque tribal masks, fertility statues, and generally disturbing primitive art. Offbeat—but not in a good way. But the joint is huge, I'll give it that. The Rattigan hovel, by comparison, could easily fit within any number of its high-ceilinged rooms. But that isn't surprising, considering what I'm dealing with. According to my customary exhaustive online research, Harvey Lieberman's a world-renowned neurosurgeon in Midtown Manhattan. You know, the kind that operates on aging actors and deposed dictators, sometimes both at once. Beaucoup bucks.

"I simply don't understand it," says a woman with frizzed-out hair, also wearing big thick glasses, who clunks down the stairs on weird wooden shoes in some flowy caftan thing. "I would have died to have gone to my Winter Formal."

Gayle Dross-Lieberman's a Professor of Child Psychology at the New School for Social Research. And from what I quickly gathered, considered a bit of a quack—even for there. Her big breakthrough? After the weaning process, breast milk can be used for cold cereal and hot cocoa. For real.

The two Liebermans squint cheerfully at me, like the insanity I've just heard is perfectly normal. I regard them quizzically. Without question, they are two of the biggest geeks, if not the biggest, I've ever met in my life. No, the word "geek" doesn't do them justice. They are dweebs.

"Celia," Gayle trills. "Your gallant knight awaits!"

No answer from above. I shrug philosophically. Easy come, easy go. As I inch for the front door, Gayle darts between me and it.

"Harvey, do something!" she demands of her husband.

"Do I have to?" he squeaks.

She gives him a look that gives me the shivers. Harvey shudders.

"Celia, this is your father speaking," he calls up the stairs authoritatively. "Come down right now! I mean it!"

"EAT SHIT!!"

Gayle turns to me apologetically. "She's just a little nervous."

I feel embarrassed for Gayle. At this point I feel embarrassed for all of humanity. I just want to get out of Dodge while the getting's good. Exit stage right. And I will—as soon as Gayle gives me the slightest glimpse of daylight to run.

"Harvey, sweetheart, the unevolved teenage mind requires insight and empathy," she says and, by way of demonstrating, calls up cloyingly. "Honey, Daddy and I only want what's best for you."

No eruption. Both Harvey and me are way impressed. Gayle continues, triumphant, on a roll.

"To build the memories we never got to have. We both missed out going to Winter Formal when we were seniors."

"I couldn't get anyone to say yes," says Harvey, misting up in painful memory.

"I couldn't get anyone to ask me," says Gayle sorrowfully, obviously still traumatized by it.

Looking at them, I can understand why.

"We've regretted not going our whole lives," Gayle says sweetly. "I swore then my daughter would go. I swore if someday I had a daughter, she'd get to dress up in frilly, pretty things and experience all the fun stuff I never got to experience." Suddenly, the mask of motherly solicitude shatters. "I'm not going to let you deprive me of that, damn it!"

"IT'S JUST A STUPID HIGH SCHOOL DANCE! I LOOK RETARDED! I'M NOT GOING! YOU CAN'T MAKE ME!"

Although I am brand-new to the Lieberman family dysfunction, if I was choosing sides, which I'm not, I'd side with Celia. I don't have to see her to know that it's got to be rough being a living do-over for two dweebs who never got to do anything fun in high school. And with good reason.

"DEVELOPMENTALLY CHALLENGED! YOU LOOK DEVELOPMENTALLY CHALLENGED!" Gayle blasts back, insight and empathy out the window. "AND IF YOU DON'T GET YOUR ASS DOWN HERE THIS INSTANT, YOUR CREDIT CARDS ARE CANCELLED AND YOU ARE GROUNDED FOR LIFE!!"

A long, ominous silence. Then, upstairs, a door opens. Gayle beams at me.

"You two kids are going to have such a way cool time, I just know it!"

So this is how Celia Lieberman makes her grand entrance down the stairs and into my life. At first glance, she's pretty much what you'd expect. Frizzed-out hair like Gayle, awkward like Harvey, but not without physical merits. I mean, she wears dippy glasses, but she's got good contours and is just fine—or would be if her makeup wasn't runny and smeared and she wasn't encased in what can only be described as a long pink poofy sack, which Gayle had to have picked out. I mean, there's curlicues and ribbons and crap sticking out all over the place. It belongs in an episode of one of those British shows on PBS, the ones chicks love to watch even though they're set back when women were treated as *chattel*—noun, property. And even then the thing would still suck.

"Oh, don't you look stunning!" Gayle exclaims, clasping her hands. "Doesn't she look stunning, Harvey?"

"She looks radiant," Harvey says, actually meaning it.

"I want you to know that you are psychologically scarring me for eternity," Celia says, then grimly vows, "Someday when you're both old, sick, and feeble I will get you back for this humiliation. You will both pay for this. I will never forgive either of you."

"Yes, you will." Gayle glows. "Someday you'll even thank us."

It's like I'm watching my very own rendition of *Long Day's Journey Into Night* performed for me. I've never seen or read *Long Day's Journey Into Night*, but if I had or I did, this is what I picture it would be like. Aghast, I cough politely.

"Hey, how about a few snapshots for the Lieberman family album?"

– – –

A Prius. In fact, they have two of them. It so figures that all they drive is hybrids. As we putter off in the seriously underpowered vehicle, Gayle and Harvey wave after us from the front door.

"Go wild, kids! Knock yourselves out!"

She ignores me. We drive in stony silence. Although I am at the wheel, I have no clue where I'm going. We reach the corner.

"Left or right on Maple?" I inquire.

"Left," Celia Lieberman says in a choked voice. She huddles miserably against her door, fighting tears, sniffling, wiping her nose on a ludicrous puffy sleeve. Poor kid, she can't help who she was born to any more than me. I'm actually feeling sorry for her. Shows what a sap I am.

"Hey, how about a little music to brighten the mood?" I suggest.

"Hey, how about you shut the hell up?"

What the fuck? Not sure if I've heard her correctly or am simply hallucinating from my ordeal, I switch on the radio. Celia Lieberman immediately snaps it back off.

"What's your problem?"

"You," she snarls like a caged beast. "You're the goddamn problem!"

"*I'm* the goddamn problem?" I can't believe what I'm hearing. If anyone's the injured party in a twisted plot I didn't ask to step into, it's me.

"If you didn't exist, I wouldn't have to be going through this farce!"

"Hey, whose parents called who?" Again, I'm simply astounded by her attitude, not to mention the general tenor of the conversation. I'm just an innocent bystander to her admittedly shitty plight and, considering the bizarro circumstances and tribal art I've been subjected to, she should be thanking her lucky stars I hung around.

"My parents don't know any better. But you! You're pathetic!"

Struggling to maintain my professional composure, I brake the Prius at a stop sign. "Left or right?" I ask.

"Right," she answers.

I turn right, chuckling loudly to myself. "*I'm* the pathetic one? Oh, that's a laugh!"

"What kind of a loser are you, anyway?" she actually has the nerve to say.

"*Me?* I'm the loser here?" I'm beyond indignant.

"I mean, Jesus Christ, there's gotta be better ways to turn a buck."

"I happen to perform a public service," I inform her.

"Oh, I'm sure you do!" she laughs knowingly.

"All of my clients have been extremely satisfied!" I shout, losing it.

"Clients? You mean victims, don't you?" she screams back.

Nose to nose, each of us shaking with rage, we reach a fork in the road.

"LEFT OR RIGHT??!!!"

"RIGHT!!!!"

– – –

By the time we make it to Chez Pierre, this big-deal French steakhouse, Celia Lieberman and I are no longer on speaking terms. I pretty much hate her guts, and the feeling's definitely mutual. But a man's word is his bond, and I resolve to try to make the best of it.

"Look," I say. "I don't like being with you any more than you like being with me. In fact, I don't like even being in the same state with you. But can't we try to get along before we never ever have to see each other again?"

I think it's an exceedingly reasonable offer, but apparently not because when the valet opens Celia Lieberman's door, she leaps out screaming: "STAY AWAY FROM ME, SCUMBAG!"

She storms to the entrance, which two doormen dressed like coachmen impassively swing open for her. Meanwhile, the parking valet's glaring down at me. He's big and giving me the stink eye like he's ready to call the cops on me.

"We're crazy about each other," I reassure him, holding out the fob to the Prius.

He looks less than convinced but takes it. I scurry away before he changes his mind. The doormen do their thing. Inside, the Chez is way fancy: chandeliers, polished wood, and red velvet. When I catch up with Celia Lieberman in the reception area, I'm seething.

"You know, I don't need this crap! I happen to be a very busy guy!"

She stomps on my toe with a spiked heel. As a dignified-looking maître d' in a long coat glides up to greet us,

I'm hopping about on one foot in agony.

"I already had a booking for tonight when your dad called," I hiss at her. "The only reason I said yes was because he sounded so desperate. Now I realize why!"

"You're so full of it!" she says, raising her voice.

"I was doing a good deed for humanity!"

"Is that what you call this?"

"No, I call this torture!"

The maître d's gone all pale, listening. I smile at him.

"Lieberman, reservation for two."

"Right this way, sir." Keeping a safe distance, he warily leads us across the main dining room. Following, Celia Lieberman won't let it go but has to get the last word.

"You made my dad pay an extra twenty-five dollars to lure you out of New Jersey! I heard you guys on the phone!"

"Yes, there was the money too," I'm forced to concede. "But that was a secondary consideration . . ."

"But nothing!" she shouts. "YOU SUCK SHIT!!"

Knives and forks cease their clatter. Staff stops. Seated coifed heads swivel in unison across the length and breadth of the elegant chamber. The majority of them are teenage heads. Girls, all prettified up, and guys, all slicked down, in small clusters at candlelit tables dining before Winter Formal. By the beads of sweat that have suddenly sprouted on Celia Lieberman's forehead, I can tell she knows them all.

"Holy fuck, half my class is here!" she whispers, stricken.

Under the collective scrutiny, her face freezes in a forced, hideous approximation of a smile.

"Quick!" she says out of the corner of her badly painted mouth. "Pretend you like me!"

"I can't!" I spout. "It's beyond my range!"

Celia Lieberman clutches my arm. I can feel she's trembling. The girl's genuinely terrified.

"Please, if anybody finds out the truth about us, I'll be the official joke of senior year!" she pleads, actually going all weak-kneed and unsteady against me. I have to prop her up.

Now I've always considered myself a reasonable person—imperfect, yes, yet all in all, a compassionate sort, fundamentally generous in nature, quick to forgive—but after the abuse I've been taking, I'm sorely tempted to let Celia Lieberman take the fall and roast in the raging fires of high school hell. But I've got a business to run and a so-far unsullied rep to maintain. Besides, I'm afraid she really might faint.

"Promise to mellow out?" I bargain.

Celia Lieberman vigorously nods. I pin on a fiendish grin.

"Smile, darling, it's showtime."

She smiles sickly. I take her clammy little hand in mine and tug her out of the spotlight. We're directed, rightfully so, to the worst table in the entire establishment, exiled in the way, way back, well apart from the others. You know the one, by the hall to the johns. Normally, as part of the package, I'd pull out her chair for her to sit down. But tonight, no way. Celia Lieberman can pull out her own damn chair. Settling in, I scan the menu for the most outrageously expensive combination of items. However much the Liebermans are paying me, it's not nearly enough.

As I decide on the lobster, I catch her sneaking a quick sip from a plastic water bottle filled to the brim with gross orange-colored liquid. By the way she's gagging as she guzzles it down, it can only be one thing.

"Hey, easy there!" I snatch the bottle from her and grimace when I sniff its contents. The fumes alone could make a small- to average-sized person pass out. "What's in here?"

"Carrot juice and vodka."

The concept alone makes me nauseous.

"I like carrot juice," she says.

"Yes," I reply witheringly. "You would."

She snatches back the bottle. "Isn't that what you're supposed to do at these things? Get really drunk and stupid?"

"No, actually, you're supposed to have a good time," I snap. "Now put it away."

"I'm ruined." She takes another slug. "I'm never going to live this down."

I realize she's in a tight spot, but her self-absorption's beyond measure. It bugs me.

"Don't flatter yourself," I huff. "You're not that important. Nobody cares. Nobody notices that you're even here."

Then, right on cue, from around the corner, emerging en masse from the ladies' room, we hear a cadre of gorgeous girls laughing.

"Oh my God, did you see what Celia Lieberman's wearing?" the first one snickers.

I wince. And, if Celia Lieberman weren't so downright unpleasant, I'd attempt a few diverting words, but none come to me.

"I can't believe she's actually with someone," a second beauty cackles.

"I can't believe she's with someone somewhat normal," a third one yucks.

The girls, their backs to us, in short, sleek dresses, sashay to their unpaid dates.

Somewhat normal? What's that supposed to mean? Is it the suit? I knew I should have sprung for the better blend.

"I'm living my worst nightmare," whimpers Celia Lieberman.

– – –

"Green Meadow Country Day Preparatory School, Pre-K through 12," the sign says. Green Meadow Country Prep has the appearance, air, and physical plant of a minor major university, not to mention the tuition of one. Rolling manicured grounds, expansive and park-like. Ivy-draped buildings. Quadrangles. Its own fucking art museum. I note the school logo in smaller gold-plated letters: *Where College Begins At Three.*

I've heard about places like this before, but the reality is sobering—and way off-putting. This is the kind of place where presidents have gone—of IBM, B of A, USA—with every leg up, head start, and unfair advantage money can buy. The finest teachers, the best coaches, the newest and most cutting-edge facilities, no expense spared. A venerable factory, finely tooled and geared to a single objective: getting its graduates into the very best colleges and up those first crucial rungs of the ladder to success. I bet even the food's good. No tuna surprise at Green Meadow Country Prep, more like tuna tartare. Here, I reflect, is my true competition. The kids with the inflated scores and eye-popping experiences. The ones with tutors for everything and college boot camps and guidance counselors who actually care. The ones with the means and connections. Who have it all. The very, very, very fortunate few.

I park the glorified golf cart at the far end of the lot, which looks like a luxury dealership. Rows of Audis, Beamers, Benzes. Not a Buick in sight. Celia Lieberman, who hasn't uttered a sound since I ordered appetizers, just sits there.

"We don't have to go in," I say, not unkindly and more than a little intimidated.

Just to spite me, she gets out. I'm tempted to just drive away, but I don't. Feeling responsible for her, although I don't know why, I get out and follow at a distance.

You know those kids who have it all? Well, they got one more thing I feel compelled to mention. Great genes. Snub noses, straight teeth, zit-free faces. We're in a teeming sea of seriously good-looking people. The guys in tailored suits they aren't paying for in installments, and the girls in shimmery dresses. Hand in hand, carefree and well adjusted, they stream past us toward the dance inside. I despise them on principle, the principle being they have everything I want and don't have. Celia Lieberman, however, does know them and they know her. And Celia Lieberman, if I must say so, looks ridiculous.

"What do you say we just say we went and go hit a movie?" she says, suddenly like we're friends, which we're most definitely not.

"I don't care what we do as long as I get paid in full at the end of it," I declare, even though part of me's longing to venture where I've never been.

"Great. We can sit in different rows . . . ," she says and about-faces to the car.

"We can even see different movies," I heartily agree, right behind.

Then, from the darkness, a voice rings out.

"Celia Lieberman, is that really you?"

Celia Lieberman freezes like a prison escapee caught in the crosshairs. Unlike her, I retain the ability to move. I turn. The voice belongs to a willowy, super put-together girl, smoking a cigarette and sipping champagne in a long-stemmed plastic glass. That's right, champagne, just like we do in Pritchard. Not. The girl teeters toward us on stiletto heels, obviously tipsy.

"Celia Lieberman, *why*, it is you!"

She cracks up as if it's some big joke. Three other figures emerge like visions behind her. I immediately get the distinct feeling they comprise the epicenter of the epicenter, the innermostest crowd. A tall, square-jawed guy who must be her boyfriend. Another guy, even taller and buffer. Definitely jocks, but in a different, more subtle way than I'm used to. Probably some gentleman's sport like squash or lacrosse, I surmise. They're smoking and drinking too. And finally, a second girl. As amazing as the first girl is, she's nothing compared to the second.

Because the second girl's the most beautiful female creature I've ever seen in person. Yeah, I know it's a cliché, but, no lie, she is. Legs that start at the shoulders, with the subtle curves and polished bearing of a top model. Silky, tawny skin, abundantly but unself-consciously displayed in a short spaghetti-strap dress. I can rhapsodize on and on—and will. The lips of Jolie, the sensuality of Alba, the sass of Johansson. But there's something else about her that I find even more alluring. An invisible sheen of confidence, of expecting and being accustomed to only the best life has to offer. Whoever she is, she is class with a capital *C*, the ultimate product of private everything. I'm spellbound.

"I almost didn't recognize you in that incredible dress!" says the first girl to Celia Lieberman.

I can't stop looking at the second girl. I search but can detect no flaws, no defects. She regards me with direct, emerald green eyes, which I get lost in.

"Cassie, leave her alone," she says. "You're not funny."

"Where'd you get it, Celia?" this Cassie chortles. "At a garage sale?"

As for Celia Lieberman, who, in the brief time I've had the misfortune of being acquainted with her, has never been at a loss for words—she hasn't uttered so much as a syllable. Celia Lieberman's a human statue. No, she's a turtle withdrawing into its shell to outlast the storm. A bomb could go off and Celia Lieberman wouldn't react. It's spooky. This is the reality of being Celia Lieberman. No wonder she didn't want to go to the dance.

Suddenly, the taller guy lets out a hairy—and I mean hairy—fart.

"Oh man, do I have to take a wicked dump!" he informs one and all.

"Tommy, you're terrible!" giggles Cassie. "Isn't he terrible, Brent? I don't know how you stand it, Shelby."

"I don't either," says Shelby, looking away from me.

"Yeah, yeah, you love it!" Tommy playfully traps her in his arms and grinds his hips against hers. I regard his mere touch as a desecration of her sanctity. It bothers me that he's with her because he's such a dick, but mostly because I wish I was.

"Bottoms up!" Brent drains his glass then tosses it on the pavement for somebody else to pick up, somebody like me. So do the others.

"C'mon, Celia, let's get this party started!" Cassie links Celia Lieberman's arm and whisks her inside. I tag after them like a mutt, which, let's face it, is what I am.

A NIGHT TO REMEMBER OR FORGET?

The auditorium is way tasteful—two grand pianos in the lobby, hanging chandeliers everywhere you look—but practically the size of Madison Square Garden. Of course the nanosecond we get inside, we get ditched, then Celia Lieberman disappears, which is fine with me. So I just stand there, watching how the rich get down. Now I'm not that into techno so I don't really keep up with the scene, but even I recognize the guy wearing the weasel head onstage working the knobs. Ferret-Face normally headlines big festivals in exotic locales for tens of thousands of people, not to mention dollars. Who knew he also does high school dances for the right price in select suburbs? Anyway, give him credit, the dude's really cooking it. Across the ornate arena, the teenage elite jerk and writhe in a frenzy.

Then, abruptly, our soundtrack for the night slows to a crawl and reaches way, way back, to a bygone day when people knew their places. A remix of vintage Sinatra at his most yearning and romantic. But with a bangin' backbeat. Seizing the opportunity to rub close, couples intertwine in response. I focus on Tommy, who envelops Shelby into his strong arms and gracefully twirls and dips her to the lilting melody. It pains me to admit it but, asswipe that he is, the dude's not bad on his toes. Years of lessons will do that. But I don't care about him, just Shelby. The only thing hotter than a total babe is a total babe shaking it. And Shelby sure knows how. I flinch and duck like a punch-drunk boxer at every swish of her skimpy skirt. I'm telling you, I'm ready to bust.

Plus, I could swear she's smiling at me the whole time. But it can't be me. We haven't even met. I look around. There's no one behind or on either side of me. It has to be me. I gawk idiotically back. For a fleeting, heart-stopping instant, we lock eyes and, at least on my end, sparks are flying. Then, wouldn't you know it, Celia Lieberman reappears, tugging on my sleeve.

"I want to go home," she says.

Go? We can't go. I know that Celia Lieberman's not having a good time, but she seems like the type who never has a good time anywhere. There's no way I'm going now, not when I've just been definitely smiled at and possibly flirted with by a divine being mega–zip codes out of my league. Fuck no. I'm staying put. So, to humor Celia Lieberman, I resort to truly drastic measures.

"I don't suppose you want to dance?" I ask. "I'm actually not half bad."

"I want to go," she repeats doggedly.

The song speeds up and so do the dancers. Taking Celia Lieberman's hand, I steer her into the churning thick of it. "C'mon, don't be such a wuss!" I shout above what is becoming an eardrum-popping roar. I box step us within gaping distance of Shelby.

"LEMME GO!" screams Celia Lieberman.

But on the dance floor, as in outer space, no one can hear you. Not taking any chances, I unfurl Celia Lieberman in a double cross-body lead, which I follow up with a nifty reverse turn.

"WHAT ARE YOU DOING?" she shouts.

Thankfully the thunderous electronic music drowns her out. And with all the colored laser beams and lights erupting, it's hard to see. Suddenly, Tommy swoops past in tight lockstep with Shelby. Grinning, the show-off unleashes a double inside-out move, yo-yoing Shelby in circles. Like I said, he's not bad. All right, he's good, damn good. But I'm better.

"C'mon Celia, show us what you and your new boyfriend can do!" Tommy gloats.

Bristling at the challenge, I whip Celia Lieberman in complex patterns, back and forth, in and out, fucking sideways. I've got her spinning like a top.

"HELPPPPPPP!" yelps Celia Lieberman.

Not to be undone, Tommy lifts Shelby. She spreads her sinuous wings like a swan as he whirls her above his head in a gracefully executed maneuver I've never seen, let alone attempted before. The guy's been watching way too much *Dancing with the Stars*. But my back's up.

"NOOOOOOOOOoooooo!!!" Celia Lieberman's face contorts in horror, knowing what's next.

Too late. Competitive juices flowing, I hoist Celia Lieberman over my head like a Russian weight lifter and rotate too. She's no feather, lemme tell you, and sure as hell no swan. I'm sweating and gasping as around and around we go. Centrifugal force kicks in. Everything gets blurry. I mean, I'm doing the steering and I'm getting dizzy. I can't imagine how it's going up there.

Finally, my strength gives out. I release Celia Lieberman back to somewhat solid ground, where she doesn't stick her landing but wobbles wildly, veering off-balance smack into Tommy.

"Hey, watch it, bitch!" blurts Mr. Charm-School Graduate, letting go of Shelby.

Celia Lieberman stumbles toward him. Her cheeks are bulging way out. Her eyes cross behind her glasses. Her hands clutch her stomach. I can trace the path of the coming eruption from there to her throat. So can Tommy.

"Oh fuck," he croaks.

I won't dwell on the gory details. The trajectory, duration, and velocity of the Day-Glo-orange spume. All are extreme. The chunks, globs, and rivulets that drench and dribble down all over Tommy. There are many. The shock and humiliation that ensue. Tremendous. Yes, my friends, these are the moments we live for.

– – –

I knew Celia Lieberman had been drinking, but not how much she'd been drinking. I unclasp her purse and take out the water bottle. It's three-quarters empty. I gag at the sight of the little that's left. Carrot juice and vodka. Either in large quantities is toxic. Together in large quantities, they are lethal. Especially when the person who consumed said copious amounts is being tossed like a salad around the dance floor. To some degree—okay, to a large degree—I share the blame. Trying to make amends, I tap softly on the door to the girls' room again. I've been waiting outside it going on a good ten minutes now.

"Celia, you okay?"

From inside, I am greeted by retching and heaving sounds that have me seriously considering dialing 911 and calling for an ambulance. I snap to as a flock of babes approaches for a touch-up and a tinkle. I feel it my chivalric duty to save Celia Lieberman from further scandal and them from a sight and olfactory experience they will never be able to forget.

"I wouldn't go in there if I was you," I say. Catching a whiff and my drift, they collectively turn high-heel and clomp away. I steel my senses for what I'm about to do. For I can no longer obey Celia Lieberman's repeated wishes for me to fuck off; I have go in there and rescue Celia Lieberman from herself. For what remains of her social reputation and my future financial one. Then, just as I'm about to embark into the unknown, a sultry voice stops me.

"Distant cousins, right?"

I know who it is before I turn. And it is. And up close, even more mesmerizing. Toking on a joint, Shelby appraises me openly, seriously.

"Cousins?" I repeat, at a loss at her impossible perfection.

"That's how you and Celia Lieberman are related."

She offers me the blunt. I take what I hope is a suave drag. My heart's pounding, my nether regions pumping. She has that effect on me. But I play it cool.

"We're not related," I report.

"Friend of the family then?" she asks, her emerald eyes tantalizingly near to mine.

"Nope. Sorry."

I want to reach out and touch her to make sure she's real and not some hallucination I'm having from bad breadsticks. Everything about her is top of the line. Her slender figure, the sleek, elegant cut of the designer dress that fits impeccably, the way she's not overdone like the others because magnificence like hers needs no enhancement. That would be plenty, but there's more. Her sophistication, her forthright manner. This is a girl who's done things and been places I can't even imagine. This is the complete package.

"So what gives?" she asks.

"Gives?" I extend the jay back to her.

"What's somebody like you doing with somebody like

Celia Lieberman at Winter Formal?"

She stares into my soul, searching for the answer. I meet her gaze, too entranced to feel the guilt I should.

"If you must know, I happen to be with Celia Lieberman at Winter Formal because I like Celia Lieberman," I lie through my smiling teeth.

"You like Celia Lieberman?"

"I find Celia Lieberman delightful."

Then, exhibiting her usual impeccable timing, Celia Lieberman lets out a hair-raising volley of gut-wrenching dry heaving and wet spewing like you've never heard. I've always been squeamish, so I want to sit down. Shelby, however, doesn't bat a professionally teased eyelash.

"That's what I told the others," she says. "Celia's a major brainiac. I said you had depth. I said you recognized her hidden qualities."

Hidden to me, that's for certain. But I shrug modestly, which I hope only increases my mystery to her.

"Somehow I think there's more to you than meets the eye," she says.

"You have no idea," I can honestly state.

She holds out a polished hand, introducing herself.

"Shelby Pace."

"Brooks Rattigan."

Our fingers spark from static electricity as we touch to shake hands. We both laugh, startled. It must be fate. Then Tommy, having shed his puke-soaked shirt and jacket, storms bare-chested out of the men's room. He's got the abs, pecs, glutes, and guns of a male stripper. Normally this would set off the red alerts for me to back off, but I'm too far gone.

"C'mon baby," he snarls. "Let's blow this shithole."

He reaches for her, but she springs back.

"Get away, Tommy! You stink!"

Then, cool as can be, she smiles back to me.

"Brooks, I'm having an after-party. Why don't you and Celia come?"

"Shelby, have you lost it?" Tommy yammers, wiping his chiseled torso with soggy paper towels. "I don't want that freak coming within fifty feet of me."

"Thanks, but I really don't think Celia's up to it," I say, reluctantly stating the obvious.

"You heard him!" Tommy agrees. "Let's book!"

"Look, you can't take Celia home like that," Shelby says to me, ignoring Bluto. "She can sleep it off at my place."

It's the excuse I've been praying for. I mean, I have to park Celia Lieberman somewhere. I can't take her home in this severely altered state, for her sake as well as mine. Going to the after-party is providing a service to the client. Celia Lieberman can sleep it off, thereby avoiding certain parental meltdown, harsh punishment, not to mention me having to explain things. It's the best possible rationalization.

"In that case, we'd love to."

"Awesome. You can follow us."

Tommy impatiently beeps the horn to his stepdad's Rolls. That's right, as in Rolls-Royce. I've never seen one in person before.

"Move it, douche bag!" He's referring to me. The Rolls is at the head of a caravan of ultra-luxury motor vehicles, all with their lights shining, idling, snaking across the parking lot. Shelby, checking her lip gloss in the mirror, is unamused.

"Oh, Tommy, grow up."

She leans out her window, smiling.

"Take your time, Brooks!"

Gasping, I dump Celia Lieberman in a limp heap in the front seat of the Prius. I'm winded and aching. She's snoring, totally checked out, and it's been a brutal haul to the car all the way from the ladies' room, which is actually more like a lounge with a leather couch and real cotton towels. I've been trashed in my time, but I've never before been as trashed or seen anyone as trashed as Celia Lieberman is. She's one for the books.

"*I'm* the loser?" I say to myself. "Ha!"

As I buckle her in, she burps right in my face. Lovely.

Shelby's spread is way out in the country. You know, down wooded lanes, past bucolic meadows and brooks, over hills and dales, whatever dales are. And when I say spread, I mean spread. There are barns and stables, like for horses and shit, multiple tennis courts, and what's that? A fucking helipad! Bringing up the rear of the procession, my eyes widen when I get my initial gander of what appears at the end of the long, winding road that is the driveway. The thing's gigantic, with wings and too many rooms to count. This is no mere mansion but a manor, a veritable estate with the sprawling grounds to match. Despite its excessive size and utter lack of social responsibility, it's remarkably unostentatious, tasteful, and old-school, like a plantation back in the glory days when slavery was out in the open. Whatever. This is the real thing. The fabled bastion of WASP privilege, which supposedly no longer exists but is actually going gangbusters. I've made it to the Promised Land.

And it's all Shelby's. The girl who has everything has even more. I know material things shouldn't matter, especially for those of us who don't have material things. So sue me if there's nothing more to me if you scratch the surface and I'm superficial, but material things do matter, and they make Shelby's already sky-high desirability quotient rocket off the charts. She can't be possible, but she is.

Ravenous teenagers stampede past Shelby's mom and dad to a fancy catered banquet, complete with serving stations and waiters in black ties offering trays of delicacies. Both parents look young for their age, fit and with it, in T-shirts and jeans. Dad's square jaw handsome, Mom's way smokin', the definition of a MILF. Shelby's furious to see them.

"Mummy, Daddy, upstairs right now!" she commands.

"But honey," demurs Daddy, no doubt some huge hedge-fund titan who's ripped off the common rabble for billions. "We want to meet your friends . . ."

The adult Paces do a double take when they get a load of me staggering in with Celia Lieberman slung like a sack of flour over my shoulder.

"But sweetheart," ventures Mummy, who probably runs her own fashion empire or the family philanthropic foundation or both.

"DID YOU NOT HEAR ME??!!!" Shelby thunders, going ape-shit. Man, I'd hate to get on her bad side.

Just then, Tommy stalks past on his way to shower, down to his bikini briefs, which I have to admit he can actually pull off. Mummy and Daddy look at him, at me again, aghast, then at each other, then at their daughter, who sternly points upstairs. Both pillars of high society meekly obey, ascending from view. Shelby smiles at me, switching back on to gracious hostess mode.

"C'mon, Brooks," she directs. "You can park Celia by the pool."

— — —

There are actually two pools on the premises: one outdoors, out of commission for the winter, and one in. The innie's a sleek lap pool beneath a glass atrium, aglow in the shimmer of starlight. How can one person have so much cool stuff? The mind boggles. I deposit Celia Lieberman in a jumble on a lounge chair, position her in a comfortable pose, then subtly stretch my back, which is having a minor seizure from the sustained load.

"You have an indoor pool?" I remark like an imbecile.

"Doesn't everyone?" Shelby crinkles her pert nose adorably. She knows she's irresistible, which should be a turnoff, but not on her. Nothing is. I'm even more bewitched.

"Not where I'm from," I stammer.

"Where are you from? How come I've never seen you around?"

She looks at me. I'm on the spot. How should I answer? Definitely some radically edited version of the truth, but how radically? Just then, Tommy spurts from the surface of the pool, flapping his arms, yelping like a walrus.

"ARFFFF! ARFFFF!" What style. What wit.

"Tommy!" Shelby frowns. "You scared the shit out of me!"

"I can't believe you let those deadbeats in here," Tommy says, like I'm not there and I don't exist, which I don't to him. He vaults from the water. Why is it that the biggest jerks are always so damn big? I'm just under six feet and tip the scales at about 170 and change, but he's got at least four inches and twenty pounds on me. And it's all rock-hard muscle. The guy's totally ripped. Extra-wide shoulders, tapered torso, washboard abs. A swimmer's body. Then it hits me.

"Water polo!" I gasp.

"Captain," he grins.

To me, water polo's one of those totally useless Olympic sports, like synchronized anything and curling, that have no reason for being. Those dippy caps they wear with the round padded things for the ears. What's that about? And those G-strings they wear for uniforms? Please. It so figures. But the point is that even though I'd love to flip some shit to Tommy and even though he deserves to be flipped, considering his size, it's not advisable.

"Tommy, you're all wet!" squeals Shelby in displeasure. "Get away!"

She darts from his dripping embrace. He lumbers after her, a buff Frankenstein monster.

"You love it!"

— — —

Everything's grandiose, oversized, out of proportion to what I'm used to. Each room its own museum, crammed with rare antiques. And, incredibly, none of it's off limits. Kids are partying everywhere, in various stages of carnal embrace, drinking, toking, sniffing illegal substances. The lights are low, the music thumps.

I check out the art on the walls. Even though I know less than nothing about art, even I recognize the signature styles of the paintings. The paint-splotch dude. The fuzzy-horizontal-stripes guy. The guy who does all the little dots. I do know enough to know that each is priceless.

And together worth the annual GNP of many small Third World countries. Then, hanging in a place of supreme honor over the mantelpiece, I come upon a portrait of a naked chick with tremendous knockers with her square head up her triangular ass. I peer at the name scrawled across the bottom corner. Somebody pinch me. It's a real Picasso, sticker price in the millions, and just small enough to tuck under my arm. For a second I'm seized by an overwhelming impulse to grab it and hightail it to the tropics. But then I see visions of Interpol and Turkish prisons, and the temptation passes.

"Chicken sat-aye," announces a voice with a reassuringly familiar broad affect. It belongs to a weary, middle-aged waitress with big hair who holds out a tray of appetizers to me. I look at her blankly.

"Chicken sat-aye in a peanut cumin sauce," she, again, mispronounces.

"Hi, I'm from Joisey!" mimics Brent, busy pawing Cassie on a couch.

Howls of laughter. The waitress, who is just trying to do her shit job, does have the thick, classic accent. She turns away from me, muttering, "Rich assholes."

She thinks I'm one of them. To my eternal discredit, I let her. Slipping away through the crowd, I decide to do a little research and Google the Paces on my iPhone. What pops up doesn't surprise me. Hunter Pace does run a mega–hedge fund, sits on the board of numerous major start-ups, and has indeed ripped off the masses for billions. Gretchen

Pace doesn't oversee a fashion empire but does possess a Yale law degree, which she apparently puts to ample use as head of various task forces against multiple forms of social injustice. Nothing like crusading against oneself, I muse. By the way, there is no family philanthropic foundation.

"You like Modigliani?" I hear Shelby inquire.

She's suddenly reappeared, standing beside me so close I can breathe her mother's best French perfume. And, boy, the stuff really works. I'm intoxicated. Shelby's referring to yet another painting I've been drooling over by some other famous artist whose name I should know, but don't.

"The long sinuous necks, vulva-shaped eyes, his unadorned depiction of pubic hair," she observes. "I think it's so sensual, don't you?"

Actually, at the moment, I am thinking of the bloody fortune it must cost to insure everything just for a year.

"Plus, ever see a picture of him?" she asks. "Total hunkster."

"Oh, yeah, Modie's great, one of my all-time favorites," I opine sagely.

"I should have known you'd be into art," she says. "Any guy who'd go out with Celia Lieberman has to have real substance. Not like Tommy. He's so deeply shallow."

"That's me," I state, continuing my search for any sort of physical imperfection on any part of her. "I'm all about substance."

"Unafraid to go against the crowd," she projects. "A man among boys."

"Right again," I say modestly.

"So where have you been my whole life?"

"New Jersey?" I venture.

Shelby laughs, thinking I'm kidding. I fervently wish I were. How can you be ashamed of an entire state? Somehow I am.

"No, really," she says.

"Actually, I . . . I live in the City."

"Lucky. I love the City. Where do you go?"

"Where do I go?" I'm spit-balling here, marveling how I just pulled the City out of my butt.

"To school, silly. Dalton? Collegiate? Trinity?"

I blink at her several times, at a loss. Then . . .

"The Electra School."

"Interesting name. Electra. The daughter of Agamemnon who blackmailed her brother Orestes to avenge their father's murder by viciously killing their mother."

"And here I thought it was just a kind of Buick," I say weakly.

She laughs again. She thinks I'm a riot.

"I'm surprised I haven't heard of it."

"That's because it's very small and very new. In the Village. Very experimental. Very out there." Man, am I good.

"Where in the Village? I'm down there all the time."

Jesus, I think, give it up already. What difference does it make? But it clearly does to her.

"Uh, there's no building." I grimace. That is so lame.

"Your school doesn't have a building?" She gives me a sideways look.

This is going badly. I can feel myself losing her.

"No, every day we just move around from place to place." I close my eyes, convinced I've just jumped the shark. You know, taken that one extra step too far, like plunging-off-a-cliff far.

"Wow, that is out there," she says doubtfully, but sort of buying it.

Then, out of the blue, I am rocked by a thunderbolt of inspiration.

"Actually, I'm homeschooled."

Her expression relaxes. I've struck pay dirt. Homeschooling's elegant in its simplicity. Very "in" these days, plausible, and most important of all, virtually unverifiable. Once again, I'm truly blown away by my own bullshit.

"Really had me going there," she chuckles, apparently still intrigued and entertained by me.

Things are going dashingly. More than dashingly. Because it's just now registering that Shelby has said the words "vulva" and "pubic" during the course of our conversation. With a portent like this, there's no telling where the night might lead . . .

"AHHHHHHHHHHHHHHH!!!!!"

It's a horrifying cry. The cry of a wounded animal.

The cry of Celia Lieberman.

– – –

125

I sprint back to the pool and find a Roman orgy. Teenagers in the all together, making out in the Jacuzzi, mooning—your basic indecent frolicking and cavorting. And in the center of it all, Celia Lieberman, curled up on the chaise lounge, wide-eyed in terror, as right before her, the entire first line of the Green Meadow Country Prep hockey team, hairy parts and beefy cheeks exposed, take turns belly flopping, engaged in fierce competition for most humungous crater. Even I cringe at the horrific view.

Seeing me, Celia Lieberman scrambles from the chair and across the tile my way.

"Where did you take me?" she hisses.

"We're at Shelby Pace's after-party," I say under my breath, pulling her to her feet. "Chill out. It's nothing you haven't seen before!"

But her stricken expression tells me I'm very wrong. She has just seen something—numerous somethings, in fact—that she's never seen before. Everyone who's anyone at Green Meadow Country Prep is watching us, cracking up. Celia Lieberman goes white as a sheet.

"You let me be the main attraction at Shelby Pace's after-party?"

I duck as she takes a swing at me.

— — —

Celia darts out the front door. I scramble through the crush after her, only to be intercepted by Shelby who, get this, has changed into a string bikini that leaves even less for my already over-revved imagination to imagine. Let's just say it clings and accentuates the way a string bikini's supposed to cling and accentuate.

"Leaving so soon?" she purrs.

"Uh, Celia's not feeling too good," I state in the understatement of the century. "Thanks for letting us crash here."

I hold out my hand to shake a tragic farewell. She wraps it in both of hers and doesn't let go.

"Maybe I'll see you around, Brooks."

"Doubtful. I don't get out of the City much." I'm heartsick. I know I will never see her again, let alone see her again in a string bikini.

"In that case . . ."

She leans forward and gives me the softest, sexiest, most playful, most frustrating kiss I've ever received. Exquisite tongue work. Although it's unmanly, I'm literally weak at the knees. It takes me more than a few moments to remember to show token resistance.

"Uh, uh," I mumble. "Got to go. Celia . . ."

"Nice meeting you."

— — —

As we drive, I don't dare turn on the radio, not after what happened last time I tried. But I can't listen to Celia Lieberman anymore. She's huddled against her door, sniffling back tears and snot in regular intervals. I'm in a pretty foul mood myself. The taste of Shelby's citrus-flavored gloss still tingles on my lips, and it's a tart, tantalizing taste that I sadly will partake of no more. But that dipshit Tommy will.

"I had to take you somewhere," I snap, having had enough. "You were in no condition to go home. I was doing you a favor."

She whirls at me, her face a soggy, streaky mess.

"So you made me a laughingstock!"

"Look, I'm sorry," I say, meaning it. "I didn't realize you had that much to drink."

"I NEVER WANT TO SEE YOU AGAIN!" she shouts.

"DON'T WORRY, YOU WON'T!" I return, as good as I get, braking sharply. We've reached the welcome conclusion of our wretched time together not a second too soon. I hurriedly climb out to complete my duties and swiftly escort her to the bitter but happily liberating end. But Celia Lieberman bolts from the car to the front door, which is whisked open before she can reach it by her clueless, beaming parents in their jammies. His have padded feet.

"So? Tell! Tell! Who was wearing what?" Gayle glows. "How was it?"

"YOU'VE DESTROYED MY LIFE!!" Celia Lieberman shrieks at them, shaking the walls, and then she stomps up the stairs to her room. Her door slams, shaking the walls again.

Harvey and Gayle, amazingly unfazed, turn to me expectantly. If even this doesn't warrant the parental sirens going off then I shudder to think what's considered abnormal in this house.

"Celia had a little too much to drink . . . ," I grimace by way of explanation.

"Celia was drinking?" says Harvey, shocked.

"*Our* Celia was drinking!" exclaims Gayle, clasping her hands.

"Gayle, really!" he says, scandalized.

"Oh, can it, Harvey! It's totally age appropriate!"

They look at me eagerly, wanting more details.

"Carrot juice and vodka," I inform them.

For a moment, even they recoil at the combination.

"Good God!" says Harvey.

"She threw up," I report reluctantly. "A whole lot."

"Good God!" repeats Harvey, only more emphatic. Gayle elbows him hard in ribs, making him double over, then refocuses her scarily enthusiastic gaze on me.

"And then what happened?"

I had been expecting any number of reactions to Celia Lieberman's dire, disheveled state. Outrage. Threats of the police. Demands for a refund. This is not one of them.

"Well, then we went to an after-party," I continue.

Gayle literally hops up and down in joy.

"Hear that, Harvey?" she squeals in girlish delight. "Our Celia had too much to drink, threw up a whole lot, and went to an after-party!"

"And this is a positive thing?" Harvey asks, mildly encouraged but understandably confused.

"Cataclysmic!" The woman's eyes are shining. "Our daughter's participated in a normal rite of adolescence!"

She gets all weepy and emotional. So does he. They take turns hugging me. I pretty much have to peel them off.

Harvey wants to give me a seventy-five-dollar bonus. Gayle insists he make it an even hundred.

GETTING PERSONAL

Verbal's up sixty points.

At first thought I'm flooded with relief as I stare in the still night at my glowing screen. I've been dreading just this moment for fifteen interminable days, the time it takes the fascists at the ETS to supposedly process and post scores. Personally, I think they turn them over in twenty-four hours, then get off on making millions of unbalanced kids twist in the wind. I was so sure I tanked. Yeah, I know everyone feels that way, but I really, *really* felt that way. But there it is in blue and white pixels. Sixty points. Sixty points may not be a giant leap for mankind, but it's a gigantic step for me. I overflow with gratification, brim with self-congratulation. All those pointless drills, exercises, and sacrifices at last had a point. Sixty of them! Seven-twenty Verbal, baby! Didn't think I had it in me. I reflect on that bastard Farkus. On the pain and humiliation I suffered. And suddenly the five hundred bucks doesn't sting so bad. Though if I ever see the runt again, his ass is mine.

But then second thoughts arrive, as they always do. Sixty points, as miraculous as it undoubtedly is, is not seventy-five points. Strack, who is never wrong, said seventy-five. Sixty, together with my math, puts me in the lower-mids. Columbia's median is the mid-mids. Seventy-five would have just put me there. Sixty barely touches the bottom fringes of the accepted range, down with the athletes, billionaire offspring, and legacies, the difference, of course, being they're athletes, billionaire offspring, and legacies. End result? Rattigan comes up just short again. Close but no cigar. My pathetic existence in an answer bubble. I fill with bitterness and self-pity. For the want of a few measly percentiles, my potentially Promising Future comes crashing down.

Fortunately for me, third thoughts creep in. What is it they say? Hope springs eternal? I grasp at straws. So what if I'm marginal? Theoretically, cold hard numbers are only part of the Admissions Equation. There are always the Intangibles. Every college catalog's replete with them. The mythic figures who defy the odds, who break the mold. The functional illiterate who launched a massive website in his bedroom, the girl who discovered the cure for cancer in her spare time when she wasn't working to support her starving family, the Nobel Peace Prize nominee at fifteen, and most *apocryphal*—adjective, of dubious authority—the kid who wrote seven-fifty words or less so sensitive, so moving, yet so understated, that the lives of even the most jaded members of the Admissions Committee were forever altered and all normal criteria unanimously and unceremoniously cast to the winds.

I will have to be that kid.

Which means it's back to the damn Application. It all comes down to the damn Application. My Short Answers are answered, spell-checked, and buffed to a luster. Which leaves the all-important, all-impossible Personal Essay. According to books on the subject, of which there is an astounding abundance, a great Personal Essay has to jump out at you. Unfortunately, so far, mine have kind of limped around. For the past month, I've struggled mightily for Worthy Topics. Racked my most distant memories for Major Misfortunes, Character Building Episodes, or Moments of Supreme Clarity, scoured the darkest recesses of my mind for examples of my own selflessness. The best I can come up with is the time I found some guy's wallet on the ground and returned it to him even though it had forty-three dollars in it. For a week or so, I explore the subject of my mom skipping out before I ever got a chance to know her, but, as a rule, I try not to ever really think about that because when I do it gets me all pissed off and bummed out, which I ultimately decide is way too personal for a Personal Essay.

Everybody has their Thing to make them Stand Out in some way. Drinking problems, domestic violence, self-mutilation. Again I curse myself for not being more messed up. I read about one guy who actually wrote about having a really big complex about having a really small dick. Now there's an Attention Grabber, though I'm relieved to report he was rejected everywhere, even his Safety, and is currently manning the register at his local Wendy's. There's always the Nobility of Minimum Wage and Starting At the Very-Very Bottom, subjects in which I am much too well versed, but Poverty's been done to death and besides, nobody wants to hear it. Maybe I should express my desire to earn an Ivy League degree that costs a bloody ransom in order to volunteer in the Peace Corps and serve those who have it even shittier than me? Yeah, that's the ticket. Doing Good for Others never goes out of style.

Columbia says it doesn't matter when you get your application in as long it's by the Due Date, which is tomorrow at 5:00 p.m. But the fact is, I should have submitted mine weeks ago. Anecdotally, the earlier you get your application in for Early Decision, the infinitesimally better your chances. Due to my own ineptitude and indecisiveness, I've pushed it as far as I can push it. Whatever I come up with now is going to have to be It.

Thus, I reach the grim conclusion that since I'm not extraordinary in any definable or measurable way, my Thing is going to have to be being super good at being a super do-gooder. And since I'm actually not so good at that either, I'm pretty much going to have to make something up. And quick.

Easier said than done. One more minor detail. Like so many countless other things, creative writing's not exactly a major talent either. In English classes of past, my literary efforts have been ridiculed and ripped to shreds, which doesn't help the already flagging self-confidence. The hours tick past in unrecoverable tiny increments. The blank screen taunts me to fill it. Maybe I don't have a Thing. What if I'm Thingless? I pace, I get jittery. The walls close in. To settle my nerves, I decide to partake in a surreptitious toke or two on one of Charlie's finest that I've swiped and hidden away for extreme occasions such as this.

– – –

One thing I gotta say for the old man, he smokes primo shit. To get the muses going, I cut to the chase and opt for tried-and-true mood music for my sorely needed flight of fancy. Thirteen minutes and two and a half tracks into *Dark Side of the Moon* on my headsets later, I am transfixed by the rapidly changing star patterns on my screen saver. I'm winging through the cosmos, weightlessly floating past ringed planets, psychedelic constellations, and swirling black holes as electric guitars are flailing. You know that song, "Time"? Yeah, you know the one. All those clocks are ticking faster and faster and faster, then all of a sudden they all start to ring at the same time, so loud you feel like your head's going to split in two like an overripe watermelon? Yeah, that one. Well, that's when it happens, that's when Little Billy emerges in fully hatched glory in my thoroughly baked consciousness.

Little Billy, as in the little blind crippled kid whom I've so heroically and thanklessly mentored through the years.

I fantasize that I first met Little Billy when Little Billy got trapped in a crosswalk after the light turned green. Nobody waits the like two seconds it would take Little Billy to get across, nobody cuts the poor kid a break. No, traffic blasts all around Little Billy, stranded in the middle of the intersection, stumbling helplessly in circles with his little cane. It's just a matter of nanoseconds before poor Little Billy's going to be lunch meat. People are always in such a rush, rush, rush to get nowhere, you know? So I have to do what anybody with a heart and conscience would do. Alas, there are so few of us. Risking life and limb, yours truly dashes into the line of fire and conducts Little Billy through a barrage of vehicles to sanctuary. That's right, I save his disabled behind. Me, that's who, because nobody else would. Which makes me exceptionally exceptional, if I do say so myself.

As the Floyd drones majestically on and on and on, so do my fingers, nimbly dancing across the keyboard to my laptop, almost in a trance. For this is just the beginning of my and Little Billy's mutually rewarding relationship. You see, after I dry Little Billy's little tears and buy him a large Tofutti with my last few hard-earned cents, I lead him home to the shabby rent-controlled apartment he shares with his overwhelmed, zoned-out single mom. It doesn't take a Steve Jobs to deduce that Little Billy desperately needs a Man In His Life and a Suitable Role Model. So, while my peers get to play varsity sports or build up their college applications by climbing Mount Kilimanjaro or paying through the orthodontured teeth for after-school seminars with Pulitzer Prize winners, I schlep Little Billy to his doctors, of which he has tons, to ball games, where I have to patiently give him the play-by-play, and to concerts in the park, which Little Billy especially enjoys because he can hear okay even if he can't see jack shit. When I finally get my license, I drive Little Billy to the beach. I teach the little fucker to swim.

But it isn't all fun and s'mores. I still choke up when I recall the time we almost lost Little Billy to that bad mortadella that he couldn't see was turning green along the edges. When all seems lost and it looks like there's going to be a complete loss of kidney function, I volunteer to donate one of mine. It turns out not to be necessary, which is a good thing because our organs don't match, but, by God, I was willing.

On my headsets, drums are crashing and electric organs pumping. I am on a monster roll, totally working it. For a precious paragraph or so—have to watch the ol' word count—I toy around with killing off Little Billy with some obscure, gruesome medical complication or equally horrific subway accident that may or may not have been deliberate on his part. Between you and me, as Little Billy and I age together, I am finding his incessant whining and endless wants to be seriously eroding the old love life, even if it is just as imaginary as my present one. I mean, girls don't exactly think it's a turn-on at the movies when there's a blind crippled kid constantly tugging at them, demanding to know what just happened. Of course, I don't render Little Billy's tragic demise so crudely. No, I am devastated, thoroughly grief-stricken—in fact so devastated, so thoroughly grief-stricken that, in a supremely benevolent gesture, I relent, do some major backspacing, and allow Little Billy to keep his wretched existence. Don't want to end the Personal Journey on a Down Note. And I am so glad Little Billy survives and Battles the Odds to this day. For I am inspired and will no doubt continue to be inspired by Little Billy and the Incredible Challenges he faces and overcomes on a daily basis. Mostly, I'm so glad I'm not Little Billy. I don't say that. But I do express the deeper message of my tale of someone else's woe. It's from the next-to-last Beatles song on *Abbey Road*, their last great album. Always good to sprinkle in Cultural References, don't you know. How in the end, you basically Get What You Give. And, brother, ain't it the truth.

That undeserved B+ in AP English that should have been an A– is inconsequential, I write with passion. My cup runneth over, compared to the crummy one Little Billy got served up. I'm blinking back tears as I shakily tap the last few finishing touches. Suffused with Love for All Humanity, but mostly with my own inherent goodness, I drift off into the untroubled sleep of the saintly or, in my particular case, the so-so trashed.

Needless to say, I am out like a light, dead to the planet until like two or three the next afternoon. Fortunately for me, it's some sort of federal holiday and there's no school. I groggily roll out of bed to take a mega-extended leak. For once, Charlie's up before me, and he's entertaining guests in his underwear when I stagger into the kitchen for rapid hydration of acute dry mouth. Two guys, wearing socks with sandals and sprouting tufts of hair in all the wrong places, huddle on either side of him at the counter.

"A Zap Plymell number twelve," squeals Number One. "Somebody pinch me!"

"Only 953 were ever printed," flutters Number Two. "I've actually got goose bumps!"

Comic-book geeks, what else. Middle-aged stoners whose mental development hit a wall at sixteen. Walking, wheezing cautionary tales. Just like Charlie, only unlike Charlie, they never went to Harvard or got to have a day in the sun. I'm semi-accustomed to their sporadic pilgrimages here. I'm not sure if I've mentioned it before or not, but Charlie's apparently got some to-die-for comic book collection. Not that I care. Whatever Charlie's into, I make it a point to be out of.

"Toldja it was worth the drive," gloats One to Two.

"Can I touch it?" Two tentatively asks Charlie.

"Not a chance," snaps Charlie, cradling the sacred artifact in white-gloved hands. "Bad enough you're breathing your germs on it."

The object of reverence is a primitive yellow-and-blue booklet encased in acid-free plastic. Charlie gingerly slides it back into its slot on custom-built shelves that fill an entire wall of our small living room.

"Do you have any conception what this would bring on eBay?" Two gushes.

"Last March, a Fair-condition Zap Plymell number twelve pulled down almost seven hundred," responds Charlie, who spends endless hours online tracking fluctuations because he has nothing better to do with what passes for his life. "Granted, the market's gone down considerably since then, but mine's Very Good to Fine."

"Possibly Gem!" pipes One.

"*Mr. Natural* up two and a third," I mutter, rattling off the titles of obscure underground comics that only gnomes like them would recognize, let alone appreciate, unable to suppress my scorn even in my fog. "*Fabulous Furry Freak Brothers* down half a point, *Two-Fisted Zombies* off one and an eighth . . ."

"Go ahead, scoff!" says Charlie, taking great umbrage. "But someday when you're the recipient of a minor but still significant fortune, you'll change your tune. Only I won't be around for you to thank me."

"Keep dreaming, Charlie," I yawn, having heard it a gazillion times. I open the fridge.

"Only wish I had bought more as a kid," Charlie reflects, daintily pulling off his gloves by the tips. "But Mom and Dad knew better. They said comics were a complete waste of time."

I grab the carton of juice, which, besides ketchup, mustard, and a jar of moldy pickles, is just about the only thing inside, and instantly feel that it's weightless, hollow, as in empty. So typical. So Charlie.

"Charlie, when we're out of juice, please throw away the carton," I say. "That way, I'll know to add juice to the list."

It burns me. With all the crucial shit I've got going on, it's bad enough I have to do all the shopping for us. God forbid he could lift a finger to help now and again.

"Just goes to show," he calls after me as I retreat back to my room with a cup of cold coffee. "Never ever listen to your parents!"

– – –

Caffeinated, I log on to admire last night's masterpiece.

Know how when you get high you think you're saying all sorts of super-important crap, crap so heavy and mind-blowing that it would forever change your life if only you could remember exactly what it is you said? And those few times you do remember to write the crap down, the next morning you either can't understand what you wrote because your handwriting's totally illegible or if you do understand what you wrote you can't understand why you thought it was so incredible when you wrote it?

Well, rereading my latest and greatest Personal Essay is just like that, only stroke-inducing. Little Billy, the blind, crippled kid? Talk about lame—literally. What was

I thinking? I taught the little fucker to swim? Yes, I actually used the word "fucker." My Personal Essay, which is supposed to be a model of Mega Munificence and Supreme Tolerance is, instead, a screed of Monumental Insensitivity and Mind-Boggling Political Incorrectness. Food poisoning from bad mortadella? I can't believe what a sadistic jerk I am. Volunteering a freakin' kidney? Actually, that's pretty good.

But, putting all that aside—I mean, I can always tone everything down, way down—there are always the legalities to consider. I mean, what if Columbia checks? You have to sign something that makes my offense prosecutable. On the other hand, Columbia gets tens of thousands of applications; Columbia can't check them all. But, with my luck, Columbia will check mine. Little Billy? I mean, gimme a break.

And even if Columbia doesn't check, my Personal Essay is one big fat lie. When it comes right down to it, submitting this Personal Essay is just plain wrong. In so many ways. On so many levels. Under the cold, bright glare of day, I can't bring myself to do it.

Dejectedly I press Delete.

I sit, staring at a blank screen, a shattered husk. My application is due in like an hour, and I still don't have a Personal Essay, the most essential part of it.

I am so fucked.

For my latest feat of futility, after months, after countless days and nights of sweating it out trying to write the

Perfect Personal Essay, I am going to have to write the Hopefully Barely Good Enough One in a matter of minutes. In yesterday's underwear, while brain-dead, while hungover. In a panicked frenzy, I cut and paste a collage of earlier efforts. Frantically, I cobble together something somewhat coherent with previously cast-off sentences and sentiments. Your basic Character Building that comes from being abandoned by your mother combined with the Nobility of Having Nothing but with a healthy dollop of Undiminished Optimism and a dash of desire to Improve the World. In short, I concoct something that approximates a Thing, although I have no inkling what that Thing is. All in 750 words or less.

Crawling, I cross the finish line with just seconds to spare. Screw having my Personal Essay shock and awe. The best I can now hope for is to do no harm.

The Send button pulsates. Bleakly I stare at the sum total of my almost eighteen years of earthly existence reduced to numbers, letters, short paragraphs, and a rushed, imperfect Personal Essay. Where are the little boxes for years of slaving at subjects that don't matter? I ask myself. Where's the space for trying my level best with what I have, the numerical value for acting on faith, risking disappointment, daring to dream? I can't help thinking there should be more, that there's more I can do. But there is no more. Because this, my friends, is the end of the line. The buzzer's sounded, the clock's run out. Game over.

Yet somehow I still can't bring myself to click. But click I must. Clamping my eyes, I murmur a silent prayer to a higher power I don't believe in.

Click. There, I did it. The die is cast, the deed done. There's no Undo.

On some level, despite it all, I should be relieved, but I'm not, far from it. I've been gearing up to this moment, this goal, since almost before I can remember being any other way. Instantly what I'm feeling is aimless, at loose ends, utterly without direction or purpose in life. It is the mother of all letdowns.

But I've got a gig coming up in Tenafly, so I troop into town to the dry cleaner. It's wet, cold, and gray out, which matches my mood. I check my suit pockets before I drop off.

"Hey, Brooks," Sanjay greets me from behind the counter. "The usual?"

I nod. Before my new vocation, I had never stepped inside the cluttered establishment even though it's been here forever. Now I've become a regular, and not only are me and Sanjay on a first-name basis, but we also speak shorthand. Go figure.

As I slosh back to the Beast, I have the sudden urge to celebrate my achievement, to commemorate the occasion, inconsequential as it is to everyone but me. But commemorate it with whom? Who, besides *moi*, gives a shit about *moi*? That's when I spot The Murf across the street in the front window of The Gun, waving my way.

"Seven-twenty Verbal, baby!" I proudly report, chest puffed out like I should get a gold star. I haven't seen The Murf since I got the semi-spectacular news. In fact, with my juggling act to complete my application, keep up in school, plus the late weekend hours working the various high school social circuits, it feels like I haven't seen him in eons. "I'm kinda sorta within official range."

"That's awesome, Brooks," The Murf says, vigorously spraying and wiping a table. He glances up at me. "You're on your way out of Pritchard."

"I wish," I say, noting for the first time that the place is quite a bit busier than usual. Why, there's even a small wait at the counter, where two new employees in Gun garb, kids I faintly recognize from Pritchard High, swiftly operate the sub assembly line.

"Pickles, then the peppers!" The Murf barks at them. "Idiots! They give me idiots!"

I also observe that all the tables are cleared, the floors shine, the trash cans are emptied, the napkin dispensers remarkably full. It's trippy; everything's too perfect. Like I'm in a parallel dimension or a bad episode of *The X-Files*.

"Murf, what's going on?" I inquire, more than slightly weirded out.

"I got promoted, that's what's wrong!" he groans as he rapidly straightens chairs. "You're looking at the new Night Manager of the Submachine Gun! And it's all your fault!"

"What happened to Pat?"

"They caught the asswipe stealing from the tip jar on closed circuit. With you gone, there was nobody else so they had to pick me!"

I'm sorry but I can't help laughing. The Murf as management. It's too much.

"You think this is funny?" The Murf says, now furiously sweeping a spotless floor with a broom.

"So quit," I advise.

"And give up the Opportunity of a Lifetime? What if The Gun does go National? I could be in on the Ground Floor."

I do a double take. Is this The Murf or some evil clone? Whoever or whatever he is, he's sipped the Kool-Aid if he thinks The Gun is going anywhere but down the toilet. But I don't say that.

"Shit-for-brains! Mustard, then the mayonnaise!" The Murf commands his flunkies, then turns back to me, grinning maniacally. "All this power is getting to me! And you know what, man? I fucking dig it!"

I edge away from him. It *is* an evil clone. Then, for an instant, the imposter's focused eyes glaze over and go dull and The Real Murf resurfaces.

"Oh my God," The Real Murf gasps. "Who am I? What am I saying?"

"We need to get wrecked," I prescribe.

"When?" he asks eagerly.

I whip out the iPhone, summon the calendar app.

"Let's see. I have an opening Thursday."

"No can do," says The Murf. "Thursdays are our busiest nights. But Saturdays are slow. How's Saturday work for you?"

"For the indefinite future, Saturdays are out for me."

To my surprise, The Murf whips out his own smartphone and brings up his own calendar app. We consult our respective schedules.

"Next Monday?" I propose.

"Can't. Have back-to-back meetings with potential new meat suppliers," The Murf says. "I mean, have you seen what they've been passing off as prosciutto?"

Once more, I can't believe what I'm hearing.

"Tuesday?" I offer.

"I don't know, man. Tuesdays are tough. We're launching a new Chicken Parm promotion."

"A week from Friday?" I persist. "The Pixies are playing that night in the Bowery."

"The Pixies?" The Real Murf emerges again. The Pixies are way up in The Murf pantheon.

"You think the Night Manager could manage to give himself the night off?"

The Pixies—but amazingly, The Murf still equivocates. "This place would fall apart without me," he says. Pride of ownership. Responsibility. Actual initiative. It's truly like some sort of alien consciousness has taken possession of The Murf's brain. "C'mon, just you and me," I implore. "Being stupid. Hanging out. Like old times."

"Like old times." He looks at me, himself again. We both sense something dark and foreboding. It can't be possible, not for the two of us. But it is. The Murf and me are losing touch.

"Okay, buddy," The Murf relents. "The Pixies. You're on."

Bumping knuckles, we seal the deal.

- - -

Bruce cranked to the max, I drive aimlessly, pondering the vicissitudes of life. And although I have tons of homework, I resolve to take the day off, something I haven't done for so long that I am at a loss as to what to do. Maybe I'll pay a surprise visit to the gym and shoot a few jumpers with my homeboys or hit a really bad movie or just cruise by more rich people's houses. Sleep is always an attractive option. Then I hear the familiar refrain:

"HEY HO, LET'S GO!!"

I switch off the tunes, click on speaker without looking, and assume my most professional voice.

"Rattigan and Associates. How may I direct your call?"

"Brooks, Harvey Lieberman."

Harvey Lieberman? Just the word Lieberman causes a spike in my blood pressure. This is a most unwelcome intrusion.

"I realize it's kind of last minute," he says. "But Celia's been invited to a dinner-dance at the Green Meadow

Country Club this coming Saturday."

I can hear Gayle right beside him. "First, an after-party!" she squeals. "Now a restricted country club!"

I picture her brandishing some fancy engraved invitation, doing a gleeful jig in those awful shoes of hers around all that disturbing primitive art. Not a pleasant image.

"No way, Dr. Lieberman. No chance," I reply firmly. "Forget it."

"Why not?" Then he actually says: "You two kids had such a blast last time!"

Just the memory of last time gives me the chills. The prospect of there ever being another time with Celia Lieberman is beyond consideration.

"Repeat business is strictly against company policy," I inform him, although there is no such policy or any company policy, for that matter. "Sorry, no exceptions."

"Harvey, give me the phone! You're doing it all wrong!" I hear grunting and bumping as Gayle wrestles her smaller, weaker mate for possession of the receiver. "Let me talk to him!"

"You bit me!" he yelps. "You broke the skin!"

Again, the sheer scale of the Lieberman insanity sweeps over me. Although it means a black mark on the brand name, I'm going to hang up on them. I must, for the sake of self-preservation.

"It's the eighteenth birthday party for a classmate of Celia's!" Gayle, the victor as usual in these struggles, shouts into my ear. "Maybe you know her!"

So long forever, Liebermans. Parting is such sweet sorrow. Not. My finger lowers on the red hang-up button.

"Shelby Pace!"

I'm not going to lie to you. In the past week or so, I've had one or two thoughts of Shelby Pace, mostly late at night with the door double-locked. Some mornings and afternoons too. Often in the shower or waiting in drive-throughs. Okay, pretty much all the time, everywhere. Although we'd exchanged but one fleeting kiss, it had been exchanged with the hottest babe in existence in a string bikini in her mansion with a real Picasso. Any one of these factors is stupendous. Together they are mind-numbing. And soul-depleting. For I'd resigned myself to the grim fact that the all-too-brief, incredibly wondrous experience will just haunt me for all of eternity. Because those stars will never realign and there'll be no return engagements to Green Meadow. And yet here, suddenly, they have.

"Brooks, you still there?" Gayle's grating voice brings me back to my senses.

I tell her I'll make an exception just this once. The regular fee.

THERE AGAIN

Celia Lieberman is alarmingly calm and composed when I collect her.

There's no big scene. No deafening displays of Lieberman family dysfunction, no embarrassing personal confessions, no vows of vengeance. No, strangely it's all sweetness and sunshine, hugs and kisses.

"Goodnight, Mummy," Celia Lieberman chirps, exchanging air pecks with Gayle in the front doorway. "Goodnight, Daddy Dearest. Don't wait up!" she trills, fondly patting Harvey on his bald head. "Come along, lackey," she says airily to me. I tag after her to the Prius, maintaining a wary distance, certain I'm the victim of a ruse that could well end in my violent death.

"Oh, Harvey," Gayle sighs loudly after us, holding his hand. "It's the youth we never had."

"Only better," he glows. "Because we don't have to go through it."

– – –

"I just want you to know this wasn't my doing. It was my parents' idea and I've decided to humor the poor, deluded darlings," Celia Lieberman says as we begin our night's journey together. "Hang a left at the corner."

Celia Lieberman's in this ugly-ass grannyish plaid number that ends mid-calf and starts at a neckline that is actually at the neck. She switches on the radio and turns the volume way up. Me, I'm on edge, I'm expecting the anvil to drop at any moment on my head—I'm finding Celia Lieberman's civility that chilling.

"Woo!" Celia Lieberman sticks her head out her open window. "TAKE A WALK ON THE WILD SIDE! YEAH, BABY!"

"You're in a surprisingly fine mood," I observe when she pops back inside, keeping her fixed in my field of vision at all times.

"Yes, I am!"

"Dare I ask why?"

"I got in Early Decision to Stanford."

The news slams into me out of left field like a ton of bricks. I mean, I'm completely blindsided. The shock's so great that I veer out of our lane into the opposite one right in the path of onrushing traffic. A chorus of horns yanks me back in the nick of time and I wheel us sharply to safety. But it's a close call and we're both rattled.

"Jesus, you trying to get us both killed?"

"You got in Early Decision to Stanford?" I croak, gulping down air. Stanford! You know how Columbia's acceptance rate is in the high sevens? Well, Stanford's is even more impossible. Try low fives. That's lower than even Harvard's, the lowest in the country, probably in the whole world. And that's not 5 percent of just-anybodies applying, but 5 percent of the very best and brightest, the ultra-achievers who have the stats and muscle to think they might actually have a realistic shot. I mean, to these jokers, schools like Columbia, Penn, and Northwestern are Safeties. But even supersmart, well-prepped, and well-connected as they are, most don't get in. 95 percent will be crushed like bugs on a speeding windshield.

Celia Lieberman got in Early Decision to Stanford! It's amazing to me that I could know anyone who got into Stanford. But Celia Lieberman? With the way she dresses? Stanford! Somehow it's the ultimate cosmic joke on me.

"How could you already hear?" I bray, refusing to believe. "It's the middle of November, and no one hears back until at least the first week of December!"

"Well, I did. Almost a week ago," she says, smiling broadly, bopping to the music.

With my increased marginality thanks to my Personal Essay, I won't hear from Columbia until the last possible second, like the late, late dog days of December when they can't put it off anymore and then who knows what I'll hear? Stanford. Fuck. Celia Lieberman!

"Do you know what this means?" grins Celia Lieberman.

"That your SATs were astronomical?" I squeak.

"No, it means that, come September 15, I'll be more than three thousand miles away from my goddamn parents. That's why I picked it!"

– – –

Green Meadow Country Club's the size of a small principality and just about what you'd expect from a private playground for the mega-wealthy, only much more so. I pull up the Prius behind a caravan of arriving Audis, Infinitis, and Benzes. A parking guy in a uniform with epaulets swiftly opens Celia's door. She prances out, pumping her hips and fists, howling.

"PARTY ON! LET'S ROCK, DUDES!!!"

The valet looks at her and then at me. I give the keys to the thoroughly startled fellow, along with an explanation since I feel he's owed one.

"She just got in Early Decision to Stanford."

We're directed through the glittering lobby into a vast ballroom with high ceilings right out of some sort of English palace. There, beneath the crystal chandeliers, in their natural habitat you might say, in full regalia and glory, are the crème de la crème of Green Meadow Country Prep teenage society. The girls beautiful, sophisticated, thin; the boys tall, trim, handsome. Future shot-callers, string-pullers, movers, shakers. Dancing, laughing, joking. And why not? I would be too.

"God, I hate attractive, well-adjusted people, don't you?" Celia Lieberman says. "Oh, almost forgot, you're one of them."

But I'm not, not by at least twenty turnpike exits. Then, like a vision, I spot the birthday girl herself from across the room. Shelby, in a short, sheer clingy dress with pronounced nipple outlines, gliding our direction through the crush.

"Listen, Celia, one thing . . . ," I whisper to Celia Lieberman. "I kinda sorta told Shelby that I live in the City."

Celia Lieberman turns to me questioningly. "Why in hell would you kinda sorta say that?"

"I, uh, didn't think it'd look good for your image to be with somebody from Pritchard, New Jersey," I stammer, increasingly nervous as Shelby nears.

Even though I look away, Celia Lieberman can see right through me. "Oh, how very considerate of you."

"Just play along, okay?" I plead.

"God, you are *such* a phony!" she marvels.

Then Shelby's upon us in beat to the throbbing music, overwhelming in her perfection. "Hey guys, you made it! I was hoping you would!"

"Thanks," yells back Celia Lieberman. "I can't believe you invited me!"

"Oh, it wasn't *you* I was inviting!" Shelby hollers back, shooting a smoldering look past her. I turn around. Again it has to be me by process of elimination. Thankful for my continued unexplainable good fortune, I return Shelby's look with the most meaning I can muster. I can see the whole sordid scenario slowly dawning on Celia Lieberman as she realizes she's been had. Been used by both Shelby and me for our own selfish devices. I cringe like the sleaze-ball I am, certain that my cover is about to be blown.

"Celia, you don't mind if I grab Brooks for a dance, do you?" Shelby asks, slipping her creamy arm through my clammy one.

"He's all yours." Celia Lieberman pinches my cheek really hard. "The poor boy could use some exercise after the long commute from the City."

Blinking back tears of acute pain, I mouth a fervid "Thank you" to her as I'm led away.

"I'll be in the bathroom throwing up," Celia Lieberman remarks after us, instantly causing both me and Shelby to whip around back at her, freaked.

"Just kidding," Celia Lieberman laughs, this time the one to do the leaving.

"That Celia Lieberman has such an interesting sense of humor," Shelby notes, watching her go.

"Yeah, she's a regular laugh-fest." I rotate my jaw, the sensation just returning to the left side of my face where Celia Lieberman pinched it. "But enough about her. Shall we dance?"

Shelby knows all the moves and then some that can't be taught. Smooth and sensuous, she coolly anticipates my every thrust and gyration and ups the ante with a few provocations of her own. Coming close, but never quite touching, we ride the cresting waves of electronic music washing over us. Her emerald cat's eyes fix on me, teasing, taunting. I want to grab her, devour her, consume her. I lust for her, for all *this*.

"So how's it going with Celia Lieberman?" she calls above the din.

"Couldn't be better!" I shout back, the music masking my bitterness. "She just got in Early Decision to Stanford!"

Shelby loses a step and we bump into each other. Stanford. Even she, she who has everything, is impressed. And envious.

"Nice!" she shouts.

Just the thought of Stanford and Celia Lieberman in the same sentence clause puts a damper on my disposition.

"Let's not talk about Celia Lieberman!" I holler. "Let's talk about you!"

Suddenly, I do a double take. For there, behind Shelby at the buffet table, gnawing on a giant lobster claw in each fat fist, is goddamn Burdette, of the blubbery Pritchard High starting front line, the first domino that started them all. My eyes jut out like in a cartoon, my throat goes dry. Before I'm discovered, I swiftly pull Shelby by the hips toward me and spin us dizzily around, deploying her as a visual shield.

"Boy," she gasps, taken by surprise but not displeased. "And here I've been thinking you weren't the type that messed around."

My heart's pounding like a bass drum as I furtively peer over Shelby's bare shoulder at the buffet. Burdette's no longer there. There's no sight of him anywhere. Maybe it was just an illusion, I reason, a hallucination brought on by surging hormones, which mine definitely are since Shelby's twirled around in my arms and is rubbing her tight little ass softly against my bulging groin. Can this really be happening?

"So, uh, how's it feel to be eighteen?" I wheeze, trying to keep it together.

"Great!" she smiles, turning to face me again. "Now I can legally vote and fuck!"

This should get my attention in a major way, but it doesn't because it *is* goddamn Burdette at eleven o'clock, double-dipping like the pig he is at the chocolate fountain. Again I swing Shelby around.

"*That* is great!" I exclaim, my brain misfiring on all cylinders, trying to plot escape.

"Which?" Shelby asks, confused. "Voting or fucking?"

"Fucking, then voting! Thanks for the dance!"

I dash off, leaving her high and dry. It's a full-tilt disaster.

– – –

Scrambling about, I spy Celia Lieberman coming out of the women's room, followed by Cassie.

"You must really put out," Cassie says after once more appraising Celia Lieberman's woeful outfit, trying to figure out the appeal. I motion urgently at Celia Lieberman, who sees me.

"Oh, I do," Celia Lieberman proclaims loudly for my benefit. "I'm a total slut."

"Really?" Cassie's mouth drops, incredulous.

I'm trying to be cool and wait for their inane conversation to finish, but the risk of public exposure is just too immediate.

"C'mon, we're leaving!" I command, tugging Celia Lieberman by the hand.

"But we just got here," she protests.

"I can't wait!"

I drag her away. Cassie's floored, thinking the worst as usual.

"Man!" I hear her whistle to herself.

I rapidly steer Celia Lieberman to the front door. When we're out of sight of Cassie, she pulls free of me.

"Hey, what's with the caveman routine? You and the duchess have a spat?"

"No, I just had a close encounter with the cousin of my first client!"

She looks at me, still not getting it. "So?"

"So he arranged it. He knows what I do!"

The color drains from Celia Lieberman's badly made-up face as she registers the potential implications, all catastrophic.

"I'll get my coat!" she yelps.

"Meet you at the car!"

We dart off in separate directions. Ducking and pivoting like a tailback, I charge through the crowd. Just as I detect a sliver of daylight between me and the front door, my path's blocked by the blond hulking form of Tommy. He bunches up my tie and pulls down, cutting off my wind. Way, way pissed.

"Listen, maggot, nobody disses Tommy Fallick and gets away with it!"

Tommy what? Could my ears, like everything else, be deceiving me?

"I beg your pardon," I sputter, unwinding from his grip.

"No one poaches in Tommy Fallick's personal preserve!"

"Your last name is Phallic?"

I'm intrigued, despite the extreme precariousness of my situation. *Phallic.* Adjective. Of, relating to, or resembling an erect penis. As in, what a dick. My night, indeed my year, has been made. Tommy Phallic! So pithy, so apt. I know I shouldn't, but I can't help smiling ear to ear.

"With an "F," Tommy burns. "F-A-double-L-I-C-K!"

"Even so, you'd think your family would have changed it," I guffaw, losing control. "A long time ago."

Just as Penis lunges to throttle me, I catch a glimpse of Burdette again and bolt. Outside, I ambush the same parking guy as before, shaking him desperately by the collar.

"Blue Prius! And for the love of Christ, hurry!"

He takes off like a rocket, whether to retrieve my vehicle or call the cops, I don't know. I dart behind the shelter of a large Grecian urn, but alas, I'm a moment too late.

"Rattigan?"

I freeze. It's over. Cringing, I poke out my head, which Burdette, behemoth that he is, immediately clamps in a crushing headlock. He chews on a leg of something in one hand as he smothers me under his sweaty armpit.

"Sack of shit!" he booms. "Thought it was you!"

I squirm and claw in his stinking death-hold, kicking in midair. My eyes begin to loll back from the stench and lack of oxygen. I'm rapidly losing consciousness.

"I . . . can't . . . breathe . . ."

Burdette releases me but comes up with new abuse by heartily pounding my back. I almost collapse beneath the repeated blows.

"Hey, Burdette, what an unpleasant surprise," I say, nimbly slipping from his reach. "What are you doing here?"

"This Shelby chick went to camp in France or some shit with some honey I'm trying to bang. What the hell are you doing here?"

"Just getting off!"

The Prius skids in front of us. I open the front door for Celia, who tears past and dives inside. Interlocking both hands, I club Burdette as hard as I can in the gut. He crumples in half. Tossing the valet guy a fiver from my bankroll, I clamber behind the wheel and floor the battery. As we slink off in a clean getaway, I watch Burdette's hunched-over, shrinking figure in the rearview mirror.

"Go for it!" Burdette shouts after me, grinning. "Sack of shit!"

For the next twenty minutes or so, we drive in somber silence. Public exposure would have been ruinous for us both, but much more for Celia Lieberman, who, if word got out she had to pay to get it, so to speak, would be a social pariah, Early Decision to Stanford not withstanding. Me, because if Shelby ever knew who and what I really am, it'd be over before it could start, which it damn near had. She'd been in my arms, looked me right in the eyes, talked of fucking. The biggest come-on in history by the most desirable girl on the planet. And I'd given her the brush-off. It's all too tragic. I think if Celia Lieberman weren't there to gloat, I'd actually cry.

"Now what?" she asks.

"Now, you go home and I go drown my sorrows in copious amounts of cheap alcohol," I grunt.

"What sorrows?"

Try never having Shelby Pace when I maybe might have. Try never knowing if it could have really happened. Try almost hoping that Shelby had just been a cock tease and toying with me and that it couldn't have really happened. Because if it could have really happened, which deep down I think it could have, well, I honestly can't imagine what it would have been like being with a girl like that. But I'm fairly damn sure it would have been beyond fucking amazing. I can't go on, it's just too painful. Indeed my sense of loss is so vast and voluminous that

I'm pretty much incapable of expression.

"Not that it matters anymore," I do manage to say. "But thanks for not letting on to Shelby about me back there."

"No worries," Celia Lieberman shrugs. "When it comes to Shelby Pace, all guys are idiots. You can't help yourselves."

Somehow I blame her. Somehow I blame Celia Lieberman for everything wrong in my life. If I could, I'd blame her for nuclear proliferation, world hunger, and the continued lack of decent health care. I know it's irrational. For Celia Lieberman, Celia Lieberman has behaved impeccably, even admirably. But the fact remains that if it weren't for Celia Lieberman, I never would have set eyes on the sublime experience that might have been Shelby Pace. And I'd be much, much better off if I hadn't.

"It's nine sixteen," chatters Celia Lieberman, oblivious to my demoralized state. "After my last social triumph, you can't take me home for at least another three hours minimum. The parental units would be all over me."

"You shouldn't put down your folks all the time," I say, supremely annoyed. "They're only wrecking your life because they care. I mean, at least they want what they think's best for you."

"Oh, and yours don't?"

No, Celia Lieberman, they don't. One took off right after I was born and the other doesn't give a shit about anything, least of all me. But they don't know about stuff like that in Green Meadow, where all the parents have the time and the means to be overly invested in their offspring. But it's hopeless to try to explain, she's hopeless, they all are, so I don't bother.

Changing the subject, I ask, "What would you be doing at nine sixteen on a Saturday night if it weren't for your parents?"

- - -

A bowling alley. It's the last place I'd ever predict Celia Lieberman would take me. I can't remember the last time I was in a bowling alley and now I remember why. I don't know if it's the heady aroma of moldy shoes, stale beer, and rancid food, or the migraine-producing clang and clatter of balls rolling and pins toppling, or the sensory overload of crisscrossing lasers and flashing fluorescence, or all of the above that is such a turn-off. No, bowling's not really my bag; that plus that I really suck at it, which I find secretly both infuriating and humiliating. Thankfully Celia Lieberman hasn't taken me to the lanes to bowl—or to the snack lounge or the bar—because I follow her past them to the game room at the very rear of the circus of wholesome family fun.

I stumble into abrupt pitch blackness. As my vision slowly adjusts, I discern the arcade's overrun with obnoxious brats, which, by definition, qualifies as anyone more than six months younger than me. Screaming and shouting for no apparent reason, gathered in shadowy clusters at various vibrating multimedia units. I turn to see Celia Lieberman pretending to play foosball at one end of a long, chipped table.

"Isn't he dreamy?" she sighs, face rapt, staring ahead, twirling and jerking sundry knobs and handles ineffectually. I strain to see through the dim chaos.

She's referring to a tall, prematurely balding string bean who's pulverizing a little girl in what I recognize as *Bludgeon XIII*, the newest, most extreme edition of an especially vile, exploitative, totally reprehensible video game in which I've been known to more than occasionally indulge.

"*That* guy?" I look at him, then back at her, then at him again. Surely Celia Lieberman cannot be serious.

"Franklin Riggs," she breathes. "Just got in Early Action to Caltech."

"That guy?" Jesus, I think, everybody's getting in everywhere.

Franklin sadistically finishes off the little girl, pummeling her video self into a bloody welter of severed limbs, squirting arteries, and spurting organs until there are no virtual body parts left to lop off or obliterate. Triumphant, Franklin holds out his palm for payment.

"Fork it over, punk," he crows. Charming lad.

"We're in the Chess Club together," Celia Lieberman continues, all radiant. "He's president. I'm secretary-treasurer."

I look again at Franklin Riggs. Besides no hair, he has no chin. Caltech not withstanding, I just don't see it. The little girl forks over what must be an entire month's allowance to him. Franklin mercilessly pockets every last cent.

"Next victim!" he sneers.

An even smaller boy takes the little girl's place.

"Sounds like a match made in heaven," I comment, at my most diplomatic.

"He barely acknowledges I exist," Celia Lieberman says dejectedly, giving up all pretense of playing foosball. She waves to Franklin, demonstrating to me.

"Hey, Franklin!" she smiles brightly.

Franklin, aglow in electronic gore, merely contorts in a sickly grimace by way of response.

"Yeah," I say. "I see what you mean."

– – –

Back in the Prius, Celia Lieberman declares she's ravenous and there's still another hour to kill so we strap on the feed bag at an ancient diner she knows about, which she says no one else from Green Meadow Country Prep ever goes to. I can believe it 'cause the place is kind of a dump, the kind of place you'd find in Pritchard. Great chow, not so big on the décor and ambience. After the deprivations I've suffered, a double cheeseburger and chocolate shake go down easy.

"So tell me about your parents," says Celia Lieberman, seated in the booth across from me. "They can't be worse than mine."

"Parent. My mom's out of the picture," I answer, chomping into greasy goodness. "It's just me and Charlie."

"You call your dad by his first name?" Celia Lieberman's already plowed through her—of course—veggie omelet, hash browns, and toast in record time. I can see her greedily eyeing my fries.

"Charlie's not much of a dad. Not much of anything really." Celia Lieberman helps herself to my fries. Without asking. "Listen, forget what I said. Your parents are messed up, okay? I guess everybody's are."

"What does Charlie do?" asks Celia Lieberman, now grabbing my fries by the handful.

"Mostly he gets high and reads comic books. But when he's not doing that, he delivers the mail." I'm very particular about my fries. You see, I parcel out my fries so there are always still some left after I've finished the rest of my repast. Fries are like dessert to me. The tiny reward I've saved for myself. How so like Celia Lieberman to spoil my treat. Suddenly, I reach the breaking point, thwacking her hand hard with a spoon.

"Order your own fries," I snarl.

"Hey, that really smarts!" Celia Lieberman complains, rubbing the sting out.

"Good," I say. "It was meant to."

Celia Lieberman watches me eat for a while. I take my own sweet time.

"Your dad's a mailman?" she asks, picking up the thread. It's almost amusing that the idea is so out there for her. That the mailman, the butcher, the tailor, all the little people who make life so convenient might have kids of their own. So, just for the hell of it, I decide to blow her mind.

"Oh, it gets better. He's a mailman who went to Harvard."

"Your dad's a mailman who went to Harvard?" Her mind is blown.

"He wasn't always a mailman. Before I came along, Charlie was an up-and-coming young novelist."

I know, impossible to believe, but it's true. Before I was born, Charlie had actually been somebody, had actually accomplished something of actual note.

"I've never met a novelist," remarks Celia Lieberman. "Doctors, lawyers, investment bankers, too many dentists, but no novelists."

"*Skies of Stone* by Charles Rattigan," I inform her. I don't think I've ever talked to anyone about Charlie's semi-illustrious past. There has never been anybody who it might matter to. "*The New York Times* named it one of the top ten new works of fiction in 1995."

"So then what happened?"

"Then 1996 happened, then '97 and '98. Nothing happened. Then I happened."

The subject's a bummer. Because I don't know what happened. Was it me that happened? Was I the reason that Charlie lost the talent and drive or whatever gift he once had? "Listen, can we talk about something else?"

"Is that why you do this—take money for being a stand-in?" Celia Lieberman persists. "To get away from him?"

I stop eating, my appetite suddenly gone. Charlie's a riddle that I'll never solve. And though it pains me to admit it, Celia Lieberman has articulated something I'm just realizing that I've long felt but never quite faced up to.

"You know, I've never thought of it that way, but I probably am."

"Amazing. We have something in common after all." She eyes my fries again. "Are you through with those?"

Defeated, I push my plate toward her. She digs in without shame.

"Actually, I'm trying to save money to go to Columbia."

"You have to pay for college yourself?"

"If I get in, which Charlie actively hopes I don't," I say gruffly. "Most likely he's gonna get his wish. My cumes are still twenty-five points below the median. And my Personal Essay's a train wreck."

Celia Lieberman's expression softens, seeing a new side of me, a side I make it a rule not to show, but I figure I'm never going to see her again so why not spill my guts a little?

"Anyway, this, as you call it, beats the hell out of getting paid minimum wage at a sub shop."

"I've never met anyone my age who works for minimum wage," Celia Lieberman muses. "Actually, I've never met anyone my age who works, period."

Not a single one? Can it really be? Although it's what I expect, somehow it's still beyond comprehension.

"Well, they do in Pritchard," I laugh bleakly.

– – –

The drive back is silent. Celia Lieberman's questions have churned up stuff I do my best not to think about because thinking about things doesn't change anything. Charlie's still a bum and I'm still on my own. I'm at a fork in the road. And if I can't hop on the train hurling by, I'm never getting my ass out of Pritchard. As for Celia Lieberman, I have no clue what she's thinking, which is normal because I never do. But I do know she's thinking about something because she hasn't made a peep for a good ten miles.

"You know anyone with pull at Columbia?" asks Celia Lieberman out of the blue.

"Are you kidding?" I answer. "I don't even know anyone who knows anyone who knows anyone."

"Are you great at anything?" she inquires. "Any talents you're keeping hidden? Sports? Music? Computers?"

"I've got nothing special going for me," I report mournfully. "Actually, if I was Columbia, I wouldn't take me either."

"My uncle's a professor there in the physics department," Celia Lieberman states.

"For real?" A physics professor isn't exactly what I have at the top of my wish list of connections, especially when I have no intention of ever again taking a physics class. I'm hoping more along the lines of a nationally elected public official or prize-winning somebody or other or just your basic filthy-rich alum. But hey, a professor at Columbia. It's a fingerhold, something, better than nothing.

"Uncle Max. Mommy Dearest's older brother. But they haven't spoken for years."

Great, just when I'd really psyched myself up about the guy. Just my luck.

"But I think he's still speaking to me," Celia Lieberman adds. "I bet I could arrange an interview if you think that'd help. He's a bit of a crank."

I'm sure he is, I think.

"I don't care if he's a serial killer, I'll take anything," I say, but not believing she'll follow through. People never do.

We slow to a stop, having reached the Lieberman abode. I pull up the Prius in the driveway beside the Beast. Celia Lieberman gets out. I do too.

"You don't have to walk me to the door," she says. "My parents aren't home to make a scene."

"They aren't?"

"They went into the City. Pops is getting some big-deal award for saving the life of some president of some West African country. They're being put up in a penthouse at the Plaza."

The whole night she's been telling me we have to stay out all night because of her parents and now it turns out they're not even around to invade her privacy? Are you shitting me? Why, that little stinker! I glare at her in mute outrage.

"Might as well get them their money's worth," she smiles innocently. "Speaking of which . . ." Snapping open her purse, she pulls out a thick folded envelope filled with cash. "Paid in full plus a little something extra."

She tosses the wad underhanded at me. I snag it.

"We'll be in touch," she says, strolling to the door.

But I know we won't.

DECEMBER

December 7, to be exact.

Pearl Harbor Day. A day that will live forever in infamy. Man, I hope not. Because, more auspiciously, it's Early Decision Notification to Columbia Day. Today the verdict is finally rendered. Applications have been processed, numbers crunched, achievements quantified, intangibles categorized. Today, young lives will be judged. And most will be found extremely wanting.

I picture the cart stacked high with the sealed fates of thousands as it's wheeled from the Columbia admissions office across the ivy-draped quad to the campus post office. The mountains of thin, identically stamped, officially embossed envelopes bringing disappointment and despair to those who gave it their all and still couldn't pass muster. The smaller stack of fat packets bulging with forms to be filled out by the cream of the crop, the lucky stiffs who have whatever it is it takes. By three thirty, great news and terrible will have been sorted and loaded into trucks, fanning out across the length and breadth of the land like a virus.

Which brings us to one minute before five, which is what it is now. In less than a minute, in addition to snail-mailing the letters, Columbia will post thumbs up or down online. In less than a minute, the Future could be determined. In less than a minute, I could be bestowed with instant status, become an esteemed member of the elite, claimant of an ancient pedigree. In less than a minute, the past, modest and pedestrian as it's been, could no longer matter. In a less than a minute, I could begin again at square one. Everything could change for me. Everything. I'm not old, but I'm old enough to know that defining moments like this are few and far between. Thirty seconds, twenty-nine . . .

Twenty-seven seconds and the Shelby Paces of the world become a possibility. Twenty-three seconds and Pritchard becomes a distant memory. Nineteen seconds and I'm one of them . . .

My hands are shaking, my throat's dry, my heart thumping.

Single digits. Five. I've worked so hard, waited so long for this, for now. Three, please God, two, please God . . . One.

I can't open my eyes. I can't breathe. Actually I feel like I should probably lie down, but I don't. Instead I stare at the flickering screen before me. My student ID number's already been entered and I'm logged onto the Columbia website. Sure enough, I have an email from the Office of Admissions. *The* email.

Summoning all my remaining strength of will, I click on the tiny envelope icon.

It opens and unfurls, expanding into a neatly typed letter on official university stationery. At first the electronic words are indecipherable, like Egyptian hieroglyphics, but gradually they resolve into context and meaning.

"*Dear Brooks,*" I am greeted.

It quickly goes downhill from there.

Because there's no first paragraph beginning with the hearty exclamation, "Congratulations!" No second sentence saying, "We are pleased to inform you." Nope, none of that good stuff for the likes of me. Instead, there's mention of record numbers and smaller percentages than ever. The same old bullshit about how they've had to turn down legions of eminently qualified candidates. It's over. I didn't make the grade. I've been rejected.

I sit there, numb. I taste ashes. Feeling the fool for ever daring to hope.

Then I notice the letter hasn't ended, but goes on longer than it should if I was rejected because I haven't been rejected. Well, I have, but not totally.

I've been Deferred.

A final decision will be made in late March or early April, at which time I will be notified. Oh, those mothers.

I try to fix on the positive. I've been given a reprieve

from the crushing demise that might have been. There's a shaft of hope. I'm still alive!

But, in truth, it's a tremendous body blow and devastating setback. Early Decision was by far my best odds. Almost a 20 percent acceptance rate. Now that I've been cast adrift into the general applicant pool, my chances are reduced to a shade under seven. I'm one of the clamoring hordes. Oh, those mothers.

I curse my own mediocrity and catalog of inadequacies. Nothing quick and easy for Brooks Rattigan. No, for Brooks Rattigan, the ordeal will be dragged out indefinitely to a most likely bitter end. But as long as there's a particle of a prayer, I'll dangle in limbo, a pawn in their vicious game. The hell of denial would be better than the purgatory to which I've just been sentenced. My agony will continue for months. Not only that, it will grow, it will fester, it will burn like acid. How much can one single adolescent male endure? In the next few endless months, I'm about to find out.

– – –

The Gun's discernibly busier and tidier than it was the last time I visited. There's a steady line at the counter; the tables are filled with a cross section of what passes for Pritchard society. Your basic just-off-from-work, too-tired-to-cook moms and dads having a quick bite with their kids, the guys from the fire station killing time, ballers replenishing after hours of hoops, stoners satisfying munchies, a homeless dude taking temporary shelter over a cold cup of coffee. Also, I notice minor physical touches have been made. Red and white checkered curtains hang from the windows, and cheaply framed glossy photos from *The Godfather* adorn the walls. Frankie Valli's falsetto croons from a just-installed used jukebox. I don't want to go overboard—I mean, The Gun's hardly a major dining destination—but I have to say that in a remarkably short time, The Murf's transformed it from a disgusting dive to avoid at all costs into a comfy neighborhood hangout with decent food. Who knew he had it in him? I most certainly hadn't.

"I could have been rejected," I tell The Murf, who's intently polishing the new self-service soda station with a toothbrush and a chamois mitt. "I mean, if I wasn't somewhat in the ballpark, they could have just axed me. That's what they do to most people."

Is there anything more pitiful than somebody who's desperate to be consoled while at the same time refusing to admit there's anything to be consoled about? Well, say hello to the New Me.

"So I'm actually no worse off than if I was just applying for regular admissions," I maintain, persisting in presenting my very best-case scenario. "In fact, you could say I even have a slight advantage because now Columbia knows they're my first choice and that I'll go if they let me in. Colleges like knowing that."

"That's awesome, Brooks," replies The Murf, hustling to open the front door for some departing customers. "Thanks, folks. Come again soon."

Suddenly, The Murf goes pale, staring ahead in shock.

"It's Her," he gasps, going unsteady.

I turn to see what could have caused such an extreme reaction. It's Julie Hickey, bouncing our way after Pom Pom practice with her almost as bountiful co-captain Mandi Piddick. Stepping back inside, The Murf quickly shuts the door, shouting:

"CODE RED!! STAT!!!"

I watch in amazement as the two flunkies instantly mobilize into action. One unfurls a white linen tablecloth over a center window booth, which I see is always kept available with a "Reserved" sign. The other produces a vase of plastic flowers and candles. The Murf resets the jukebox with a bump of his hips. His own personal mix of romantic classics begins. Darting back and forth past me, the flunkies converge on The Murf. One positions a mirror in front of him so he can recheck the hair, the other holds out a sport jacket, which The Murf nimbly slips into. One brushes The Murf's shoulders with a whisk broom, the other dims the overhead lights. All part of the drill and accomplished just in time for The Murf to casually swing open the door and greet the object of his most hardcore desires.

"Arrivederci! Welcome to The Gun. We aim to please!" Cocking his fingers, he blows imaginary smoke from the barrel gangster-style. "Murphy. Peter Murphy, Night Manager."

"Julie, you know this creep?" Mindi asks, giving The Murf a dubious once-over.

"Don't ask," Julie answers, rolling thickly lashed eyes.

"Right this way, ladies," The Murf directs, unflappable. "Best seat in the house."

He ushers them to the now candlelit booth and makes a great show of removing the *Reserved* sign on it. Next, in a much rehearsed gesture, The Murf dramatically waves away the menus that the flunkies present, bowing and scraping all the while.

"If you'll allow me," says Mr. Suddenly Slick. He snaps his fingers with commanding presence. "Two *Vito Gargantuans* on rosemary ciabatta, extra peppers, extra cheese! The works! Pronto! Move your asses!"

The flunkies bolt back behind the counter. Despite my self-imposed misery, I'm curious to see how the new and improved Murf's going to play with Julie, but he shoots me a sharp look that makes sticking around out of the question.

"See you Saturday," I say.

He nods. Saturday. Then he spins back to Julie, clasping his hands, smiling slyly.

"Usually I'd recommend a crisp Chianti to go with the Vito, but since we're still waiting to hear back on the liquor license and you're under twenty-one anyway, we offer a wide variety of nonalcoholic beverages."

"Just water," replies Julie.

– – –

The lights blink on up and down Main Street, or what's left of it. Most of the storefronts are boarded up, long abandoned, their faded signs epitaphs to misplaced toil and dashed endeavor. A cold wind chills me to my bone-weary soul as I trudge back to my car. I am so tired of it. Of me. I begrudge The Murf nothing, wish him only the best, but his newly acquired sense of purpose accentuates my utter lack of one. Because I have lost mine. Fucking Deferred. I'm spent, the tank's dry. Besides, what difference does it make? Why keep banging my head against an impenetrable ivy-draped wall? Why not just give up, take the path of least resistance, go with the flow? It's not like someone's keeping track or even gives a flying fart. There's no one out there to monitor my misbehavior, acknowledge my struggle, or sympathize with my plight, no one in my corner to cheer me on, to push and prod. It's just me, always has been. And I'm feeling it more than I ever have before.

"HEY HO! LET'S GO!" my cell phone taunts. Yeah, right. What a joke. You ain't going nowhere, chump. Purely out of reflex, I take the call.

"Yeah," I answer dully, too dejected to ply on the professional facade.

"I want you to know I had to beg, grovel, and generally debase myself," a girl's voice announces from the other end of the line.

I recognize the voice. I never expected to hear it again.

"Celia Lieberman?" I say. I've had no contact with Celia Lieberman or any other Lieberman for weeks. Hearing her voice brings back painful memories of Shelby and the Good Life, both of which are farther than ever out of reach.

"Uncle Max will see you at his office at 10 a.m. sharp on Saturday," she informs me proudly. I can hear Gayle shrieking in the background. "Celia! Come see the darling dress I just bought you!"

Then it dawns on me what Celia Lieberman's going on about. Uncle Max. The physics professor at Columbia. The potential fingerhold that I never thought would happen. Could Uncle Max be the edge I lack and so sorely need to tip the delicate balance my way just once? I press the phone closer, not sure if I've heard right.

"He will?" Renewed commitment to my own slim cause courses in my veins. Instantly I'm recharged, remotivated.

Gayle screeches again in the most annoying way possible. "Ce-lia!"

"I'll meet you in front of Low Library at nine forty-five," Celia Lieberman says to me, then shouts at the top of her lungs: "LEAVE ME ALONE! I'M ON THE GOD-DAMN PHONE!!"

My right eardrum's blasted out. The pain's penetrating and intense. I stagger back from the shock waves ricocheting in my skull.

"Eight months, eleven days . . . ," Celia Lieberman mutters to herself. But I can't much hear her. I can't hear anything except a tremendous ringing that doesn't seem to be going away.

"You're coming with me?" I croak finally.

"I can't let you walk into the lion's den alone," she says.

"What do you mean, lion's den?" I ask suspiciously.

She clicks off before I can get an answer.

UNCLE MAX

No matter how many times I experience it, it still floors me. That first distant glimpse of the shimmering City on the northbound train. It comes at you all of a sudden, out of nowhere. A massive mountain range of glass, steel, and enterprise, towering past vast marshlands, beyond the glittering Hudson. It's like that scene in *The Wizard of Oz* when Dorothy, the Scarecrow, the Tin Man, and the Lion go skipping merrily across the fields of poppies toward the Emerald City sparkling ahead—except I don't pass out stoned on opium. I stare out my window in awe. I haven't been around much: Boston and Philly a couple of times, Baltimore once, but no great world capitals like London, Paris, or Beijing, but even so, I somehow know in my soul there's no City like mine. And nothing gets me stoked like just diving into it. Because in the City, you never know what's around the corner. In the City, any and all things are possible.

— — —

When I arrive fifteen minutes early, I discover Celia Lieberman's already there. Perched way up at the top of the great granite stairs to Low Library, sitting cross-legged, absorbed in a book. I almost don't recognize her because it's the first time I've ever seen her when she wasn't wearing a doofy gown or fluffy outfit that Gayle's picked out for her. Bundled in a knit cap, parka, and jeans, Celia Lieberman actually appears somewhat normal. She quickly tucks away the book into a pocket as she spots me approaching. She stands. I hold out my hand for her to shake. She takes it. Looking her steady in the eyes, I shake her hand firmly for a full five seconds, then release it. Her arm flops limply at her side.

"So how was it?" I inquire by way of greeting.

"How was what?" she responds, mystified.

"The average college interview lasts a mere 6.3 minutes," I explain. "Every second counts. Thus, the handshake, as my one PPC, assumes enormous importance in the Admissions Process."

"PP say what?"

"Physical Point Of Contact. It's in all the self-help books." How so like Celia Lieberman not to know. But then anybody who gets in Early Decision to Stanford doesn't need to know much about the gentle art of kissing ass like the rest of us mere mortals.

"A short, weak handshake exposes a lack of confidence,"

I explain in all seriousness. "But squeeze too long and hard and you might come off as a pushy jerk. The secret's a comfortable middle zone."

"You're scaring me, dude," she says, stepping back.

I thrust out my hand again.

"Go ahead," I instruct. "Give it another whirl."

"If I must." Celia Lieberman reluctantly re-shakes my hand. I give her the full treatment again—steady look in the eye, count to five, release.

"So how was it?"

"Weird," she answers. She plucks two cups of hot Starbucks from the steps and presents one to me.

"Better not," I beg off. "I'm wired enough as it is."

"You're nervous?" she asks, surprised.

Yes, I'm nervous. What does she expect? The lion's den? What's that about?

Dwarfed by immense edifices of higher learning on all sides, we wend our way through the bustling campus. This is a serious place, full of serious people thinking about serious things. It's almost like you can hear all the brain cells humming. And you know what? I love it.

"So why do you want to go to Columbia?" Celia Lieberman drills me.

"Because it's the closest Ivy League school to my house that I have a prayer of getting into," I answer lamely but honestly.

"No, dummy, not the real answer. Authority figures totally get off on lofty, altruistic horseshit."

Tell me about it. I think of Little Billy and what almost was and smile secretly. Celia Lieberman has no conception of just how lofty and full of altruistic horseshit I can be.

"Especially Uncle Max. He considers himself quite the intellectual giant, though he's a bit lacking in the social graces," she advises. "What did you say in your Short Essay?"

"I ended up writing about what a buzz I always get coming here."

"Here?" She looks at me, not following.

"Here. Columbia. Van Am Quad."

I stop, taking in the whole view. The Rotunda, with its weathered, chiseled words of wisdom from some forgotten notable. Taint Gate with its ancient clock that still works. Old school, understated, stately. An oasis of calm and reason in an increasingly crazed planet. Oh, to be just a tiny part of it.

"You come here a lot?" Celia Lieberman asks.

"Whenever I get the chance."

We resume our trek. I expound, though I'm not sure why.

"I know it sounds hokey but I always picture the people who were once late to class on the very concrete we're walking on. Alexander Hamilton. Jack Kerouac. Rodgers *and* Hammerstein. Even Lou Gehrig. Only when they were young like us and just anybody. Both Roosevelts, James freakin' Cagney, Barack Obama. Before they did their things and made their marks. I don't know, but it's . . . it's like touching greatness. That's kind of what I said in my Short Essay, but better because I did like a thousand drafts."

"Wow," she says. "Good one."

"And, actually, it's not bullshit," I admit a little shyly, wondering to myself why I am telling her any of this. Probably because I'm never going to see her again.

"Uncle Max will eat it up," Celia Lieberman predicts, trotting ahead of me. "Just be sure and mention Enrico Fermi. He was a member of the Physics Department here when he worked on the Manhattan Project."

"I know who Enrico Fermi is," I object, even though I don't, hurrying after her.

— — —

Uncle Max is a real bundle of charm. Craggy and gray, in a fraying sweater-vest, and out-of-control bushy eyebrows, which I have this tremendous compulsion to forcibly pluck. By the way he's glowering at the prearranged interruption, Uncle Max must have been on the brink of some cosmic breakthrough. And I can kind of believe it, judging from the stacks of thick scientific texts piled everywhere and the twin blackboards crammed with hastily scrawled calculations of dizzying complexity. I can see what Celia Lieberman means now about the lion's den. I'm way intimidated.

"Thanks, Uncle Max," Celia Lieberman twitters nervously. "I really appreciate . . ."

"C'mon, let's get it over with," Uncle Max barks. What was it Celia Lieberman said? A bit lacking in social graces? Try totally lacking. He opens his office door all the way, brusquely motioning her out into the hallway, and double-locks it after her.

"The daughter's as batty as the mother," he grumbles, settling behind a cluttered desk. "You have a name?"

"Brooks," I stammer. "Brooks Rattigan." I hastily remove a surprisingly heavy centrifuge from a dusty chair and sit.

"Well, Mr. Brooks Rattigan, I'll tell you what I tell everyone who asks for assistance for admission into this august institute of so-called edification. I'm a professor of physics, which doesn't rate very highly around here. I have absolutely no influence with admissions whatsoever. So if you don't mind, I'm an extremely busy man . . ."

Then, swiveling around in his seat, he surveys the two blackboards, picks up a nub of chalk, springs up, and resumes furiously jotting and erasing jumbles of letters and numbers. I sit there, stunned. That's it? I got my hopes up and schlepped all the way to Morningside Heights not to get my 6.3 minutes? Uncle Max could at least pretend not to give me the brush-off. I'd like to mess up his equations. I'd like to tweeze the hairs in his brows one by one by the roots. Giant intellect, my left testicle. Try giant asshole.

But I don't say this.

"Enrico Fermi!" I do blurt, desperate not to waste my only chance at a chance.

He turns to me, curious. "What about Enrico Fermi?"

As I rack my brain for a follow-up, Uncle Max's cell vibrates. He grimaces at the number on the display.

"Close the door on the way out," he mutters to me. Shuddering, steeling himself, he picks up his phone and clicks on. "What now, Marion?"

I've been dismissed. I will get no audience, no consideration, let alone glowing recommendation. Dejected, I stand and heft the centrifuge back on the chair.

"What do you expect me to do about it?" Uncle Max growls into his phone. "Take her myself?"

I reach for the doorknob. I start to turn it.

"Don't yell, Marion!" yells Uncle Max. "I understand it's her senior year. But be reasonable. In the overall scheme of the universe, the Winter Formal hardly rates . . ."

Winter Formal? I perk up. I linger, sensing opportunity, smelling fresh meat.

"That's not fair. But . . . yes, but, but . . ." Uncle Max wages a losing battle to get a word in edgewise. "Of course I'm all broken up about it. Gravity's our only child, but she'll live."

Suddenly I'm hearing electric guitar solos and a choir of heavenly voices. Dark clouds are parting, blinding celestial light is pouring down on me. I'm illuminated.

"Get a grip, Marion! It's not a tragedy . . ." Uncle Max flinches as I hear the line go dead on the other end. He shakily clicks off, rubbing his temples, a monumental migraine coming on. He's forgotten I'm there, that I exist. I let him twist in the wind for a moment or two, which is what the old grouch deserves. Oh, how swiftly the worm has turned. Picking my moment, I pounce.

"Excuse me, Professor," I offer in my most helpful tone. "But I couldn't help overhearing that you have a daughter . . ."

"Gravity," he says miserably, reaching for a large bottle of extra-strength aspirin.

"A lovely name. Must be a very special girl."

He puts down the bottle and looks at me. For a self-proclaimed genius, the cogs sure turn slowly for Uncle Max.

"Winter Formal," I mention in passing, coaxing him with my palms to reason it out, to make the connections and arrive at the obvious solution.

"Oh, she is!" he professes fervently, finally, finally getting it. "An, uh, inspired ceramicist . . ."

— — —

Celia Lieberman's pacing anxiously when we emerge twenty-three minutes later. Me with a shit-eating grin, followed by a fawning, effusive Uncle Max.

"The Dean of Admissions is an old poker pal of mine,

Brooks," he enthuses. "I'll be sure to give him the full-court press first chance I get."

"Thanks, Max," I say magnanimously. "Anything you can do."

Her mouth drops in astonishment as Max, overcome with gratitude, crushes me in an emotional bear hug.

– – –

"You are such a sleaze!" howls Celia Lieberman, almost choking on her foot-long after I tell her what went down.

I am a sleaze. A fat, happy one. I marvel at how the winds of fate have so suddenly and so uncharacteristically blown my way. I revel in my ability to spot and seize the moment, take immense pride in my complete lack of scruples. A sleaze, you bet your sweet ass I am. And to celebrate my underhanded feat, I've treated us both to two of New York's finest, heaped high with all the fixings as we thread down the vibrant, teeming sidewalks of upper Broadway.

"I can't believe you stiffed poor Uncle Max for 150 bucks," Celia Lieberman says, mustard dribbling down her chin.

"Hey, that's 40 percent off the normal rate, and he insisted," I say, swallowing hunks of delicious animal fats and artificial additives. "What I can't believe is that somebody named their daughter Gravity. No wonder she's depressed."

Suddenly, Celia Lieberman halts, stricken. "Hey, you didn't tell him anything about me?"

"Please, I'm a trained professional," I reassure her. "Discretion comes with the job."

We come to the corner and the stairs to the subway. Celia Lieberman stops again.

"Well, this is me," she says.

What she means is this is where we say good-bye, which I abruptly realize will be for the last time. All Lieberman business has been transacted. I should be jumping up and down for joy, but I'm not. I'm appreciative and grateful that Celia Lieberman, that anybody, in fact, has come through for me. As Celia Lieberman awkwardly sticks out her hand to shake a fond *adieu*, something falls to the ground from her parka pocket. Gallantly I bend to retrieve it for her.

It's a paperback book, the one she was reading earlier. The blue cover crinkled and faded, the pages tattered, yellowed, worn around the edges. I recognize it. I should. We have a bunch just like it at home. *Skies of Stone* by Charles Rattigan.

Just seeing the title almost takes my breath away. I hand Charlie's one claim to anything back to Celia Lieberman, looking at her questioningly.

"Where did you . . ."

"Online. And let me tell you, it wasn't easy . . ." she replies uneasily, quickly pocketing it again.

"How is it?" I ask, mildly curious, but mostly weirded out that she has a copy.

"So far a real downer, but in a really good way," she informs me. She pauses. "Are you telling me you've never read it?"

And give that asshole the pleasure? No, I haven't read it. For a whole slew of reasons that I've never been able to sort out and have long ago given up trying to. Mostly I guess because I've never wanted to experience firsthand the sheer magnitude of Charlie's wasted potential. Good? I'm sure it is. But what's done is done. No use crying over spoiled talent. What's the point of thinking what might have been if Charlie could have just kept it together? Good? With my luck, I'm sure *Skies of Stone* is goddamn terrific. Read it? No fucking way.

But I don't say that.

"Well, thanks for the memories," I do say, a little more crisply than intended, sticking out my hand.

"You too," she says softly, shaking hands with me. "Good luck with Columbia."

"Give 'em heck at Stanford," I respond, sorry to have been so sharp.

We just stand there, then Celia Lieberman starts down the stairs. I watch her go with strangely mixed feelings. Glad to be rid of her, but deeply grateful, a little nostalgic too. Can't say it hasn't been uneventful. Then, as she's about halfway down—I swear to God I don't know where it's coming from—but I call after her:

"If you want to attract that Franklin guy, you have to make an effort."

She stops, teetering on a step, and turns to me, surprised. What have I done? What am I doing? We look at each other. Neither of us speaks. Finally, she picks up the conversation where I so abruptly left off.

"I've tried everything," she laments. "Laughing at his lame jokes. Dropping stuff and bending over. Listening to his incredibly awful taste in music. Get this, Franklin actually thinks the Backstreet Boys are underrated."

"You cannot be serious."

"*Seriously* underrated," she emphasizes.

"God," I sympathize.

"I even let him beat me in chess, which is hard because Franklin really sucks."

"I mean, how you dress," I suddenly say, trying to stay on subject, again not sure why. Celia lowers her eyes, self-conscious.

"That's a lost cause."

Climbing back up the stairs, she rejoins me on the sidewalk. People stream in all directions around us. We're in the way. She follows me through the fray, off by the storefronts where we can conduct a more private consultation. I turn to her, all business.

"You've got all the right fundamentals to build on," I say, "analytically speaking, of course. You just need to find your own style."

"Oh, and you're an expert," she says, ever the skeptic.

"After four months of being a stand-in, I happen to consider myself an authority on fashion," I sniff haughtily.

Actually I kind of do. In the past months, I've pretty much seen it all. Strapless gowns, backless dresses, those halter jobbies. Hair straight, teased, curled, up, down, sideways, sometimes all at once. And shoes. Don't get me started on shoes. Why the female gender's so obsessed with them is beyond me. I own like two pairs. But not them. At least three pairs of everything. High heels, flats, open-toed, the variety is mind-numbing. I won't delve into the dos and don'ts of makeup, the toners, enhancers, powders, and lotions, or the ins and outs of proper nail color. It's like each girl is her own personal work of art. Before late September, I never realized the stupendous effort, infinite choices, and extreme anxiety that go into being a typical teenage girl. And, if you ask me, they're all insane. Yeah, I know it's how society tells them they have to be. But still. Lunatics, every last one of them.

But, again, I don't say that.

"Well, maybe not," I concede instead. "But I know what guys like, being that I am one."

"My mother buys all my stuff," she says.

"What would you wear if it was your choice?"

"*My* choice?" The idea seems inconceivable to her.

"Your hair," I say. "Ever consider going shorter?"

"Like in a bob like—?" she looks at me, alarmed. "Isn't that a little radical?"

I chuckle. There's so much I could do.

"Give me two hours and I'll rock your world," I vow.

Celia Lieberman stares critically at herself in the front

window of a Chinese restaurant. Despite the flocks of drying duck carcasses dangling from hooks alongside her reflection, she seems intrigued by her possibilities. Then I read the doubts flickering on her face. Self-expression, to sink or swim by one's individual predilections and preferences, without mom and dad as an excuse and ultimate safety net, is too much for her.

"Sorry," she says, wimping out. "But I can't afford you."

"No charge."

"No charge?" She looks at me, incredulous.

This isn't exactly the way I expected to spend my precious afternoon in the City. But like I said, in the City, you never know what's going to happen. So I go with it.

"One good turn deserves another," I toss off, casual-like. "Besides, I'm meeting a friend later so I've got some time to kill anyway."

– – –

I take her to Williamsburg, the new hipster section of Brooklyn. She's never been. I've been once, but act like I'm a regular. As we stroll down funky Bedford Avenue, I recount all my adventures at the local watering holes, making them up as I go. I nod in warm greeting at people I don't know, and I'm quickly running out of material when we finally reach our destination. A techno hair salon of which I took mental note on my sole prior reconnaissance as a hotbed of super hotties. If I'm going to do a good deed, might as well soak in the scenery while I'm at it.

"Prepare to be transformed!" I announce grandly.

First, a multi-tattooed, multi-pierced beautician prepares to hack off a good six inches of Celia Lieberman's unruly locks with a giant pair of medieval scissors. Celia Lieberman pleads with me for three inches. I hold firm at five. She resorts to death threats. It's like she's possessed by Satan, only her head's not spinning around and she's not puking up green slime. I remain resolute. Five it is.

Next, the glasses. The frames, I mean. They have definitely got to go. They're earnest and clunky, and Celia Lieberman's earnest and clunky enough as it is. We move on. I take her to an out-of-the-way place I've read about in Greenpoint with cool stuff. In her newly shorn state, she blindly squints at herself in the mirror in a succession of trendy, retro-hip items. Cat eye, rainbow, aviator, oval, oblong, octagonal. Most are hopeless on her. But I keep trying, methodically winnowing through looks and affectations. As I make my final selection—horn half-rims, bookish but with just the right touch of attitude—Celia Lieberman expresses loud reservations. I tell her to trust me. She has to since she can't see a thing without corrective lenses.

By the time I practically drag her into the vintage store down the block, Celia Lieberman's in full rebellion. She gapes at the racks and racks of rumpled garments.

"But they're used!" she squawks, backing to the door.

"Oh, excuse me, your Royal Highness," I say, yanking her back in.

But it's the last time I will have my say.

For the next two hours it's like I'm a prisoner trying to escape from a music video in some chick flick. Skirts. Dresses. Ensembles. Mod. Punk. Goth. A parade of major and minor fads of the past half century. One by one, Celia Lieberman tries them on for my inspection. Why, I have no idea. Because my opinions are roundly ignored, soundly ridiculed, or summarily rejected. In a minor snit, I throw up my hands and catch up on my email. It's like a feeding frenzy, the cute little shopping bags with handles multiplying exponentially as we make the rounds. I become her Sherpa.

By the time we get to shoes, as I feared we eventually would, I'm zonked, going on fumes, but not Celia Lieberman. No, Celia Lieberman's just hitting her stride. She balances on stilettos, spins around on disco platforms, poses in checkered sneakers. About ten cute little bags with handles later, when we finally leave the store, I'm in a dazed stupor but momentarily rouse myself as we pass a large picture window displaying skimpy, kinky lingerie. Now here's a cute little bag with handles I would gladly add to my burden. I hasten to open the door for Celia Lieberman. She gives me a bemused look and marches on. A guy can try, can't he?

– – –

Greenwich Village. Fourteenth to West Houston, Hudson to Broadway. A few blocks only, but its own special vibe. In the Village, the streets aren't numbered or alphabetized or laid out logically in grids; they have names and go nowhere. MacDougal, Christopher, Grove, St. Luke's Place: each is its own story. Right from the start, the Village's been the part of New York reserved for the unconventional—the rebels, the oddballs, the outcasts. The dreamers. Super important writers composed masterpieces here. Edgar Allan Poe. Mark Twain. Robert Louis Stevenson. You can still feel their presence somehow. And Dylan Thomas, just about the only poet I halfway get. In the early sixties, when he was just starting out, Bob Dylan played the Gate and the Vanguard, both tattered and worn but still doing business. Later on, at the late, lamented CBGB, it was the Velvet Underground, the Dolls, the Ramones, the whole glam and grunge scenes. Gay rights started in the Village. So did the women's rights movement. In the Village, the stuff of legend happens. It's my favorite piece of the City, one I know well.

And the best time to be in the Village is right now, just before Christmas. It's not just the strings of colored lights strewn everywhere, the rappers rhyming, the ethnic foods frying, the clusters of demonstrators demanding this, the counter-demonstrators protesting that, or the steady buzz and bustle of holiday commerce that makes December so awesome here. It's the *all* of it. The energy, the expectation, the sense something Big's coming.

So even though I'm laden like a pack mule with Celia Lieberman's purchases, I'm feeling frisky. Uncle Max's going to put in a personal word to the Dean of Admissions about me, my self-inflicted shopping ordeal is over, the mighty Pixies await! Crossing the narrow cobblestone lane, I breathe in Café Figaro with its intoxicating aroma of steamed milk, chocolate, and freshly roasted coffee. And almost get flattened by an errant taxi running the light. We're talking inches. The asshole doesn't even honk.

"DICKHEAD!" I shout, lucky to be alive.

The turbaned cabbie flips me the bird. I cheerfully flip him right back.

"God, I dig this city!" I exclaim.

"You certainly seem to know your way around it," remarks Celia Lieberman, now having to do the scurrying to keep up.

"I come whenever I can," I say loftily, surveying my domain. "It's neutral territory."

"Neutral territory?"

"Yeah, you never know anybody and nobody knows you so the gloves are off. You can be yourself without the slightest social consequence. It's liberating."

We safely reach the other side. Another cab rockets by. I smack a forearm at it, just for the fun of it.

"FUCKFACE!!"

In Pritchard if I shouted that in public on the street, I'd most likely be arrested. In Green Meadow, I'd be beaten to a pulp by the local police within seconds. But this being the City, I don't get a single look, reaction, or objection. Not even by the beefy cop in a long coat, patrolling his beat, twirling a nightstick.

"See?" I boast. "No one gives a fart!"

Celia Lieberman looks at the cop, then at me again, a little appalled. "So this is the real Brooks Rattigan?" she asks wryly. "A seething mass of anger and resentment?"

"That's me."

Suddenly, from down the corner, I hear a familiar refrain.

"YO, BROOKSIE!"

Do my eyes deceive me? It's The Murf, just as expected, but it's The Murf of old: happily disheveled, hammered out of his mind, swinging one-armed from a lamppost. Can this day get any better? It can. He holds up a huge square bottle of wine, which God only knows where he scored.

"Manischewitz!" he toasts. "This shit's kosher!"

– – –

"It's good," admits The Murf, furiously chewing. "I ain't gonna lie. Damn good. But I've had better."

The three of us are devouring an entire extra-large sausage and peppers, standing up, squeezed at a grimy counter. John's of Bleecker Street is one of those places aficionados swear by, and who's got the best pizza is the heated topic of an ongoing debate between The Murf and me since we were five.

"Wanna real slice?" pontificates The Murf, shoveling his down. "Come to Jersey! Tony's in Neptune City. Now there's crust. Now that's a pie! Am I right or am I right, Brooks?"

Drying her fingers on a napkin, Celia Lieberman dutifully types in the name on her iPhone. "Tony's. Neptune City. Got it."

"The Murf's the world's greatest authority on junk food," I inform her.

She laughs, relaxed and not uptight as usual. She's actually having a good time with us. I hadn't intended to include Celia Lieberman, but The Murf had insisted and I'd reluctantly given in. I'm not that comfortable with having my two realities intersect. Celia Lieberman and The Murf's are very different sides of me that I've carefully kept separate from each other. But surprisingly, they get along pretty well.

"I don't know," she says, "we've got some pretty good places in Green Meadow."

"Sure, if you're looking for a nonfat, nontaste, tiny slice of nothing," The Murf scoffs. "Quiche-eaters."

"You're right." Celia Lieberman smiles, surrendering gracefully. "Give me Jersey anyday."

She's being open and nice, not patronizing and condescending. The Murf beams. I can tell he likes this Celia Lieberman.

It's getting close to concert time. Under The Murf's thoroughly amused eye, I dutifully haul Celia Lieberman's plunder outside after her, staggering beneath the tonnage, and signal for a cab.

"Your friend's nice," she notes, almost as much to herself as to me.

Little does she know that, right behind her, displayed in the front window of John's, The Murf's flashing me two emphatic thumbs up like Celia Lieberman's some kind of hot babe.

"Yeah, The Murf's one of a kind," I remark fondly. "Which is good because the world couldn't handle two of him."

Then, to up the ante, The Murf puts up paws and wags his tongue like a crazed canine, like I should totally go for it. The man's got no shame.

Go for it? With Celia Lieberman? The idea's preposterous.

A taxi skids over to the curb. I swing open the door and pile all her little cute shopping bags on the backseat. She slides in beside them and then turns to me, waiting. For what, I don't know.

"Franklin will never know what hit him," I tell her.

"It's probably still a losing effort, but thanks, Coach."

"Confidence! Positive mental attitude! Go team!" I close the door. This is it. This time I have a clear conscience and no regrets. All accounts have been settled. We part with a clean slate. As the cab rolls away, she lowers her window and leans out.

"Well, nice knowing you, Brooks Rattigan!"

"You too, Celia Lieberman," I call back, slightly surprised because I kinda sorta mean it. I watch her disappear into traffic and out of my life forever.

CLOSE CALL(S)

The Pixies are what they always are when I see them. Atomic. No gimmicks, Jumbotrons screens, or elaborate light shows with this crew. Just a damn fine band jamming, charging through straight-ahead, kick-ass tunes. In fine fettle, Black Francis growls, snarls, roars, a deranged monk. Joey's wailing, killing it on lead, and Dave's pounding the skins like he's gonna give himself a heart attack, which, at his semi-advanced age, he just might. Good, honest music. I ask you: Does it get any better?

Smooshed in front of the sold-out house, The Murf and me are buffeted in the hurricane of sound, both of us well on the way to glorious drunken stupor, me having secured a treasured colored wristband from a sympathetic elder hipster. Pumping our fists to the thunderous beat, barraged by flailing limbs, we give back as good as we get, pushing and shoving, getting pushed and shoved in return. Absolute chaos, pure abandon, unbridled release. It's been so long, the sensations feel almost brand new again.

I trap The Murf in an exuberant headlock. He counters with a hard elbow to my gut. I double over. We both grin. Like old times. Buds again. I brandish two fingers, querying if he's ready for refortification. The Murf nods enthusiastically.

It takes a full ten minutes for me to battle my way to the bar in the lobby and another ten to order up another round. I'm regrouping when I hear:

"Brooks?" The seductive voice sends tingly sensations up and down my spine. "Brooks Rattigan?"

I don't have to tell you who it is, but I will anyway.

Shelby Pace.

Leaving little to my vivid imagination in a micro-skirt that stops just short of being prosecutable. Shelby Pace, of long lithe leg, of tawny skin, of plunging neckline revealing glimpses of nothing else underneath. Shelby Pace, the beyond-attainable.

I'm speechless. Not only by her presence but by the impossibility of her. I'm a puddle, an overheated, soggy heap. Everyone is. My God, it's the freakin' Pixies! How can you not be? But somehow Shelby isn't. Even jostled in the crush, she's perfectly put together, not a hair out of place, apart from it all. It's like she's one of those Greek goddesses we studied in class, the ones who descend from Olympus to sport on a whim with us lesser beings. Shelby's lips, ripe and luscious, smile coyly. Her emerald cat's eyes tease.

"Should have known you'd be here making the scene," she says.

I look at her dumbly. Why would she think that? Then my web of deceit re-engulfs me. I'm not from Jersey, I'm from here. I'm cutting edge, ahead of the curve. My gears snap into alternate reality mode.

"I . . . I practically live next door," I shrug, nonchalant. "You alone?"

A tremor in the crowd presses us together. I breathe her in again. Her scent's subtle, delicate, yet pungent. She smells like Money.

"Oh, I am," I profess. "So very alone!"

On cue, I'm handed two large, overflowing plastic cups of beer by the guy behind the counter, indicating to Shelby that I'm either an alcoholic or a compulsive liar or both.

"You?" I wince.

"Yup," she sighs, taking one of the beers and sipping it. "Just poor little *moi*."

Then, glancing over Shelby's shoulder, I spy Cassie Trask, wearing a cute little designer ensemble, being hotly pursued from the women's room by a bunch of tough, tattooed City chicks, all loudly giving her shit. Shelby's clearly not here alone. Shelby's a lying piece of shit—just like me. Somehow it only adds to her allure.

"BROOKS! YO, BROOKSIE!!" It's The Murf, glassy-eyed, shirt torn, nose bleeding. He waves happily across the tumult to me. I pretend I don't see him.

"Want to cut out?" I suggest.

"HELLLPPPP!!" squawks Cassie, getting bounced around and hassled by the City chicks. She must have said something really offensive to piss them off in the bathroom. Knowing Cassie even as little as I do, there are so many inappropriate things she could have said. Actually, she didn't need to say anything. It's easy to detest Cassie just on sight.

"Absolutely!" Shelby says, willingly abandoning her best friend to a dire fate.

We escape by taxi. I eagerly clamber in after her.

"Where to?" the cabbie grunts. I'm at a loss. Where does one take a girl who has done and seen everything?

"Seven ninety-nine Park Avenue," Shelby says.

As we pull away, The Murf sprints out into the middle of the busy street, shouting in pantomime after us. I conveniently ignore him.

Yeah, I know. It stinks, a monumental double cross on my part. Like most guys, there's an Unspoken Code between The Murf and me that all fraternal obligations are null and void if the prospect of hooking up with a hottie appears on the radar. No, taking off's not my crime. Taking off without warning or word is. But I'm guilty of something much bigger than that. It's not just that I'm afraid The Murf would blow my cover and ruin my chances with Shelby, meager as they are. There's an even deeper sin which I have committed, if just in my mind. The terrible fact is that, for the first time ever, I'm ashamed of The Murf, ashamed of who he is, what he represents. Most of all, I'm ashamed of myself. Being with Shelby does that to me.

And Shelby is all that matters.

- - -

I have a confession to make. In all my visitations to the City, I have never taken a single cab. And, as we arrive at our unknown destination, I am harshly reminded why. Fifteen bucks to go sixty measly blocks. Forty cents a block. The subway would have been almost as quick and cost a tenth. Just saying.

Shelby hops out, leaving me to settle accounts. It's not deliberate. It just that since money's not a consideration for her, she assumes it's not for the rest of the world. With anyone else, it would be obnoxious. But I'm charmed and gladly fork over, extravagantly adding a 3 percent tip.

We're on the Upper East Side, a region into which I've never before ventured because I've never before had the slightest reason to. One of the many things that gives me a rush about the City is how each part of it has its own mojo going. Wall Street. Soho. Times Square. The names alone are iconic. Tribeca. The Flatiron District. The Bowery. So diverse, so equally unaffordable. The whole damn City is. Tens of thousands to rent a place the size of a broom closet, multiple millions to buy even the teensiest square footage. Even so, there are areas that are more stratospheric than others. Well, the Upper East Side's pretty much on the very tippy-top of the fiscal totem pole. Private townhouses, luxury high rises, super high-end stores. Trends may come and go and other neighborhoods may ebb and flow, but the Upper East Side's exclusivity reigns supreme. I mean, the Upper East Side looks down on the Upper West Side, which is saying something since you practically have to run a small country or major hedge fund to own an apartment on the Upper West Side. The Upper East Side prides itself on looking down on everybody. Not just in New York. On the entire planet.

"You live here?" I gasp.

I trail reverently after Shelby to the locked entrance of one stately palace. She presses a gold-plated button beside a gold-plated door.

"It's not much," she says.

"Oh no, just Park Avenue," I observe dryly. Even within the Upper East Side there's a pecking order. Park's the shit.

Through the glass, an elderly doorman, kindly and portly like the grandfather you always wished you had, bustles up to the door and unlatches it.

"Evening, Miss Shelby," he says, tipping the brim of his hat.

"Hey, Hugh, how's it hanging?" Shelby says, breezing past him into the small plush lobby. There's a single elevator at the end of it, which magically slides open for her. I scoot inside just as it whooshes shut behind me.

"Just a little pied-à-terre for when Mommy and Daddy are too tired to make it back to Green Meadow . . . ," Shelby explains. The elevator slides open, revealing not a corridor of doors to separate deluxe apartments, but the middle of somebody's living room.

Yes, a living room. The Pace pied-à-terre takes up the entire floor of the building. Okay, it's not a huge building. But still.

"Make yourself at home," Shelby says. "I have to pee."

The place is the usual amazing. More priceless art. More antiques. More Taste, more Class. Floor-to-ceiling windows on all sides. High above the rabble, I stare out in awe at the dark expanse of Central Park, framed by the magnificent, glittering skyline. My eyes shine. For I have seen the light. This, my friends, is What Life Is All About.

"Someday," I promise myself.

"Did you say something?" Shelby says, reemerging.

"Uh, I was just saying that second places are essential to maintaining one's sanity . . ."

Using a universal remote, Shelby dims the lights, activates the fireplace, and turns on some romantic sounds. "Sex Me (Part 1)" by R. Kelly. An excellent—and encouraging—choice. I just hope there's a Part 2. "Oh, you have one?"

Me and my big mouth. Do I have a second place? Why the hell did I have to imply I had one? Now I *have* to have one. Where the hell do I have one?

"Just a little shack in the Hamptons," I stammer. "We barely use it, but it's comforting to know it's there."

Kicking off her heels, Shelby pads to a well-stocked bar and looks through an array of imposing bottles. "East, West, or South?

Does it matter? How can there be so many increments within increments of status? I mean, how do they keep track of it all? What difference does it make? They're all goddamn richer than fuck. But it does. I look at her blankly.

"East, West, or South Hampton?" she repeats, pouring us each big crystal snifters with dollops of thick golden liquid. Cognac. The label's in French. I make mental note of it.

"Uh, Midhampton. It's kind of in the center."

Shelby's brow furrows. She's never heard of it—because it doesn't friggin' exist. I grimace but brazen it through. Swaying to the throbbing, insistent music, she hands me a snifter, gently swirling hers by the stem. I take the bowl-sized glass with a teaspoon of wildly expensive alcohol in it. I've never held a snifter before and, when I swirl mine too, I almost douse myself. We're both swirling like crazy as we raise snifters.

"To new acquaintances," she toasts.

We clink. She drains her glass in one sultry gulp. I swig mine down too. Instantly, a river of hot molten lava courses through my already thoroughly buzzed body, scorching my insides, settling in my already short-circuiting nether regions. My eyes water. My head goes all fuzzy, my vision in and out of focus. So this is good cognac. I must have it. Another new necessity to add to the list I'm starting.

Shelby curls up on the couch, patting the space beside

her for me to sit. I gladly obey. We are bathed in the glow of artificial flames. I turn to her. She turns to me. Our lips are mere inches apart and getting closer. Aroused and intoxicated, I fight to control my animal instincts, to resist the overwhelming urge to just jump her bones.

"How's Celia Lieberman?" Shelby says, taking me way, way off guard.

Celia Lieberman's the last person I'm thinking about. I mean, Celia Lieberman's not even a blip on the monitor. Then I detect a predatory gleam in Shelby's eyes, and it's not entirely transfixing like everything else about her. I pull back a little as I realize that my terrific looks and sparkling personality aside, Celia Lieberman's a substantial, if not primary reason, for Shelby's astounding interest in me. Ah yes, of course, nothing beats the thrill of causing someone else's heartbreak simply because you can. And this sudden realization throws me into a brief philosophical quandary. Is it wrong to cheat on Celia Lieberman even though I'm not actually going out with her? Technically that's not two-timing, is it? But the fact that Shelby thinks it is somehow makes it not so cool to me.

"You know Celia Lieberman," I answer noncommittally. "Never a dull moment."

"So things are good between you two?" she inquires, hovering.

"Oh yeah," I say, looking away. "Just today we were strolling beneath the elms at Columbia and I was remarking to her . . ."

I can't believe what I'm saying. There are no elms at Columbia. Why am I saying this? I'm never going to see Celia Lieberman again. I'm drinking fine French cognac alone with the most beautiful and beguiling female in the world in her parents' posh Park Avenue pad with a gazillion-dollar view, and I'm blowing it. This cannot be.

"Remarking to her about the, uh, all-time greats who were once late to class on the very concrete on which we were treading . . ."

Shelby nuzzles a fragrant cheek against mine. She's making it very, very difficult for me to remain theoretically faithful. I trail off. She nibbles my ear. For love of God, I'm only flesh and blood. My resolve's cracking, about to shatter into bits.

"Lou Kerouac," I croak, "Jack Gehrig . . ."

"Well, come September, I'll be serving a four-year sentence there," Shelby says, kissing me. Her lip gloss tastes like citrus with hints of chocolate. I am too stunned to respond. I stare at her, aghast.

"You . . . you got into Columbia?"

Shelby looks at me, mystified. I'm not just giving in according to plan. I'm a puzzle and a challenge, even though what I really am is envious and jealous.

"Early Decision." She gets up from the couch and pours us both another snifter. "Not that I ever had any choice. My dad went to Columbia, and his dad and his dad. My brother, my sister. And now me."

Oh, poor baby. A fucking legacy. I might have known.

It's not enough that mommy and daddy can fund a chair or endow a library. The acceptance rate at Columbia is triple for legacies than it is for the great unwashed mob like me. Like she doesn't have enough going for her.

"Even so, it was a little iffy," Shelby muses. "Whoever invented extended time, I salute him."

"Extended time?"

"For learning disabilities. Mine's anxiety. A shrink writes a note and then you get as much time as you need to take the SATs and nobody knows."

"They can do that?" I marvel. I had no inkling that such a thing was even possible. "And no one actually knows?"

"Half the kids I know at Green Meadow get it," she says, holding out a snifter.

Extended Time. I'm floored, reeling at the enormity of it. I've heard of rigging the system, but nothing nearly as nefarious as this.

"Don't they have it at your school?" She gives me a curious look. "Oh, that's right, you're homeschooled."

Extended Time. This is beyond the bounds of my paranoia. Talk about your shadowy conspiracies. The last people who need extended time get it. And for what? Anxiety! I've got tons of anxiety, I ooze anxiety, I define anxiety, and nobody's extending me a single nanosecond of extra anything. When I think of what my scores would be with Extended Time, when I think of what I had to go through to raise them. Work Hard and Play By The Rules, we're taught. Only Rule Number One is that the rules don't apply to the people in charge because they make up the stinking rules. What a sick joke. What a complete outrage!

But I don't say that.

"I got Deferred," I do say, bitterly guzzling my cognac.

"Really? At Columbia?" she says. "Hey, maybe we'll be classmates."

Somehow I doubt it. Shelby settles beside me on the couch. Leaning in, she tries again, kissing me with extra emphasis. I'm unresponsive, still digesting the criminality of Extended Time. When she finishes, I pipe:

"My dad went to Harvard."

I wince. I sound like such a loser. Why am I so insecure? Why do I feel I have to justify myself to her? Actually I've got tons of reasons, enough to keep that shrink of hers scribbling on a little pad for decades. Try because I'm a phony and a fraud, just for starters.

"He's a writer," I mention for no particular reason.

Shelby could care less if he was Buddha. Exasperated, she belts down the rest of her snifter.

"Celia Lieberman's not the only one who can put out," she declares with grim determination and shoves me backwards on the couch. As I flop limply on the cushions, she reaches down, unbuckles my belt, and unzips me, one, two, three, all business. And . . . and I don't know how else to put this, I mean, what can I say—she shoves her hand down my pants.

It's as if I've been hit by a bolt of lightning. I writhe, shudder, and stiffen in her sure grip. Thankfully this is no hallucination. And resistance is futile. Not that I'm resisting in the slightest way. At this point I'm a hundred and one percent with the program.

I pull her to me and suddenly we're rolling back and forth making out with serious tongue action. Her manicured fist is going great guns. She's got me where she wants me. Where I've longed to be. Totally at her mercy. I'm on fire, all chemical reaction, engorged sensation. Shelby breaks away, slick with our mixed slobber, smiling in victory.

"That's more like it."

"Yes," I pant like a dog, begging, "more like it."

Shelby slowly lowers between my legs from sight. Everything about me—eyes, tongue, upper and lower appendages—is lolling in anticipation. That heavenly choir is singing hallelujah. Her lips, my you-know-what. Oh, everlasting joy!

Then lights shine, blindingly bright. Not metaphorical lights, but real actual artificial ones.

"Shelby?" says Shelby's mom, squinting in the entryway. "What are you doing here?"

Startled, Shelby scrambles up and over the couch for cover. I leap to my feet. Seeing me—or rather, it—Shelby's mom drops her shopping bags in stupefaction.

"Oh, dear."

I look down, gulp, immediately turn around, quickly tuck in and re-zip myself and then whip around again. I've got a monster—and I mean monster—pup tent sticking out from the front of my trousers. I never knew I could be that monstrous. In another place and time, I'd be rather impressed with myself. In this one, however, I snatch a fancy pastel throw pillow, shielding my massive protrusion, and grab my jacket and frantically mince to the open door.

"Nice seeing you again, Mrs. Pace!" Shelby's mom skitters from my path. I wave back to Shelby without looking. "Well, be seeing you, Shelby!"

Shelby peeps up from behind the couch. "Say hi to Celia for me!"

– – –

Epididymal Hypertension. Or what's known in the male gender as Blue Balls. Basically, boys and girls, when a guy gets really turned on—which I definitely am—the blood flows to his, well, stuff. He gets a, well, you know—which I most emphatically have—and his, well, things swell up to 50 percent beyond normal size—which mine unfortunately have. The nut sack loses oxygen and assumes a slight bluish tinge, hence the name. I haven't had a chance to look, but I assume mine's deep purple. If there is no release, so to speak—which in my case there hasn't been—these over-inflated balloons become supersensitive and super painful. Now here's the bone of contention, so to speak. Many women, in fact, claim Blue Balls are a shameless fabrication designed to elicit pity sex. A masculine myth.

Well, lemme tell you, it's no fucking myth. And Shelby's citrus-glossed mouth you-know-where was no fabrication, even if it was just for a fraction of a second. Not only do I have a throbbing hard-on the length and girth of a telephone pole, which I'm unsuccessfully trying to camouflage with the pastel throw pillow I'm still clutching, but sharp excruciating spasms rack my shell-shocked body with each delicate step. I'm traveling at a snail's pace down the bustling street, sweating in the cold, groaning, breathing heavily. Fortunately for me, I'm in the City, where I'm well within the realm of what's considered normal behavior.

You know that pervert that's always on the subway late at night making demented faces and disgusting sounds as he fondles his junk? Well, that would be me. Gripping a hand strap with one arm, clamping the tasseled throw pillow over my aching groin with the other, I dangle, moaning with every vibration of the speeding car. The other passengers give me wide, wary berth. I don't blame them.

The forty-three-minute train ride back to Pritchard is a dull haze, but somehow I make it. Leaning on the railing, I slowly limp down the stairs, pillow still strategically positioned since there's no letup in the wood department. Blasting home in the Beast, the pain arrives in huge waves now and I swear I almost pass out twice. I'm a corked-up pressure cooker. I curse the heavens, pounding the wheel in sexual frustration, my intense physical anguish compounded by even greater mental torment. It's so unfair. My blow job lasted all of a second. How much can one man take?

I burst through the door into the apartment, tossing aside the throw pillow, unbuttoning my trousers, hobbling straight to the kitchen. Flinging open the freezer, I yank out the tray to the ice maker and empty the entire contents down the front of my boxers.

"Awwwwwwwww!!!" I grunt like a Neanderthal.

I gyrate and swivel my pelvis, adjusting the ice that packs my underwear. The effect's immediate and soothing, the intense coldness numbing my overexcited, under-stimulated gonads. Well, what do you know? It really works. Cubes dripping down my pants legs, I whine, I whimper.

Then I see a small ember light up in the darkness, glowing at the table. It's Charlie in his pajamas, sucking on a blunt, clinically observing me. Wonderful. Just what I need. What the hell is he doing up? He's never up.

"What?" I snap defensively, refusing to give him the satisfaction of me being embarrassed no matter how severely compromised I happen to be. "I saw Pacino do it once in a movie."

Mustering my shredded dignity, trailing ice, I crunch to the sink and scoop out my glacial load into it. Charlie observes me in silence.

"You're out late," he finally says. "And it was De Niro."

"Greek wedding in Parsippany," I blithely lie, sticking to my catering cover story. "Those things go all night. The souvlaki was really flying."

I shuffle awkwardly toward my room. Although frozen, my equipment's still in an all too fragile state and I'm careful not to jar it more than absolutely necessary.

"Well, next time you're out until three, call," Charlie admonishes after me, asserting parental authority. This while he's got a roach sticking out of the corner of his mouth. The guy's pathetic. I haven't been home before three every Saturday night for months and this is the first time he's bothered to notice. I do what I always do and ignore him. All I can think about is the comfort of bed.

"This came for you today."

He holds up a thin stamped envelope from the table. It's embossed with a familiar crest on the upper corner. Columbia University. My official notice of Admissions Purgatory. Like most colleges, Columbia mails its verdicts as well as posts them online. Their way of providing you with the indelible experience of having your dreams destroyed twice for the price of one dime. I'd forgotten to intercept it.

Nothing like a little failure to make one go flaccid. The night's woes vanish as the bigger, darker picture redescends on me. And Charlie knowing just adds to the crushing burden.

"That's mine!" I say, springing to him in one step, grabbing the envelope from his grimy hand. His very touch taints my chances.

"I've delivered enough of those through the years to know what's inside," Charlie says mildly.

This is why he stayed up. To personally revel in my latest defeat. Asshole.

"Sorry to disappoint you, Charlie," I glare. "It says *deferred*, not rejected. I can still get in as a regular admission in April."

Charlie nods to himself, scratching the stubble on his chin. He knows he should shut up, but he just can't help himself.

"I just don't want you to get your hopes up, Brooks," he counsels. "You'll just get hurt."

He wants me to give up. Just like he has. The old, raw rage rises within me.

"Screw you," I say.

Then, storming into my room, I slam the door on him.

WINTER OF MY DISCONTENT

Countdown.

Three. Two. One.

Midnight.

Happy New Year.

In Times Square, the ball drops and thousands of normal people my age cheer and carry on. Around the globe, transcending religion, culture, and time-old enmity, all of humanity's united momentarily in celebration. But not here in Pritchard, New Jersey. Here, it's Grimsville.

Graduation. College. The Future. This is the Big One. The calendar year my whole life has been leading up to. One way or the other.

I should be happy. First semester, the last semester that matters, is over. I've aced my courses, and my Mid-Year Reports, when they are sent to Columbia, will be golden. Although there's been no word of or from Uncle Max, I should be delirious with the prospect of coasting through the rest of senior year, partying every chance I get, enjoying the fruits of my labor. And I would be if I'd only gotten in and hadn't been Deferred like the piece of shit I am.

I'm alone in my room, getting blitzed on old malt liquor that I squirreled away so long ago I can't remember scoring it. I hate malt liquor. That's how crappy my New Year's is so far. But then again, the holidays have always been kind of a drag for me. I mean, me and Charlie by the tree, which, incidentally, we've never once had, isn't exactly a cozy greeting card like most everyone else's Christmas holidays. There's no exchange of gifts, let alone glad tidings. But these holidays are especially rotten. You see, since my little outburst, the battle lines have been drawn. Charlie's room is enemy territory; the bathroom, the kitchen, and the rest of our shared quarters are a no-man's land, of which we only avail ourselves sparingly and swiftly for the absolute essentials. And even though we've hardly seen each other, our uneasy truce casts a pall over any thought of festivity.

Usually my chief joy and only consolation over the break is hanging and getting stupid with The Murf. But since I so wrongly ditched him without the courtesy of a word, I've been un'd on Facebook, Twitter, Skype, and various other apps I'm unaware of, and he won't respond to my repeated amusing texts and goofy selfies. The Murf's way pissed and I can't say I blame him. Besides, even if The Murf was talking to me, which apparently he's not, these days he's always at The Gun and thereby unavailable for much needed companionship.

Oh, Columbia, why won't you have me? I'll do, I'll say anything. Earthly existence could be so divine if only you would. Classmates with Shelby. Talk about an added bonus. But it cuts both ways. The concept of her there without me is extra torture. I must get in. I must. Because if I don't, I'll never again feel those lips wrapped around you-know-where.

Oh please, spare me the righteous indignation. Easy for you to say. You weren't there, you aren't me. It didn't almost happen to you. I almost wish it'd never almost happened to me. *Almost*. That can't have been it. It's like I've been handed a lifelong sentence of psychic blue balls.

— — —

The next days and weeks are spent holed up, perfecting the Brand. According to all the guidebooks, a supplicant is allowed one last gasp of self-promotion to the Admissions Committee in the otherwise fallow period before April. In fact, all the guidebooks encourage it. But no more than one, all the guidebooks warn; don't want to come off as too desperate. Usually it's an update of some new meaningless honor, award, or foreign adventure, a gentle reminder that you're still out there dangling, but others, I've been informed, can get quite creative. Baked goods have been sent, entire arias posted on YouTube, some have even tried nude pictures. Not the best idea. The Last Gasp is supposed to be the subtle expression of one's unique uniqueness and a pledge of one's unwavering commitment to their august institution—unless, of course, one gets into some place auguster.

Lacking a decent singing voice, culinary talent, and basic inspiration, I've decided that mine's going to be an old standby—a video profile highlighting guess who. Unfortunately there's not much to work with. As in, literally. Practically no baby photos, few candids of me playing Little League or anything else, a paucity of keepsakes from family vacations because there were hardly any. Though I've searched through shelves, drawers, and dusty boxes, there's the scantest record of me, which is kind of depressing and stokes my festering resentment of Charlie. But I do what I can with what I got and, after countless hours and after much trial and error on my computer, come up with two tightly edited minutes of the Best of Brooks Rattigan.

Thoughtful Brooks Rattigan staring up silhouetted against a blazing sunset. Young responsible Brooks Rattigan, age nine, captain of safety patrol. Brooks Rattigan's many Honor Roll certificates. Playful Brooks Rattigan banging the bongos. Outdoorsy Brooks Rattigan paddling a kayak. Brooks Rattigan, Renaissance Man, pondering at the art museum. Brooks Rattigan's various trophies, most of which Brooks Rattigan picked up at various yard sales. I add twirling graphics and cool special effects recounting my many attributes: Brooks Rattigan, National Merit

Letter of Commendation Winner. 3.83 Overall GPA, 4.14 Weighted. 720 Verbal, 760 Math. 680 Writing, but everyone knows that section's bullshit. For inspirational music, I try everything from "The Star-Spangled Banner" to Ween to the theme from *Rocky*, but nothing does the trick. I know I need more.

Let's face it, My Brand is lackluster.

– – –

Another Saturday night. A huge one. I'm forty-seven minutes late picking up Gravity Dross for Winter Formal and I'm a nervous wreck. Not wanting to blow my last, best chance for Columbia, I've allotted myself a good two hours to make the foray from Pritchard to Westport, but with all the snow and ice there's a big accident on the GW Bridge and so it's taking almost three, and that's with me driving like a maniac, screaming and yelling like the guy in *The French Connection* but doing him one better because I'm consulting Google Maps on my phone the entire time. When I finally skid up to the wooded manor nestled on its own meandering stream, I'm twitchy and foaming, in dire need of a prolonged time-out in a padded cell. You'd think Uncle Max might cut me just the teensiest bit of slack, but no. He's ready to strangle me because Aunt Marion's ready to strangle him. As for Gravity, she could care less, off in the adjoining spacious room absorbed in an old *SpongeBob* I've seen like six times.

"Gravity, he's here," trills Aunt Marion, trying to make the best of it but giving me the stink eye.

"OK," answers Gravity, dutifully turning off the TV.

Being Celia Lieberman's cousin, she's not what I'm expecting. First off, she looks nothing like Celia Lieberman. Gravity's tall, whisper-thin, very pale. You could say she has a calm, ethereal quality about her, which Celia Lieberman definitely does not. And she dresses a hell of a lot better. In a sleek, stylish gown that accentuates her assets, she's actually striking and, unlike Celia Lieberman, seems to possess a remarkably agreeable disposition, which again makes it hard to believe they're related.

"Say hi to Brooks," Aunt Marion beams at her daughter, adjusting a stray strand of Gravity's otherwise perfectly done locks.

"Hi," Gravity greets me, smiling pleasantly.

"Brooks is your date tonight. He's going to show you a good time."

"Okay," Gravity says.

"He'd better," adds Uncle Max too meaningfully, giving me the instant impression he hasn't had his little chat with his buddy the Director of Admissions about me quite yet.

"How about a few snapshots for the Dross family album?" I hurriedly suggest, trying to pick up the pace and make up the clock.

"Great idea, Brooks!" enthuses Aunt Marion. I must say she's surprisingly pretty and well-adjusted to be married to a grump like Uncle Max. If she wasn't so stressed she might even be nice.

"Okay," says Gravity.

Okay's pretty much the extent of the conversation on the ride in Uncle Max's battery-underpowered Tesla (more oomph than the Prius, but still not close to a good V6, let alone a V8) to the naturally superexpensive restaurant that practically had to be bribed to hold our reservation. Gravity's smiling and in good spirits, but I'm not exactly sure that she knows what's going on or what she's doing with me. She's got this vacant look in her eyes that I find unnerving, until I remind myself that many of the finest-looking babes do.

But when Gravity orders a grilled cheese sandwich and potato chips off the menu, which is all in French, I'm getting the sense that somebody hasn't been telling me the whole story. Because Gravity's not all here or there or any-where on this temporal plane. She's in her own head, what's known in the brain trade as *on the spectrum*. I think maybe she's autistic. No joke.

Parents, I brood as I saw into my Chateaubriand, which is getting to be not such a novelty. Poor dumb rich parents. They think if they spend enough money they can fix any-thing for their kids. But there are some things that can't be corrected, like crooked teeth or an extra-large probos-cis, some things beyond even their purchasing power. And sweet, happy Gravity's one of them. And maybe even if she could be repaired, she shouldn't be. What the fuck do I know.

By the multitude of strange, curious looks of which I'm on the receiving end as I escort Gravity into the plush auditorium, my suspicions are confirmed, but I decide to just roll with it. It's all good. Bowing gallantly, I ask Gravity if she'd care to trip the light fantastic, and of course she's amenable. What the hell, I figure I'll teach her a few simple steps, but guess what? If anybody can teach anyone a thing or two, it's her. Gravity's an amazing dancer. Like a prodigy, even. Gracefully she follows where I lead, anticipates my every move, takes me where I've never been. We spin, prance, and twirl almost without stop, with abandon. She laughs. So do I. We go for hours.

It's late as we drive back in contented silence through a frosted landscape softly glowing in the night. For the first time in a long time, I'm at peace with myself. I'm feeling like I'm the one who should be doing the paying.

Aunt Marion and Uncle Max are waiting, faces drawn and anxious, in their bathrobes by the front door as we come up the walk. Aunt Marion emotionally hugs her daughter.

"So how was it?" she asks benevolently, as if she's bestowed some great gift on us, which she just might have.

"Okay," Gravity answers brightly.

Aunt Marion lets out this big sob and breaks down crying and I think I kind of know where she's coming from. There is no magic, no miracle cure. Pretending Gravity's normal, whatever that means, doesn't make it so.

"Good-bye, Brooks." It's the first time Gravity says my name. Then she gives me a kiss on the cheek, goes into the other room, and switches on the wide-screen, resuming *SpongeBob* where she left off.

"I told you this was a bad idea," Uncle Max whispers to Aunt Marion, who just keeps sniffling. "Why must you keep torturing yourself?"

"We actually had a really good time. Gravity's an incredible dancer," I say, thinking it might give them a lift.

But they don't hear me. And I realize that I've been the unwilling subject in an ongoing experiment with the same heartbreaking result. The evening's been more about the two of them than the one of her. Uncle Max is in a sour mood as he wordlessly pays up. There's no tip, not one red cent, not that I really care, but I take it as an ominous omen. It's like it's my fault Aunt Marion's a wailing puddle.

The drive back to New Jersey is long and sobering. Uncle Max is supposed to be my edge, my big benefactor. As the miles pile up, so do my doubts that his chat with his pal the Director of Admissions will ever happen. Back to Square Zero, Brooksie.

— — —

Meanwhile, The Murf's boycott against me continues without letup. He must have gotten a sizeable bonus or substantial raise at The Gun because The Murf's bought a used pickup—a cherry 2004 Ford F-150 with a V8 that rips—and now chauffeurs himself to school. We don't have any of the same classes, and on the rare occasions when we pass each other in the hallways, he makes a point to cross to the other side. At lunch he gets up and moves to another table if I sit down next to him. After a while, all the cold shoulder treatment gets me ticked off right back at him. I mean, I've admitted I was in the wrong, made repeated attempts at amends and redress. What more can a person do? What does he want? Fucking flowers? Hmmm, not a bad idea. A guy giving another guy flowers? Am I really that far gone? In any case, I ask you, is my crime so grievous that it's worth chucking a lifelong friendship over it? Evidently The Murf thinks so, and that makes me that much madder.

But despite the fact that he's being a complete dick, I still miss my bud.

So maybe that's why one frigid afternoon I find myself at the Reservoir with my old blue bucket drum. The Reservoir's where The Murf and me used to convene jam sessions of the Pritchard High Ethno-Percussion Society. The landscape around the parking lot's patchy, bare, and bleak, reflecting my flagging spirits. This winter seems especially brutal and endless. I'm hoping a good pounding, even if solo, might be therapeutic. Nothing else is working.

As I tread down the path through the somber woods to our spot, I hear something ahead. A lone, hollow thumping. Sounds like . . . hands beating on plastic. Could it be? Quickening my step, I soon come upon the large rock outcropping overlooking the vast frozen expanse. And sure enough, there's The Murf, swaddled up like an Indian chief, nursing a Guinness, listlessly whacking his blue bucket. A forlorn figure if there ever was one.

He sees me but doesn't react, just takes a deep sip of his stout.

"You're not at The Gun?" I observe in surprise.

"I gave myself the afternoon off," he answers gruffly, continuing to beat his instrument.

"Mind some company?" I inquire tentatively.

"Free country," he replies tersely. "Or so they keep telling me."

I perch on the rocks opposite him, position my bucket between my knees, and begin pounding along. It's not much of a duet. Neither of us is feeling it.

"Murf, it's been over two months," I finally offer.

"Seven weeks, three days," The Murf corrects.

"You're going to have to talk to me sometime."

"You ditched your best friend for some superhot chick, man," The Murf says, brushing me off. "Nothing to talk about."

"Yes, but don't you want to know why I ditched my best friend for some superhot chick?"

The Murf stops banging and looks straight at me. "I'm all ears."

This is it—the moment when, if I had any balls or speck of character, I should come clean, confess my many hang-ups, deficiencies, and insecurities. Problem is, the truth hurts. Him. More importantly, me.

"She was superhot," I declare, not meeting his eyes.

Like I said, normally according to the Unspoken Code that would be ample explanation. But The Murf, whatever his College Board Scores, is no dummy. He senses there's something more because there is something more.

"That's all?" he asks, still staring right into me.

"Swear to God." I'm such a lowlife scumbag. He knows I'm lying and I know he knows I know. But good, simple soul that he is, The Murf gives me the benefit of the doubt and takes me at my word. That's part of the Unspoken Code too.

"Did you at least score?" he smiles, resuming thumping.

"Kind of, if you count a two-second blow job. Her mom barged in."

For some reason The Murf finds this hilarious. Laughing, he thwacks with renewed energy. I eagerly jump in. We pound in syncopated unison.

"Actually more like one," I admit sheepishly above the rising din. "When I got home, I had to pour ice cubes down my pants to get rid of an extreme case of raging hard-onitis."

"You dog!" The Murf howls, delighting in my misery. We beat our buckets faster and faster, then he slows up again. "You still could have told me, Brooks."

I look away uneasily. He extends his forty to me. I take a long pull.

"It's this whole Columbia thing," I maintain. "It's got me all crazy."

We cheerily pound away for awhile. From our high

vantage point, I notice a bunch of little kids at the other end of the Reservoir playing hockey where they shouldn't, where The Murf and me once played where we shouldn't have too. Back when the Future was a non-factor. Could it really have been just a few short years ago?

"How is the college derby going?" The Murf asks, making conversation.

"Pretty much stuck at the gate," I say.

Closer below, a crooked rusted sign protrudes above a thin frozen sheen about twenty yards or so from the shore, warning in big red letters: "DANGER! THIN ICE!" Every two or three winters some yahoo drowns in the Reservoir, usually when loaded out of his mind. It's kind of a Pritchard tradition.

"Hey, it ain't over 'til it's over," The Murf says by way of encouragement. "And there's always Rutgers. It's a friggin' good school. I mean, I couldn't get in there if my life depended on it."

"No, it's over, Murf," I state conclusively, giving up, giving into the moment. We continue thwacking our overturned buckets. Our palms sting from the impact. We're cooking, our beat tight, complex, and furious.

"Why's it mean so much to you, Brooks?" The Murf asks. "What's out there that we don't got right here in Pritchard?"

I grimace. This is where me and The Murf unapologetically part ways. I may be going nowhere fast, but at least I've got my eyes open and know what's what. I can't settle for less like The Murf even if I wanted to, which, now more than ever, I desperately don't.

"Oh, c'mon, Murf, Pritchard's a shithole," I say in exasperation.

"True." He laughs ruefully. "Pritchard blows the big one. What am I saying?"

We pound harder, each of us turning inward. Across the Reservoir, the kids whoop and holler, skating back and forth. The tilted sign flashes at me like lit-up neon. "DANGER! THIN ICE!" An idea forms and grows with each thump on my can. If my life depended on it, The Murf said. A dastardly, diabolical notion, one that I shouldn't even let myself consider, but one that just might work.

"Well, if there's anything I can do, I'm here for you, dude," The Murf vows.

"Well, actually there is something," I announce, suddenly galvanized with evil purpose.

The Murf looks at me, a little startled that I'm so rapidly taking him up on what he thought was a token offer.

"I need you to let me save your life."

The Murf stops drumming, stunned. "*What*?"

"You fall through the ice, I rescue you," I explain rapidly before principles and reason can set in. "I guarantee you'll be totally safe. You just have to look like you're in mortal jeopardy. Five minutes, ten tops!"

"Are you off your nut?"

"I need an update on my application. Something major, to put me over the top."

The Murf looks down at the sign, then back at me. "Like now?"

"You mind? The updated forms have to be postmarked by Monday."

— — —

"It's no good if nobody sees us," I brief The Murf as we slither through the gaping hole in the chain link fence, which everybody uses and which has never once been repaired in my lifetime. "So yell like crazy."

We emerge on the slanted concrete lip of the flat, open reservoir. A long, rectangular lake of ice expands before us. It looks pretty thick and secure except for the soupy patch around the rusting sign. Only a complete imbecile would go out there. Or a best friend.

"You're really going to make me go through with this?" The Murf asks uneasily.

But I'm not listening. Instead I'm playing the video clip in my mind:

"I saw the whole thing. It was righteous, man," an adorable bundled-up little kid on skates tells an off-screen interviewer. "The dude ran out and saved the other dude," another one chimes in. "He was like a superdude!" Then we go to me, shivering, coatless in the bitter cold. "I never thought about my own safety for an instant," I state. "My only concern was for my fellow man, right Murf?" Quick shot of The Murf, wrapped in a thermal blanket, lips blue, skin pasty, sipping a hot cup of coffee. "R-r-r-ight," he chatters. Back again to me because I'm the main story. "It was nothing," I shrug modestly. "Really." Then Chuck Spencer, our local burnt-orange, toothy anchorman, steps up beside me, blocking out The Murf. "Brooks Rattigan," he resonates deeply into his microphone. "Pritchard's own superdude." Superdude, cute touch, huh? I mean, where's the harm? Take that, fucking Columbia!

"Couldn't we just say we did it?" The Murf equivo-cates, tugging me back to the immediate situation at hand.

"Oh, don't be such a pussy." I shouldn't, but it is Columbia at stake, so I shove The Murf way out to sea. He careens across the ice, sliding to a stop about ten feet from the sign. The slick surface creaks precariously under his weight.

"Stomp on it!" I direct, darting a look at the little kids skating.

The Murf does a little hop. The ice splinters, then cracks beneath him into an intricate spider web of fractures but, remarkably, stays intact. Bummer. He looks happily back at me.

"Okay, I stomped!" He scuttles back toward shore. Suddenly, he slips, flails in midair, and crashes back-wards on his ass. The ice shatters. The Murf goes under. Excellent!

"HELLLLLPPPPP!!" The Murf shrieks, spurting like a seal back up into view. I glance at the kids. They don't notice. How could they not notice?

"Louder!" I command The Murf. "Act like you're drowning!"

"WHO'S ACTING? HELLLLLLLPPPPP!!!" The Murf splashes frantically in a crater of frigid water. He keeps trying to grip the ice to climb out, but it keeps breaking off. Talk about dramatic. But those idiot kids still haven't noticed. At wit's end, I holler:

"HEY, YOU LITTLE DIPSHITS!! HELP!!!"

This gets their attention. They stop their collective pursuit of the puck.

"MAN DROWNING!!" I announce, pointing at The Murf thrashing in the ragged hole of icy water. Here's my cue to spring into heroic action.

"HOLD ON, MURF!" I proclaim, stripping off my coat, which I plan to use as a rope while remaining comfortably safe and dry. "I'M COMING! I'LL SAVE YOU, PAL!!"

I race out across the ice to the edge of the crater of swooshing gray water. But when I get there, there's no Murf. Just shards of floating ice.

"Murf?" No, God no. Not The Murf. What have I done? "MURF?"

I dive headfirst into the crater. The churning liquid's the consistency of just-mixed cement, the cold instant and excruciating. The next few seconds are a dull blur. I can't see a thing but am somehow able to reach out and latch onto something somewhat solid. An elbow. Lungs bursting, I sink, touch bottom, and launch back upwards. At this temperature, the water doesn't even feel wet, it's just a searing cold sensation. Pulling The Murf by the arm, I thrash through gelatinous murk. Finally, just as I can take no more, we jet up through the surface, into light, into chilling, polluted but still life-sustaining air. Gasping, gulping it in, I grip The Murf's limp, petrified figure, making myself his personal flotation device.

"I GOTCHA, BUDDY! I GOTCHA!"

Frantic, I shake him, unsure if he's really dead or merely comatose. Then both his eyes flip open and his pupils lower from his head. Glory be! The Murf lives! The Murf grabs my neck and starts choking me. The ingrate throttles me.

"HELLLPPPPP!!!" I splutter.

The little kids have skated up. Mostly boys, a few girls. All miniature, like Munchkins, around six or seven years old and indeed adorable, straight out of Central Casting. Gathered around us, they raptly watch our titanic, life-and-death struggle.

"Far out!" one exclaims.

"FUCK FAR OUT!!" I shriek at the pipsqueaks as The Murf tries his feeble, sluggish best to shove me back under. "DO SOMETHING!!!"

"Spread out!" their fearless leader orders. Instantly the little kids skate into line.

"HURRY!!!" I yelp.

"Sticks!" The little kids extend their hockey sticks. Each clutches the blade in front of her or him, thereby doubling the length of the rescue chain. A nifty maneuver, if I do say so myself. At the head of the line, the commander, gripping onto the stick behind him with one mitten, extends the curved portion of his tiny hockey stick with the other so it's just able to reach a few inches beyond the perimeter of the open, surging crater.

Grabbing The Murf by the collar, I propel him toward the hook. He clamps a petrified claw around it. In turn, I lock onto his ankle. He tries to kick me loose.

"GO!!!" I shout.

"Hey, I give the orders around here!" the leader glowers at me. "GO!!" he shouts at the others.

Holding onto the sticks between them, the string of little kids skates cross-foot in perfect step backwards. Turns out they're all members of the same Cub Scout troop and have just earned merit badges in teamwork. If I wasn't barely clinging to survival and The Murf's foot, I'd be saluting the good ol' red, white, and blue.

Our frozen hides are dragged out of the water across rock-hard ice. My head clunks up and down on the jagged surface and I almost black out. But we are saved. When The Murf regains partial use of his vocal cords, he tells me if I ever talk to him again, he'll kill me.

I figure he'll cool off once he thaws out, but he doesn't.

GOING PUBLIC

Spring has sprung, buds are budding, sprouts are sprouting, but for me it might as well still be cold stark winter. I have no home, no safe place to rest my weary brow, just a demilitarized zone I co-inhabit with Charlie. My bestest, closest pal in the world has expressed the fervent desire to kill me. I will never again partake in the perfection that is Shelby Pace and, most tragic of all, I have no edge with Columbia. My money-market account with 0.093 percent interest does continue to steadily climb, however, as in a show of blind faith I continue to take any gig that comes over the transom. Paramus. Cherry Hill. Piscataway. None, thankfully, are particularly memorable.

Basically I'm a wreck. I can't sleep, can't concentrate. I exhibit sundry physical symptoms too. Wisps of hair float at my feet when I shower. There are dark circles under my eyes. My gut's doing flip-flops. Don't want to get too graphic but, doctor, I'm all bloated and gassy and haven't had a satisfactory bowel movement in what seems like months. That's why I'm on the throne, losing at Angry Birds on my iPhone, huffing and puffing, when I get the call. Recognizing the number on the display, I eagerly click on.

"Dr. Lieberman?" I announce in surprise.

"Hope I'm not getting you at a bad time," Harvey says.

"Not at all," I claim, calling it a day, reaching for the TP.

"It appears we have another birthday party. A Cassidy Trask. This Saturday. I'm calling because the invitation was addressed to you and Celia both."

Cassidy Trask. Why in God's name would Cassie Trask invite me and Celia Lieberman to her birthday party? She detests us. There's only one obvious answer. Shelby. Shelby put her up to it. She still lusts for the old Rattigan bod. It ain't over. There will be another inning. Hope glimmers at least on one of my horizons.

"I'm on the case, Dr. Lieberman."

We hang up after agreeing on the usual terms. I am smiling. My mood has lifted and so, apparently, have my intestines. Oh, sweet relief!

– – –

The next few days and nights are filled with dancing visions of me and Shelby doing it in an amazing variety of exotic locations and positions. Then a new cloud descends.

For there looms, I realize, a most inconvenient complication. Celia Lieberman. I can't connect with Shelby as long as Celia Lieberman's part of the picture. I can't two-time Celia Lieberman. My conscience and sense of business ethics, slender as they are, forbid me from exposing her to embarrassment and scandal, however illusory. If Shelby and I are ever to reach the next level—which we must—Celia Lieberman has to be deleted from the scene. Ergo, I must break up with Celia Lieberman.

As I nose up the Garden State Parkway to collect Celia Lieberman, I rehearse how I will gently break the devastating news to her. I plan to use a few of the old standbys. It's not her, it's all me. I don't want to be unfair to her. She deserves better than the lowly likes of me, which she does. The fact that we're not actually going out barely registers.

— — —

Celia Lieberman clops out the front door in high heels as the Beast rattles up the driveway. Adorned in Gayle's latest hideous, poufy approximation of high fashion, she's seriously regressed since our last meeting. We convene in the front seat of the Prius.

"What are you wearing?" I blurt in horror. "I thought . . ."

"Mommy Dearest insisted and I didn't feel like getting into it with her bitchiness," she cuts in breathlessly.

I activate the golf cart and back out. We glide down the street. "It's not that bad."

It is. It is that bad. It's horrible.

"Jesus, Celia," I say. "When are you going to stand up for yourself?"

"Never mind that. We have to talk!" She brushes me aside, apparently having more urgent matters to discuss.

"I agree," I say, summoning my tired litany of excuses for our impending permanent separation. "Ladies first."

"We have to break up!" she announces, eyes shining.

"Exactly!" I beam until the indignity of it hits me. "Let me get this straight, *you* want to give *me* the ax?"

"Franklin's jealous!" she exclaims, all aglow. I've never seen her so aglow.

— — —

She tells me the whole sorry tale. Apparently it happened late Wednesday afternoon at Chess Club practice. I know, Nerd City. Celia Lieberman's humoring Franklin, letting him think he's winning as usual. Then, after gleefully taking one of her castles, Franklin finally speaks.

"You look different," he says. "What have you done to your hair?"

Celia Lieberman brightens. It's the most Franklin's ever said to her. I know, pitiful.

"It's the new me," she informs him. She tells me she was wearing one of her recently purchased vintage dresses, a short, kind of turquoisey one, which she had taken in and was feeling quite très cool, if you please.

"You like?" Celia Lieberman asks Franklin.

"I hate," he grunts.

"You hate?" she says, crestfallen.

"You're trying to fit in," he states. "I liked you better before."

"You liked me better before?" Celia Lieberman sneak-attacks and decimates Franklin's bishop with a knight, then smacks her timer. "You never said two words to me before! Check!"

Franklin stares at the board, aghast. He's in deep doo-doo.

"It's that guy you were with at the mall, isn't it?" he says, frantically protecting his king, then taps his timer. "He's the one turning you into a mindless clone!"

"After three years, this is your idea of a first conversation?" Celia Lieberman thunders, her queen pulverizing his king. "To demean and insult me!"

Franklin goes white as a sheet as he fully realizes the fix he's in. He's trapped, hemmed in, and besieged by Celia Lieberman's rampaging forces on all sides. Without releasing his hand, he makes a rapid series of theoretical moves, before deciding to shift a pawn one measly space.

"Franklin, sometimes you are such an asshole! Checkmate!"

Franklin stares total, crushing defeat in the face. He

was doing so well. How did it all suddenly go so wrong? Grabbing her stuff, Celia Lieberman storms away.

"Celia, wait!" Franklin whimpers, rushing after her. Fade to black.

Needless to say, I'm delighted by this latest development. But more than that, I'm profoundly gratified. I mean, it didn't go down exactly the way I planned, but you can't argue with results.

"Am I a genius or am I a genius?" I boast.

"Don't get cocky," she grins. "Franklin hates what you've done to me. He considers you an evil influence."

"Hey, I got the job done, didn't I?"

She laughs. Like I said, I've never seen her so glad.

"What about you?" she asks, now that her item's been dispensed with. "What did you want to tell me?"

My item on the agenda's just been preempted by her item. Fine, she can delude herself that she's the one breaking up. My ego, fragile as it is, can take it. So instead I merely state, "No biggie. Just if I don't bone Shelby Pace soon, I'm going to spontaneously combust."

I know, in retrospect, probably not the best choice of words. But since when are Celia Lieberman's sensibilities so delicate? I mean, you've heard her. The girl has a mouth on her like a fucking truck driver.

"That's terrific, Brooks," she says, the smile gone. "Guess we're both getting what we want."

– – –

We putt up to the entrance of the country club and, strutting out like a fully paid-up member, I toss the key to the parking guy. Although I'm raging with heightened expectations for the evening, I politely motion Celia Lieberman ahead of me.

"Then it's agreed," she says, roughly taking my arm, propelling me with her into the revolving door. "I dump you tonight. Publicly and dramatically."

"Sooner the better!" I rejoin enthusiastically.

All of the sudden, Shelby, in tears and in a dress that's mostly slits and missing slots, sweeps past in the rotating glass door going in the other direction. My target sights spin and lock on her. I'm telling you, I'm ripping, raring to go, a snorting bull unleashed at last to awaiting female pasture, but still, exercising remarkable discipline, ever the gentleman, I turn back to Celia Lieberman.

"Excuse me," I say. Pushing her into the lobby as our door compartment passes it, I continue revolving without her. Back outside on the red carpet, I dart after Shelby, who's giving her ticket to a different parking guy.

"Shelby!" I gasp. "What happened?"

She turns and looks at me, her impossible beauty marred with little streaks of makeup that somehow make her even more must-have-able. "I just broke up with Tommy!"

I erupt into a huge smile. Another auspicious omen. Tonight the impediments to consummation are coming down fast and furious. It's clear sailing, all systems go, full speed ahead. Shelby dries her tears with a crumpled cocktail napkin that has Cassie's initials embossed in gold letters on it.

"I know he's deeply shallow, but Tommy was my first real boyfriend," she sniffles adorably. "This is an extremely traumatic moment for me."

"There, there, Brooks is here," I soothe, taking the napkin and gently dabbing. She lets me, obediently still. "Poor, poor baby."

"I feel kind of bad," she allows sadly. "He just got a tattoo of my name."

I bust out laughing. I'm sorry, but I can't help myself. I mean, what kind of nitwit gets a tattoo of his high school girlfriend? Your high school mascot, maybe. Let's get real here.

"Oh man, that's so great!" I chortle in deplorable delight.

"Oh, you enjoy seeing me in mental distress?" she inquires coyly, her luscious, glistening lips mere centimeters from my thirsting ones.

"No, I mean it's so great you're single."

I stop dabbing. We're down to millimeters. I breathe her ultraexpensive scent in. She says in a husky voice, "Why, Brooks? Why is it so great that I'm single?"

"Because you can do tons better," I stammer, lost in her unblinking cat eyes, drowning in a vortex of desire. "Tommy Fallick doesn't deserve you. Especially with a name like that."

"And who does deserve me, Brooks?" she presses against me, knowing the answer but insisting I say it, which I'm all too willingly about to do when, over Shelby's shoulder, I spot Celia Lieberman glowering behind her, arms folded sternly, impatiently tapping a pointy-toed shoe that looks like it could do real damage.

It occurs to me with thunderous dismay that not all impediments are gone. Not officially. Celia Lieberman has yet to break up with me.

"I can't tell you now," I tell Shelby, which I can tell doesn't go over too well.

"When can you tell me?" she demands.

"Could I tell you in, say, twenty minutes?" I query, signaling spastically with my eyes at Celia Lieberman to bug off.

This, of course, causes Shelby to turn around and see the same Celia Lieberman who, to add salt to the wound, gives her a little wave.

"How about ten?" I implore.

Shelby's Beamer screeches up. The parking guy clambers out of her way as she leaps into it. Meanwhile, Celia Lieberman marches to me, indignant.

"You mind?" she glares. "You're still my boyfriend!"

As I'm yanked hard by the hand inside, I watch in quiet devastation as Shelby floors the gas and zooms into the night. Yessiree Bob, there's nothing like the acceleration of a precision-tooled internal-combustion engine. Sure as hell not a battery-powered motor.

The ballroom churns with scions of privilege, the tunes are tight, and I'm fuming. I don't know if and/or how I'll ever recover my losses after this latest setback with Shelby, but, damn it, I'm sure going to try. I won't let it end, not when I was oh-so-close. But first and foremost I must divest myself once and for all of Celia Lieberman.

"Go ahead," I prompt. "It's showtime, folks. Let me have it."

"But we just got here," she says, sipping a Coke.

"Why waste time?"

"Listen, Rattigan, you can't be dumped by me one minute, then chase after Shelby the next."

"So I bounce back fast."

"You could act a little upset," Celia Lieberman demurs, bopping to the beat, determined to draw out my agony. "It wasn't all bad, you know. We had our moments as a fake couple."

"Oh yeah, thanks to you, she left," I grumble with profound bitterness. "Now we may never hook up!"

"I HATE YOU!!!" Celia Lieberman suddenly shouts just as the band arbitrarily decides to take five. A sea of coifed heads turns to us. However, I'm too steeped in self-pity to care.

"*Now* she hates me!" I beseech the vaulted ceiling and the cosmic forces that somehow continue to conspire against me. "She couldn't hate me like twenty seconds ago!"

"YOU ARE SUCH AN ASSHOLE!!!" Celia Lieberman roars, all flushed, veins sticking out, expression twisted. I'm riveted and more than a little taken aback by the intensity of her performance.

"Celia, I really like where you're going with this," I whisper, smiling all the while, playing to our riveted audience. "But could you bring it down a notch . . ."

"ALL YOU THINK ABOUT IS YOUR DICK!!!"

Livid, Celia Lieberman throws her drink in my face and stalks away. I stand there, dripping. Coke, no less. My dry cleaning bill is going to be exorbitant.

— — —

The drive back, as you can imagine, is interminable. We're both brooding, although what Celia Lieberman has got to be sore about is beyond human comprehension. I ask you, who's the aggrieved party here?

"The dick remark was effective enough," I finally say as we pull into her driveway. "Was the drink-throwing thing absolutely necessary?"

"All part of the act," she says stonily, staring out her window.

"Well, you were very convincing."

"Actually I couldn't be more delighted that you and Miss Homecoming Queen can finally screw your tiny little brains out."

"Really? Shelby was Homecoming Queen?" I ask,

quite pleased by this tidbit of information. I mean, come on, what guy doesn't nurse a secret hard-on to score with a Homecoming Queen?

The second the Prius halts, Celia darts from it.

"You are such a putz!"

"Now what did I do?" Genuinely mystified, I trot after her.

"You are so superficial!"

"Oh yeah? Shelby thinks I'm deep!"

As Celia Lieberman charges up the walk, the front door swings open for her. Gayle and Harvey, again in their jammies, hover in it, beaming expectantly.

"So? So?" they chant.

"Oh, God, would you two get a life!!" shrieks Celia Lieberman, plowing inside between them and slamming the door right in my face.

– – –

Free at last. At last I can proceed with a somewhat clear conscience.

Instantly I mobilize into action. The first thing I do when I get home is scrub the Web of all remaining traces of my name and image, which isn't that hard to do since, fueled by scurrilous rumors of College Admissions Committees checking out applicants online for incriminating posts and compromising pictures, I've long been scrupulous about limiting my social media exposure. During free period, at ten sharp the next morning, I'm waiting in the Beast in the parking lot for the cellular phone place to open.

"Let me get this straight," the overweight put-upon salesman guy says. "You want all your calls forwarded to a 917 area code?"

"That's right," I reply. I'm there to upgrade to a new phone and new cell number with a Manhattan area code. I can't communicate with Shelby without one.

"But you live in 732?" he questions, giving me the dirty eyeball.

"That is correct. Yes," I affirm a bit sheepishly. Great. Why do I get the guy missing the self-edit button?

"What's wrong? Is 732 not good enough for you?" he asks, hitting my bull's-eye.

– – –

Back safely in the Beast and properly if reluctantly equipped, I punch in the digits to Shelby's cell number, which I secured from her Facebook profile, and type in the letters to the text that I've been composing in my mind over and over again. Here goes nothing.

"Me," I tap with trepidation. "I deserve you."

Actually I don't deserve her on a million different levels, primarily because I'm not who and what she thinks I am. But no matter. I press Send anyway.

Who knows if she'll respond, but at least I've launched my initial salvo. But she does respond. Out of the blue, two hours and thirteen minutes later, in the middle of Statistics class.

"What about Celia Lieberman?" reads her text.

Celia Lieberman. Always Celia Lieberman.

"Ancient history," I hurriedly transmit back.

"Yeah, I heard," her message bubble pops.

Pretty short. Pretty cryptic. Could mean anything. I tense up, all nervous, unsure what to write next.

Then another bubble pops on my screen.

"☺"

Yes! The Brookster lives! The journey to ultimate ecstasy continues!

Shelby texts more. She's with Cassie in the sauna at school and they're shaving their moist appendages. The image makes me shift and cross my legs. Cassie's told Shelby all about Celia Lieberman's big breakup with me, having witnessed the whole debacle. Shelby hears it was brutal. Cassie, not Shelby mind you, thinks if anyone was going to do the dumping, it would have been the other way around.

I'm inclined for once to agree with Cassie, but I can't. Instead I'm philosophical.

"It was time," I type.

Shelby surmises a different scenario. Her theory is that it was really all my doing, and I gallantly fell on my sword and allowed Celia Lieberman to have the honors to save her minimal standing. Is she right? Is that true?

To my eternal discredit, I allow it to be true.

Since Spring Fling season's just getting into full swing and I've got three bookings and she's flying out, private jet of course, to the villa in St. Barts for break, it takes a little back-and-forth before we're able to coordinate our schedules.

We make a date for dinner two weeks from Friday. I can't wait. It's first down and I'm on the ten-yard line, the goal finally within reach.

THE WORD

"April is the cruelest month," the poet I was so unfortunately assigned once famously poeticized. Well, he's wrong. March is. Late March, to be semi-exact.

That's when I finally hear. After taking the better part of an entire school year, *They* can't give you a specific date or approximate time. No, that would be considerate, that would actually be humane. Instead, *They* want you to writhe in suspended agony. And I do, second by interminable second. "*Late* March." What does "*Late* March" even mean? The last two weeks? The last week? The last few days? Oh, those miserable mothers!

So starting the sixteenth, I'm online like every ten minutes to check if thumbs up or down's been posted, and naturally it never is. By the twenty-third, I'm a basket case, constantly muttering non sequiturs to myself, nails chewed down to bloody nubs. By the twenty-ninth, I'm climbing the walls, triple-checking like every ten seconds. Logging in and out, out and in, over and over again, in a mindless trance. Hours go by. And this is all night, three, four in the morning, because I can no longer sleep because I've basically morphed into a walking zombie.

So there I am, ebbing in and out of consciousness through AP English, when the news floats through the ether that just this moment Phil Chen's gotten into Columbia, which doesn't surprise me, and that he immediately flipped off the principal, which does. I bolt upright. My last check online was a full twelve minutes ago. I curse myself. How could I have let so much time go by? Frantically I bring up my keyboard on my iPhone and attempt to log on to the official Columbia University website but the official Columbia University website doesn't come up because the official Columbia University website's freakin' down. The reason the official Columbia University website's freakin' down is because across the continent and around the globe, all 34,929 regular admissions applicants are frantically clicking just like me on the same link at the same time.

Which leaves the letter, or what's known in the college racket as the "invitation" if you're in and the "eat shit and die" if you're not. Columbia times its letters to arrive the same day that decisions are posted online. My fate's signed, sealed, delivered, and lying on its side in our mailbox. Even though there's still another ten minutes of class, I am out the door with my teacher's sympathetic acquiescence.

The drive back's a frenetic blur. This, my friends, is

finally it. The Word. What I've worked and sacrificed for. The years swirl around me. The endless hours studying subjects I could care less about, the tedious books I slaved through, the grueling months of preparing for the SATs. The few ups, the many, many downs. The constant anxiety. All for one single purpose. Columbia. I don't want to know and have to know at the same time.

Double-parking, I explode from the Beast and sprint into the dingy lobby of our building. PO boxes fill an entire wall. I dash to ours. Hands trembling, I dial the combination and swing open the little frosted glass door. My fingers grope inside, find nothing. Kneeling, I anxiously peer into the metal compartment. Empty. I can see all the other boxes have stuff in them. The mail's been delivered for the day. Which can only mean one thing.

Charlie. A wave of horror engulfs me as I realize it's Friday. Charlie gets afternoons off on Fridays because he works Saturday mornings. God, no. Charlie's got it!

I clamber up the stairs, three at a time, all the way to the fourth floor. Tear along the shabby hallway lined with doors to identical cubicles. Fumble for my keys, only to see the door is open a crack. I barrel in, breathless.

"Did it come?"

Charlie's slumped at the table in his blue postal uniform, which isn't unusual. What is unusual is the open bottle of whiskey. Charlie's a stoner, not a drinker. Guzzling brown liquid from a glass, he grimaces as it goes down, obviously in distress.

"It's not important where you get in, Brooks," he says softly. "It may seem like it is, but it really isn't."

Then I spot the printed piece of embossed paper spread out in front of him. He's read it. He knows before I do. I'm beyond pissed.

"You had no right opening it!"

I snatch the letter from the table. The world's spinning. It's over. I can't bear to look. My legs go all wobbly. I have to sit down.

"The least you could do is let me get rejected first-hand," I whisper in defeat.

"You didn't get rejected, Brooks," he says, pouring himself another slug.

"I didn't get rejected?" I look up at him, stricken. "No, please don't tell me I've been *Wait-Listed*!"

Wait-Listed. First Deferred, now Wait-Listed. Is there no end to this misery? I give up, I can't take anymore. Oh, those mothers!

"You got in, Brooks," Charlie says.

"What?" I say, barely listening.

"You got into fucking Columbia," he states.

"I got into fucking Columbia?" I repeat, incredulous. Can it really be true? I read the first paragraph of the letter. It starts with "the greatest pleasure." None of that let-you-down-easy bull about receiving more applications than any time in recorded history, blah, blah, blah, before they give you the old boot. Instead, *They're* inviting me, Brooks Rattigan, to join the Columbia community. It's not the thin envelope. I got the big fat thick one. I'm in. It's true!

Instantly Queen's "We Are the Champions" is pounding in both ears. I'm up on my feet, dancing around, shadow boxing and flattening any and all comers. I rock, baby. I am the shit!

"I GOT INTO FUCKING COLUMBIA!" I exult. "I GOT INTO FUCKING COLUMBIA!!"

I cannot believe I got into fucking Columbia. I thank Farkus, my lucky stars, but most of all Uncle Max who, it turns out, is a man of his word and must have tipped the scales in my favor.

"You're getting twenty thousand a year toward tuition," Charlie says, gulping down another belt of whiskey.

"Twenty grand! All right! I'm going to fucking Columbia!!"

"Which leaves us, or rather me, owing a mere $44,144. And that's just for the first year."

But the numbers aren't sinking in. Nothing is. I just keep feinting and punching thin air. I'm in the club, one of the select few! I made the cut! Me! I made it!

"Tuition, $46,846," Charlie reads through the list in a dull monotone. "Room and board, $11,978. Love it how they've got it down to the exact dollar. Fees: $2,292." He laughs mirthlessly. "What the hell are fees? Like tuition's not a fee? Books and personal expenses: $3,028. For a grand total of $64,144."

As swiftly as it arrived, the joy drains out of me, but I stubbornly continue my celebration.

"Take off room and board," I declare grandly. "I'll commute from here."

"Okay," Charlie sighs, pained that he's not getting through. "That still leaves $32,166."

I creak to a crawl. Thirty-two thousand? Thirty-two thousand's serious.

"Can't we get a loan?"

"The twenty grand is a loan, Brooks."

"Then we'll get another loan," I persist. I always knew money would be an issue; I mean, I've been working and saving since I was sixteen. But I always figured somehow it'd take care of itself. The all-important thing was to get in. Which I just fucking did, damn it. I've done my part.

"With what? For God's sake, tuition alone is what I make in a year." Charlie suddenly stands in agitation. "I mean, what universe have you been living in? Wake up! I don't own this place or have any savings to speak of. I lease my car. I have nothing."

Silence. He looks down, unable to look me, his son, in the eyes. He has nothing. He is nothing.

"I've tried to tell you, Brooks," he says. "But you just wouldn't listen . . ."

"I don't need your help," I say angrily. "I've got my own money! Almost ten grand!"

"You have almost ten thousand dollars?" he says, surprised.

"And I can make more!" But I'm reeling, flooded with helplessness.

"It's still not even half, Brooks," he says. "And that's just this year. What about next year and the two more after that? We're talking hundreds of thousands. We can't swing it. I don't know what else to tell you. I'm sorry."

I shakily sit at the table, my dreams dashed just as they come true. Charlie picks up another opened envelope.

"The good news is that you've been accepted into the Honors Program at Rutgers with almost a full ride, which leaves just room and board, which is doable . . ."

Choking back emotion, blinking back bitter tears, I look at him. I feel so tired, so old.

"You are sorry, Charlie," I say. "A sorry excuse for a father."

It's like I hit him. He flinches, backs from me, turns away to block the barrage but I'm relentless.

"I'm your only kid. You could have put something aside. You could have planned. You could have at least fucking tried. Most parents want better for their kids. But not you, Charlie, you want me to have it even crappier."

I say it. I say it and a lot more. I tell him as soon as I can I'm leaving and never coming back, just like Mom did. I tell him to take a shower, that he smells. I tell him I hate him. Everything I never said before. I let him have it with both barrels right between the eyes. And then I leave.

I drive and drive and then drive some more. I don't know where I'm going, I just go as fast as I can. Away from Pritchard, from Charlie, from grim reality, away into the waning light. Eventually I find myself cruising up and down the stately, impeccable streets of Green Meadow. Past the glittering palaces safe and snug behind their imposing gates. How can some have so much and others so little? It's all about Money. My place at Columbia will be taken by some rich snot whose family can afford it. So much for a level playing field, for so-called equal opportunity, for the concept of fairness. To the victors go all the spoils. I reach the driveway to Shelby's spread, where I fight the urge to witness its splendor just once more, but that would be too painful.

I need to talk to someone, to pour out my crushed heart to a sympathetic ear, but there is no one. No one who'd get it anyway, who'd give a flying fart. Not even The Murf. 'Cuz there is no Murf for me anymore. I've seen to that. For a second, I actually even consider calling Celia Lieberman. Yes, I am indeed that far gone.

It's getting late. I keep driving, away from the place I have no reason being, speeding toward the towering, shimmering skyline of Manhattan, to the chaos and refuge of the City.

Van Am Quad's dark, quiet, and still when I get there. Smoking my tenth cigarette in a row, I settle heavily on a bench beneath the softly glowing Rotunda. Unscrewing a pint of cheap vodka wrapped in a crinkled paper bag that I picked up at a dump I know that doesn't card, I take a long, gut-burning swallow. I stare out at the majestic rectangle of green lawn ringed by the massive stone and brick edifices that constitute just a small part of what makes Columbia University. Touching greatness. It was all such a cruel joke.

My iPhone blips with an incoming text. Forcing down another slug, I absently check the display.

"Hey," a bright green thought bubble announces, followed by a little smiley face.

It's from Shelby.

Do I answer? Dare I tell her what has happened, who I really am? Where and what I truly come from? And if I did, is there the remotest chance she'd understand?

I don't answer.

– – –

"Hey!" a harsh voice intrudes through the murk.

There's a sharp, hard poke in my side. I sit up with a start. It's later but still night, and I've passed out, stone cold on the bench. My vision's fuzzy but clear enough to make out the shape of a beefy campus security guard prodding me with a billy club.

"What do you think you're doing?" he glowers.

"Drinking myself into oblivion," I answer truthfully.

"Well, do it someplace else!" he says.

– – –

Shelby texts again the next day and Snapchats me twice the day after that. But as much as I want to, I still don't answer. I mean, come on, what am I going to tell her? That I'm a phony and a fake? That the game's been rigged from the start and there never was a chance in hell we were ever going to be classmates? That, unlike her and all her friends in their gilded, gated bubble worlds, I'm going nowhere? No thanks. Better to take the coward's way out. To just melt away like the mirage I am. I tell myself it's for the best. For her. For me.

A chatty email arrives in my inbox on Wednesday, playful and flirty, filled with all the latest juicy gossip from the hallowed halls of Green Meadow Country Prep. Tommy's being a big baby, threatening certain death to any member of the male persuasion who gets within five feet of her. Trent and Cassie are on again-again after being off again-again. Gwen Visser's father is getting divorced for the fourth time in like five years. Brittany somebody's wicked stepmom got another nip, lift, *and* tuck. Not exactly Pritchard fare. I don't answer. I feel shitty about it because I'm being a total prick, but I know it's for the best, that it's what I have to do.

By the end of the week, all attempts at communication from Shelby have ceased. Although it's what I expect, my ego's bruised all the same. Deep inside, I'd hoped she'd give me at least until Friday afternoon or early Saturday. Late at night and numerous other times, I try not to picture those full lips, those endless legs, that toned body doing all sorts of nasty things to me in various configurations. I fight to suppress what could have been, if only I was the someone else she believed me to be. It'd be different if I was going to Columbia, I reason. Then I could have somehow eased the truth on her. But Rutgers. Let's be real here, girls like Shelby don't go out with guys who go to Rutgers, Honors Program not withstanding.

Spring Fling season staggers to its wobbly conclusion, which means Prom's next up on the social schedule. Prom. The mother of all events, the final blow-up, signifying the end of the line, the point of no return. If you ask me, Prom's right after being a bride in a girl's fashion existence. I mean, the chicks go all out. Hair, toes, and every inch in between, sculpted, primped, and primed. And the get-ups. The plunging gowns, revealing backs, slanting shoes, sparkly accessories. You'd think it was the red carpet at the Oscars, not a high school dance.

Missing Prom's the ultimate FOMO, so the calls keep pouring in. I'm like a switchboard, juggling dates. My calendar rapidly fills in, Friday and Saturday by Friday and Saturday. Hackensack. South Amboy. Keansburg. All over the map. And I take them. Because even though it's hopeless, I haven't given up hope. Besides, as the man once said, I needs the money.

In preparation for the coming campaign, I bring the Armani tux I've bought on installment at a consignment store in Metuchen to the cleaners for alterations and, while I'm at it, drop off the ol' suit for one last fluff and dry before I retire it for the duration. I've grown quite fond of the suit. It's proved to be a trusted friend and sturdy companion. My suit has served me well. Checking through the jacket pockets like I always do, I nod to Sanjay, who, reeking of cleaner fluid, faintly waves back. I pull out a little crumpled cocktail napkin. The name *Shelby* is embossed in elegant gold letters on the lower corner. It's from her birthday gala at the club. The vision of that night returns. Her. Gliding in slow motion through the twirling bodies in the glittering ballroom. The short, sheer, clingy dress. The pronounced nipple outlines. Beauty, smarts, class, but more than that, radiating a supreme confidence that can only be inherited. Shelby's the whole package. Mine, all mine. That is, of course, if I'd just been lucky enough to be born the right kind of person. The injustice of it roils through me.

HEY HO, LET'S GO! HEY HO, LET'S GO!!

It's my iPhone. I resolve to buy a new ringtone. It refrains again. No doubt another frantic put-upon father. I click on.

"Rattigan and Associates," I announce by rote over the rattle of rotating clothes racks.

"Hey," a subdued female voice whispers.

Oh God, it's her. It's Shelby. She must have added my phone number to her address book when I called. I go cold. My heart stops. I hesitate.

"Hey, you," I finally manage. "I've been meaning to call."

"Haven't heard from you for awhile," her voice wavers. She's trying to be nonchalant but failing. She's confused and upset with me. I would be too if I were her. Actually, I'd be nuclear. What's surprising is that she isn't. "Everything cool?"

"Dandy," I lie.

By the very fact she's degraded herself by calling, I realize Shelby's a finely tooled high-maintenance machine, not used to such a marginal level of attention, let alone outright rejection, which perversely only increases my attraction to her and hers to mine. She's got everything in life worth having, but she's still a chick. And chicks always go for the self-centered douche bags. I'll never understand it.

"You know, usually I'm never the one who has to call," she jokes mildly.

Usually she wouldn't have to. Usually I'd be panting after her like a rabid dog, like every other red-blooded teenage male in Westchester County. Which I suddenly further realize means usually I wouldn't have a chance with her even if I was being me. Ironically, the fact that I'm not who she thinks I am and can't act like I usually would is my biggest appeal. It's insane.

"Sorry, I've had a lot on my plate," I maintain, noncommittal.

"We still on for Friday?" she ventures.

Friday? I've forgotten all about Friday. What to do about Friday? The target's within sight, yet somehow I can't pull the trigger. Not under false pretenses. Okay, I'm a dick, but not that much of a dick, as too often I wish I could be. But what if I'm wrong about her? What if it's the real Brooks Rattigan, the sensitive, considerate Brooks Rattigan deep underneath that Shelby instinctively yearns for? I'm not a bad-looking guy, I've done all right. A little uncouth around the edges compared to the fair-haired boys she's used to, perhaps, but not without my charms. The industrial-sized washers churn around me. I'm in the cleaners. I interpret it as a metaphor, a portent on how to proceed. What if I come clean with her? Lay it all out there. Not about being Celia Lieberman's paid escort. Never. But all the other stuff. What I'm really about, what I hope to become. What if by some miracle it doesn't matter that my father's a postal worker and I go to Pritchard High in New Jersey or that I'm matriculating at Rutgers? If there's even an infinitesimal possibility, shouldn't I reach for the grand prize? I must be out of my freakin' mind.

"Well?" she presses.

I stare at the dainty napkin in my hand, conflicted. A beat, then . . .

"Absolutely."

COMING CLEAN

Ablutions commence extra early Friday afternoon. I shower for like forever, shampoo, cream rinse, scrub in places I rarely if ever scrub. Shave twice so the cheeks and chin are baby soft. Towel and talc. Slap on the expensive cologne, topside and bottom. Sucking in my gut, I flex the abs and pecs and stare at my fogged-up image in the mirror. I'm looking and smelling mighty damn fine. With so much at stake, I have to be at my absolute best tonight.

I review the many eminent New Jerseyites I plan to run past Shelby when I make the Big Confession. The Boss. Sinatra. Bon Jovi. Jon Stewart. Whitney Houston. I mean, when it comes to celebrities, New Jersey takes a backseat to no state, except maybe New York, California, Texas, and possibly Tennessee. Edwin "Buzz" Aldrin, second man to walk on the moon, born and bred right here in Glen Ridge. Thomas Edison invented the lightbulb in Menlo Park and it doesn't get any more historical than that. Sherwood

Schwartz, creative genius behind *Gilligan's Island* and *The Brady Bunch*? Proud native of Passaic. Not good enough for you? Try Supreme Court Justice Antonin Scalia—actually, strike him. Okay, General Norman Schwarzkopf then, whoever the hell he is.

"Yeah, I'm from New Jersey," I defiantly declare at myself. "What's it to ya?"

Pumped, I swing open the bathroom door only to come face to face with stark, semi-naked reality. Like the Reaper himself, Charlie, woollier, groggier, and more stoned than ever, slouches in wait for me to emerge. I've barely seen the asshole since the blow-up. Just the unavoidable, fleeting glimpse here and there that comes with co-existing in such close quarters even as we endeavor to completely avoid the other. The sudden awful sight of him thoroughly demoralizes me.

"Least I was here," he slurs. "Least I put a roof over your head and food on your fucking table."

Apparently in his book doing the absolute minimum makes him some kind of hero, at least compared to the specter that is Mom. But not in mine.

"Don't worry," I say, brushing past him. "You won't have to much longer."

"Brooks, we need to talk," he says, now all serious-like.

"You and me got nothing to talk about," I snarl. Talk to him? I can't stand even looking at him. Well, I'm not going to let him and his shit rub off on me. Asswipe's not going to ruin my chances. Not anymore. Not this time.

"Mind explaining the almost ten grand you have saved up?" he says, lurching behind.

"I don't have to explain anything to you."

"If you're dealing pot, Brooks, I swear I'll . . ."

The irony of this halts me dead in my tracks. I turn to him.

"What? You'll buy some? Sorry, Charlie, I don't give family discounts."

Then I slam my door on him.

Fifteen minutes later when I come out of my room, dressed and groomed for battle, Charlie's still rooted where I left him. He looks away, ashamed as I step around him.

"Don't wait up," I state flatly. "I'll be out late."

– – –

Shelby and the Truth await, both equally terrifying. Traffic's as crappy as my mood, so it takes almost two hours to reach Blue Meadow and another twenty minutes to find the train station. It's just after six thirty. Fortunately, not leaving anything to chance, I've allotted myself plenty of time. I park the Beast. I've thought it all out. Blue Meadow's just two stops from Green Meadow, but I still can't chance anyone I know spotting me there in a late-model American-made clunker, especially one with Jersey plates, so I park at the far end of the lot. Unlike in Pritchard, the Blue Meadow terminal's tidy and upscale, with a cheery medieval theme. Alone on the platform, I feel like a spy going undercover deep into enemy territory. When the northbound five thirty-seven groans up, I hurry on.

The doors slide shut conclusively behind me. The train lurches forward. The car's deserted. An old guy knitting a dog sweater. A tired mom with one comatose kid and one hyper one. And, in the back, piled high on a seat, a small mountain of cute little shopping bags with handles, and sitting cross-legged beside them is none other than Celia Lieberman, intently reading a book cradled in her lap. She looks different. It's the glasses. She's got on the studious yet slightly retro frames we picked together. Okay, I picked. But I stand by my choice. And I note with equal approval the short pleated skirt I foisted on her, which she swore she'd never ever wear. I find myself smiling. I am glad to see her. I am actually glad to see Celia Lieberman. Then, to my great dismay, I relive the drink tossed and front door slammed in my face. Our last parting wasn't exactly on the friendliest of terms.

Before I can decide on an appropriate course of action, I recognize the faded blue paperback that she's so absorbed in. Sensing she's being observed, Celia Lieberman looks up from *Skies of Stone* and sees me. Taken off guard, she quickly slams shut Charlie's opus and, for good measure, sits on it. I pretend not to notice. Composing herself, she returns her frosty attention to me.

"Brooks."

Exploiting the fact that she's too flustered to remember to be pissed at me, I trundle down the aisle. "Pardon, Madame," I bow debonairly, "but is this seat taken?"

If I was truly forgiven, she'd remove her packages so I could sit beside her. She doesn't. But she doesn't tell me to eat shit and die either, which I take as promising. I plant myself onto the bench right behind her. Now that the ice has been accidentally broken, she can't exactly act like I'm not there.

"Brooks," she repeats frostily, keeping her back to me. "What are you doing here?"

"Meeting Shelby," I answer.

"You didn't drive?" she inquires, her back like a wall.

"I live in the City, remember? People from the City take trains."

I don't need to see Celia Lieberman's expression to know that she remembers all too well my web of deceit and furthermore doesn't much approve of it. She pointedly changes the subject.

"So did you hear from Columbia?"

"I got in."

She immediately whirls around to me, smiling widely, genuinely excited by my momentous news. Could it be that Celia Lieberman alone recognizes what I've accomplished, how much it means to me?

"That's so great, Brooks!"

"Yeah, yay me," I smile wanly.

"It's not so great?" she asks, registering the deliberate tepidness of my response.

"Can't go. Don't have the dough, baby," I say, doing a lame Bogart. I shrug like it's no biggie, but she knows better.

"But you have to go!" she protests, suitably outraged on my behalf. "Isn't there something you can do? What about all the money you made?"

"I'm not even in the ballpark," I laugh harshly. "Hell, I'm not even in the neighborhood."

"What about your father?"

I feel myself go cold, so cold it scares me.

"Fuck my father."

I look away from her. She nods, not pushing it.

"Hey, hating your parents. That's my line," she observes.

"Yeah, well, guess you're rubbing off on me," I say gruffly. "What about you? Everything good with Franklin?"

"Couldn't be better," she says, motioning at her array of acquisitions. "Just returning from the City where you can see I picked up a few essential items for Prom."

"Franklin asked you to Prom?" I ask, astounded.

"He read me a sonnet he wrote, then gave me a long-stemmed rose and everything," she beams. "It was dippy, but quite sweet."

I'm speechless, totally floored. Franklin putting on the moves? Has the universe shifted that much? It can't be.

"We're meeting up tonight to go to a zombie movie," she giggles girlishly, disturbingly pleased. "What is it with guys and zombie movies?"

"The same thing with girls and vampire ones." My eyes narrow suspiciously as I reappraise her pile of cute little bags. Now that the picture's clearer, I can just imagine what's wrapped inside some of them.

The train grinds to a halt. The doors open and close. We vibrate forward again. Next stop, Green Meadow. Celia rises and collects all her stuff.

"Brooks, something will work out with Columbia," she says. "It has to."

"Thanks," I say, meaning it, but I know something won't. "Don't forget your book."

She blushes, turns around, scoops it up, and tucks it into one of her bags. I shuffle after her to the doors. We stand together, waiting. Then she looks up at me.

"Brooks, there's nothing wrong with being from Pritchard."

"You've never been there," I say stonily. And she never will. Places like Pritchard don't exist to people from places like Green Meadow.

"Can't be any worse than this barracuda tank," she says softly.

Through the windows, the impeccable hamlet of Green Meadow appears, laden with shops and wares way beyond the grubby grasp of the mere likes of me. A filtered world, populated exclusively by the well put-together and the well preserved. It's like no human frailty's allowed within town limits. I get that old familiar knot again in the pit of my stomach. She has a point.

"If Shelby really cared about you, it wouldn't matter if you were from Kathmandu," Celia Lieberman continues. "Not that I have anything against Kathmandu. I mean, from what I've read, Nepal's a very cool place. Extremely scenic. The entire Himalayas in fact, although you have to watch out about drinking the water . . ."

She trails off, awkwardly. Up close, I can see that she's wearing makeup. Not much, just a little bit to accent the amber highlights in her eyes. And is that a touch of gloss making her lips glisten so appetizingly?

"So you think I should tell her?" I murmur.

"You should," she says, staring back at me. "That is, if you really, truly care about her."

The train shudders to a stop. Green Meadow. The doors whoosh open for us to disembark onto the platform. I hold up a warning hand, caution coming before gallantry.

"I'd better go first," I explain apologetically. "Shelby has this thing about you and me."

"I know," Celia Lieberman says, mystified. "I just don't get it."

"Yeah, me neither," I say, but I actually kind of do.

– – –

Shelby honks for me as I emerge into view. Illegally parked at the curb, behind the wheel of daddy's cream-colored Bentley convertible with the top down. I don't know which excites me more, her or the car—that's how hot she's looking. No joke. But somehow I manage to keep it together enough to saunter over to her without tripping or drooling all over myself.

"Hey, you made it." Shelby smiles dazzling white straight teeth, shaking her long silky tresses, which caress smooth tanned shoulders. She's molded into a short, thin one-piece halter number, which would be oh-so-easy to untie and remove. I'm utterly captivated.

"You had doubts?" I say.

She leans over the passenger door, lifts two gold-bangled wrists, and pulls me down to her. She kisses me open-mouthed, with intensity and every indication of much more to follow, before breaking off, leaving me weak-kneed and breathless.

"It's a new sensation," she admits. "I'm not sure I like it."

– – –

Shelby never asks me about Columbia. I guess she just assumes I'm going, that I had someone arrange it for me like she always has someone arrange it for her. Either that or she just doesn't care. I prefer to believe the former.

"The carpaccio and then the lobster ravioli," she decrees, handing back her menu. "Thanks, Alfredo."

She's insisted we go to *Le Petit* something, her favorite restaurant in Green Meadow, and the prices are heart-palpitating. Did she really have to order lobster? It doesn't even have a number listed beside it, just the initials "MP" as in market price as in I don't even want to think about it. We haven't established who's paying, but I've got a pretty strong hunch it's me. And why not? She thinks I'm just like her, loaded. In her galaxy, everybody is. Needless to say, I order the chicken.

Got to tell her. Got to tell the Truth. Got to.

But how to do it? And when? Just the right opportunity never seems to arrive as Shelby chatters about her summer plans over most of dinner and all of dessert.

". . . Venice, Mykonos, a quick pit stop back in Paris again," she says, barely touching her twenty-two-dollar tiramisu.

Italy, the Greek Isles, France. Pictures in books to me, but not to her. I mean, I'll be lucky if I make it to Atlantic City for a weekend. Now there's a segue.

"Then two weeks in Barcelona. I think that's my favorite city on the entire continent. Then back to reality . . ."

Reality, that's a laugh. She's living a fantasy. Mine. Got to tell her. Got to. Got to.

"What about you?" she asks.

I don't answer. I can't. Shelby misinterprets my silence.

"Am I boring you?"

"Not at all," I protest, although she actually is a little. I mean, do I really have to hear an hour-long recitation of all the amazing places I've never been and most likely will never go? But that's not her fault. Among the smart set, summers abroad are a post-graduation rite of passage, don't you know.

"Guess my level of conversation can't match a mental giant's like Celia Lieberman."

"Would you cut it out with Celia Lieberman?" I say, irked to be thrown off my mental stride. Why does she always have to keep bringing Celia Lieberman into everything?

In a huff, Shelby gets up to go the ladies' room, giving Alfredo his cue to discretely present me with the check. My eyes almost pop out of my skull at the final tally. I knew it was going to be bad. But $171! For that? A spoonful of pasta and a tiny piece of chicken, scrumptious though it was. We didn't even have wine! Alfredo hovers. I furiously peel off twenties from my college bankroll.

"I expect change," I seethe.

The valet fee's fifteen bucks. I could have parked on the street for free, but that would be too déclassé. Fifteen bucks right out the window. Fifteen bucks is two hours mopping floors and cleaning toilets at The Gun. Fifteen bucks is a quarter tank of gas. Nevertheless, I fork it over. What the hell, just more ill-gotten gains I won't be spending to go to Columbia.

As we cool our designer heels for our uber-luxury mode of transport, the sales tax of which is more than most people's mortgage, Shelby touches up her lips. As if those lips need enhancement. I can tell she's ticked off at me for not fawning over her. A breeze blows her hair and sheer little dress, outlining the incredible curves of her figure. She looks like a supermodel on a runway. What am I doing with her? I am in so over my head in so many ways. Got to tell her. Got to. *Got to*. Now or never, boy . . .

"Shelby," I say. "I'm sorry if I've been so out of it. It's just that there's something important I need to tell you . . ."

Before I can utter a single incriminating word, two large veiny hands clutch me from behind by the throat and lift me bodily until I'm squirming half a foot off the ground.

"Nobody dumps Tommy Fallick!"

I twist around. Tommy's eyes are wild and bloodshot and he reeks of booze and cigarettes. Never good signs.

"Tommy Fallick's always the dumper, Tommy Fallick's never the dumpee!"

Even though he has me by at least four inches and can probably out–bench-press me by several hundred pounds, I'm pretty sure I can take him. I mean, I've been in a few scrapes in my time. Okay, two, and one was in kindergarten. Okay, I give me even odds.

Barely.

"Oh, Tommy, stop being so Jersey!" says Shelby.

"I am not being Jersey!" bellows Tommy, applying tremendous pressure on my windpipe with his oversized thumbs, cutting off all oxygen intake.

"You are too!" Shelby shouts, walloping him with her nine-hundred-dollar Versace purse. "You are being so Jersey!"

Yes, folks, that is what they say. I only wish I was making it up.

Twisting hard, I slip from Fallick's soggy grip. And then I get up right into his face, ready to rumble. I'm seeing red. Stupid, rich, undeserving, lucky Fallick's the living embodiment of everything that's messed up in my world. His very name's a personal affront to me. So what if he can pulverize me? Just one good punch, that's all I'm asking.

"And quit following us!" Shelby says, shoving him away. "I'm gonna call the cops. I mean it!"

Tommy's dull eyes glaze in self-pity. He steps back, goes slack, then meekly stumbles back to whatever rock he crawled out from under. Shelby coolly turns to me.

"You were saying?"

Jersey. So Jersey. The ultimate put-down. To say the wind has been knocked out of my sails would be a vast understatement since there wasn't much wind to begin with. I will not be speaking the Truth anytime soon.

"Barcelona's mine too," I say, meaning my favorite city on the continent.

I'm bestowed with that radiant smile again, restored to good graces. The night's young and so are we.

– – –

Ragtop down, constellations shimmering above, overlooking a vast empty beach on the Long Island Sound. Untouched, undeveloped private beach, I might add, passed along for generations. The-Dream thumps softly on satellite radio from a state-of-the-art sound system. The weed's kicked in—hers, heavy duty, better than I'm used to. I'm so buzzed. And the cognac, pungent and piercing, is not helping the old impulse control.

Which I am in dire need of because, my friends, I'm dry humping the most beautiful girl in the world in the backseat of her father's Bentley. Her flesh pressed against mine, supple, yielding. Our limbs interlocked, mine wandering, hers playing zone defense. Our lips and tongues partake in a torturously slow, multicourse feast of delicious sensation, parceled out by a master temptress. She knows how. And how. For a flicker of an instant, I actually sympathize with Fallick. To receive such divine gifts and then to be deprived of them forever. No wonder the dude's falling apart at the seams. My loftiest expectations are exceeded, my wettest dreams surpassed, which, considering how warped I am, is pretty astounding. I can't believe it's really happening, that at last she—this—is all mine.

"You're perfect," I whisper in awe.

"Everyone says that," Shelby responds, suddenly pushing free. "It's super annoying."

Apparently I've struck a nerve without intending to. She sits up, hair disheveled, dress mussed, unaligned, an even bigger turn-on.

"And it's not true," she says. Then she smiles coyly. "I have a mole."

A little bird tells me this is going to be good. So, despite my raging hormones and throbbing hard-on, I play along.

"*Do* you?" I inquire innocently. "*Do* you really?"

"Wanna see it?"

"Oh, *could* I?" I say, pressing my palms fervently in prayer.

Shoving me back on the plush leather seat, she straddles my hips. Her hands reach for the string bow behind her neck, the main target in my sights for the past half hour. She tugs one end, the bow unravels, and praise be, the pearly gates are swinging open. The thin straps so tenuously holding up what little there is of her halter dress slide down. She turns, giving me the full effect.

"See?

I not only see, I gawk, I gander. But mostly, I lo and behold. Decorum forbids me to tell of the twin glories that rise before me. Let's just say remarkably firm, gravity defying, the size and shape of small cantaloupes. As for the mole. Well, for a mole, it's perfect. It's a perfect mole.

She's a drug and every ounce of my being craves a fix of her. I pounce. We lock mouths again. She clamps around me. Her exquisite naked mounds are pressed hard against my shirted chest. We roll off the seat to the thickly carpeted floor.

"No, Brooks, not here," she gasps. "Not like this."

"What's wrong with this? This is good. This is excellent!"

She's topless in the back of a freakin' Bentley on a friggin' private beach. I ask you, am I missing something?

"Prom night," she whispers between steamy kisses. "We can get a room at the Ritz. Do it in style. Bubble bath. Champagne. Scented candles. An actual king-sized bed. Like the semi-adults we're supposedly about to be."

Prom. The be-all and end-all. Deep in the swamp that's my addled brain, I know I shouldn't. To ask her is to ask for trouble.

Then she reaches down. I whimper, putty in her slow, steady grip.

"How about the Comfort Inn?"

"Sorry, but you'll have to do better than that," she grins, thinking I'm joking. I'm not. She increases the tempo.

"The Marriott?" I squeak, eyes lolling.

"That is, if you're not busy that night. You still haven't asked me." Her hand halts, leaving me hanging. She looks at me, all business.

The Ritz. The Taj Mahal. At this pivotal juncture, I'd agree to anything.

"Will you go to Prom with me?" I rasp, insane for relief.

"I'll think about it."

But then she sinks between my knees. Words fail me.

THE BIG NIGHT

After serious deliberation, I settle on the Hilton. Not quite the Ritz, but the best place within a ten-mile radius of Green Meadow that takes AAA discounts. Even so, it's a giant pain in the behind, since if you don't have a credit card, which I don't, they make you leave seven hundred dollars—yes, that's right, seven hundred smackeroos—in either cash or a cashier's check as a deposit before they'll book it. Which means early one Saturday morning I have to drive an hour and a half to deliver their blood money.

On the way back, I make a quick pit stop at a Bed Bath & Beyond, where I have a plethora of five dollar and 20-percent-off coupons. There, I purchase the most expensive bubble bath they carry and stock up on scented candles. There's a whole section of them. Three full aisles. *Morning Rise. Afternoon Surprise. Raging Sunset.* I never before realized that there were so many olfactory moods to pick from. I select *After After-Party Humpathon.* Just kidding. Try a six pack of *Deep Penetration*. Waiting in the checkout line, I see they're having a special on dried rose petals, so what the heck, I spring for a sack of them too. No expense spared for The Great Consummation.

The Great Consummation. I have mixed feelings about The Great Consummation. Guilt, because The Great Consummation, if there is indeed one, will only transpire because I'm a lying piece of crud and complete tool. I all-too-fully realize that I can't keep the balls in the air indefinitely and anything beyond Prom's an impossibility for Shelby and me, but I figure where's the harm in one measly night? One scorching hot, beyond incredible night. Okay, technically I'm using her, but in a twisted way she's using me too so that means we cancel each other out, right? I mean, I still don't get Shelby's fixation with Celia Lieberman, but why look a gift horse in the mouth? Anyway, soon Shelby'll be traipsing off to Barcelona and Mykonos and I'll just be a beautiful memory. I hope. I pray.

Because the other even stronger feeling I'm feeling is Lust, with a capital *L*. Our close encounter in the backseat of the Bentley hounds my every waking second and haunts my most fevered dreams. We did everything. I mean everything. That is, Everything But. And lemme tell you without getting too specific, Everything But was earth-shattering. I can't wait for what But's going to be like. I am a man possessed.

I can't sleep the night before the Big Night. Besides the endless loop of erotic fantasies, I'm as nervous as a schoolgirl on her first date. Despite all the Homecomings, Winter Formals, Spring Flings, and Proms I've attended in the past year, in some ways this is a first for me. First time it's mine. First time I'm going as me. Kind of. First time I'm paying out of my pocket, that's for danged sure.

- - -

I arrive at the hotel two hours before tee time. Park the Beast at the very top of like a ten-story garage, where it's most out of the way. When I get to the room, it's got twin beds. I practically have to pitch a hissy fit in the lobby for the promised king and end up with a queen with a view of the air-conditioners. I unpack the bubble bath, strategically arrange the scented candles, sprinkle the rose petals. Then it's a quick shower and another shave. I lay out the trusty tux on the bed and then collapse in my boxers besides it. Everybody's supposed to meet up at Cassie's at seven sharp for assorted beverages and photos before we collectively embark in the super stretch limo. But that's not for forty-five minutes and she lives like a three-minute cab ride away. Plenty of time to cool out. I switch on the Yankees. Top of the fifth, we're up by two. I need to refortify. Truth be told, with all the preparation and anticipation, not to mention the constant white noise and angst about Columbia, I'm pretty beat.

Next thing I know, I'm drenched in a puddle of my own drool and it's the bottom of ninth, Yanks down by three, two outs, nobody on. I bolt up, peer into the shadows. What the hell? That game was in the bag. I realize I've nodded off. Question is, for how long? Holy crap! Seven sixteen! I'm late! So late! Maybe too late!

I'm still yanking on my pants and misbuttoning my shirt as I streak from the Hilton. There's only one cab in the cab line and five people waiting for it. I have to frantically debase and demean myself by begging and groveling and then bribing them each a twenty to butt in first. I scream at the driver to step on it. He doesn't appreciate the attitude and I have to apologize before he'll move an inch. Then, just to add salt to my gaping wound, he deliberately goes a full three miles under the speed limit the whole ride there.

– – –

The circular driveway to the Trask manor's a jumble of valet parked high-end imports. I jump out without tipping and sprint, windmilling around to the back patio, where there's a big circus tent under which everyone is gathered. Up front, obscenely well-to-do, normally with-it parents are elbowing and jostling each other like crazed paparazzi, grabbing shots of a long chorus line of their begowned, bejeweled daughters. Arm in arm, their pampered little princesses vamp, giggling and smiling bashfully as expensive digital cameras whir and flashes flash. They know they're hot. Each more done-up, more gorgeous than the last. And in the center, the most ravishing, most regal of them all. Shelby. My date for the evening. Lucky, lucky me.

Or am I? Even though she's grinning ear to ear like Heath Ledger in *The Dark Knight*, I can tell Shelby's not exactly a happy camper. I haven't exactly helped my cause by leaving her to fend for herself for the past twenty-six minutes of phony pleasantries and rampant speculation about my whereabouts and then strolling in like the cock of the walk. It's pretty much inexcusable. But then again, being a dick's part of my inexplicable charm for her, so maybe I still have a shred of a chance at redemption.

"Okay, now girls *and* boys!" directs the hired professional photographer, the same annoyingly chipper gay guy in the pink bow tie who's snapped me from time to time at sundry events on the senior year social circuit. I'm too relieved to be suitably alarmed.

For all is not lost. I haven't missed the couples shots. That would have been irreparable. I've made it just under the wire, without a nanosecond to spare.

The guys in their tuxes take their places in the chorus line beside their dazzling dates. I take advantage of the frenzy to nimbly slide in beside Shelby.

"Sorry," I murmur. "Death in the family."

"Where have you been?" She smiles a frozen smile at me as the cameras continue to flash. "I thought you had stood me up!"

"Smile for the birdie, everybody!" yells Pink Bow Tie.

Then he pauses, glances up from the view finder, and looks at me quizzically.

"Hey, weren't you at the Prom in Bronxville last weekend?" he asks.

Actually, it was the weekend before and in Larchmont. But of course, I shrug like I don't know what he's talking about.

"Not me," I demur, darting a look at Shelby. Fortunately, she's too relieved that I'm there to take notice.

Scratching his head, Pink Bow Tie returns to his task.

"All right, boys and girls. It's all downhill from here! On three!" he chirps. "One, two . . . !"

I bare my incisors and smile for posterity. One of them.

Instantly I'm swept in the mass migration to our awaiting carriage. Tearful parents stream in a herd after us. Their babies, all grown up, leaving the feathered nest and all that. Hunter and Gretchen Pace swoop at me from out of nowhere, beaming, wanting to converse, however briefly, with their daughter's date for such a landmark occasion.

"Hi, Brooks, I'm . . . ," Hunter gasps, thrusting out his hand.

"MUMMY, DADDY, WHAT DID I TELL YOU BEFORE?" thunders Shelby.

Whatever she's told them before must have been a real doozy, because both titans of their respective fields immediately evaporate back into the ozone.

— — —

To rousing adult clamor and the deafening cannon-fire of confetti, we pile inside, eleven dashing couples, twenty-two stars and starlets in all. Although our motor craft's about the length of a lap pool, it's still a tight squeeze and Shelby has to perch on my lap. I don't mind, not a bit. Primped, powdered, and perfumed, molded into a sheer backless, strapless designer gown, wearing Mummy's diamond earrings, she's never looked more glamorous—and probably never will. She's at her apex. She *is* the apex. And she's mine. All greedy mine. Or can be—if I can just manage to suppress my scruples and not to screw it up, which so far I seem bound and determined to do.

Honking obnoxiously, we pull away. Within seconds it becomes Party Central. Kanye's blasting from surround speakers, colored strobe lights are crisscrossing. Yes, there's a laser light show inside the limo. Flasks are produced, fatties the size of Cubans proffered. Gratefully and greedily I partake of anything that comes my way. So does Shelby. She brushes into me when we round a corner. I detect major wood forming. So does Shelby. She presses down against it—uh, me. All is forgiven. It's fuckin' Prom.

There's only one large-sized fly in my ointment. Fallick. Busting out of a Valentino, he stares daggers at me from his seat directly opposite the rectangular compartment. Booze dribbles down his chin as he swigs, the sight of me with Shelby eating him alive. I mean, if looks could kill, I'd be dead meat a thousand times over.

Vicuna Munson, Fallick's consolation date, strokes his heaving chest. And she's some consolation, lemme tell you. Taut, tawny, bountiful where it counts. But nevertheless a distant second to Shelby—just like every other girl. The weird thing is, though, this Vicuna chick's staring right at me too, like we know each other, like she's trying to place me. What's weird about that is I've never seen this Vicuna chick before tonight, because if I had, I definitely would have stored this Vicuna chick in the memory banks, her bounty is that bountiful. Anyway, I have no clue why she's staring, but it's kind of unsettling.

Suddenly, still glaring at me, Fallick lets out the terrible guttural cry of a wounded animal.

"AHHHHHHHH!!!!"

I mean, he just howls. The others interpret it as simple high spirits and join in. I know for a fact it's simple homicidal rage and don't. Guys, girls, everyone's whooping, hollering, yowling. A rich, ever-ravenous-for-more pack. Totally unhinged.

"AHHHHHHHHHHHHHHHHHHHHHHHH!!!!"

Even Shelby's howling. In her case, adorably, with her little button nose crinkled up. The air's electric with expectation. For this is it. The final blowout. The end of an era.

And then I howl too. Part of it all, even though I'm not. And why not?

It's fuckin' Prom.

— — —

Fully baked and starving from the stimulants, not to mention the primal screaming session, we arrive en masse at Chez Five-Dollar-Signs-On-Every-Review-Site, where we're stampeded by a particularly snooty maître d' to our own plush private banquet room in back. Even in my stupor, it remains staggering how much one meal for two's going to set me back. In the musical chairs scramble for cushioned seats, I momentarily and uncomfortably find myself next to this Vicuna chick, who continues giving me the eyeball.

"I know I've seen you before," she says.

"I don't think so," I respond quickly, ushering Shelby to the far end of a conveniently long table.

"Westport!" she declares decisively.

Westport! Westport was the night with Gravity Dross, the night we mind-melded and I joined her some place remote on the spectrum. No wonder this Vicuna chick doesn't register on the Rattigan Scale. That night I was so lost grooving in inner space, an alien invasion wouldn't have.

"Never been," I grunt haughtily, like Westport's a teeming cesspool right on par with the Black Hole of Calcutta. Best defense is an offense, right? But my heart's suddenly thumping like one of The Murf's crazed solos.

She looks at me doubtfully, but not a hundred percent sure so she lets it slide for now, allowing Fallick to drag her away Neanderthal-style back to his drunken jock pals. Shelby looks at me like, what's that all about? I shakily pull out a chair for her. What the hell's going on tonight? First Pink Bow Tie Guy, now this Vicuna chick. I'm telling you, I'm living on borrowed time.

Shelby orders the Beluga caviar for starters. There is no chicken. Casting financial fate to the winds, I say fuck the pheasant and go for the steak. It takes both appetizer and salad courses for my nerves to settle sufficiently to digest Shelby's ongoing conversation.

"So then Daddy says, 'Honey, you sure you don't want to go?'" she's saying. "'I'd hate to have you miss it.'"

"Go?" I ask absently, sawing into my grass-fed slab.

"To Prom, silly rabbit," Shelby smiles, barely nibbling on her truffles. First the twenty-two-dollar tiramisu, now the thirty-one-dollar truffles. Why does she order the crap if she's not going to eat it? "When I wasn't sure you were going to have the balls to actually ask me."

"Oh yeah," I observe, infantilely titillated that she just said "balls." Remember, I'm severely buzzed at this point.

"Anyway, for a while there it looked like I wasn't going. I mean, nobody at school would dare ask since Tommy's running around threatening certain death . . ."

I nod, chewing vigorously. Sixty-plus bucks and they can't even cook it right. My meat's overdone, tough as shoe leather.

"So my dad, get this, he tells me that at his office the other day," she titters, finding it so hilarious that she can only speak in disjointed pieces. "At his office, he heard about this kid who could take me."

I stop in mid-chomp. Somehow I know where this is going.

"Very discrete, he says. Great dancer. Comes highly recommended," she guffaws. "A stand-in!"

"A what-in?" I rasp.

"A stand-in," she says, cracking up more. "A professional escort. Can you imagine?"

Yes, I can imagine. That and many other things. Like being roasted alive on a spit over a bonfire in the town square of Green Meadow as hundreds of super-fit villagers with torches and shotguns cheer.

"So I tell him, please, I'm not that desperate," she chortles, shaking with merriment. "Allow me some small semblance of pride."

She laughs uproariously, the idea ludicrous to her. I chuckle along at the absurdity of my own existence. She's way stoned too so we're just chuckling like a couple of morons when suddenly sirens and red alerts are going off because a thick un-masticated hunk of overcooked beef has just lodged tightly in my narrow passageway.

The effect's immediate, a jolt to the system. It's like being trapped in one of Burdette's headlocks, only there's no Burdette to beg to stop. This blockage has a sense of permanence. I leap up, clutching my neck, thrashing and flailing. Dishes go crashing, chairs topple, Promees scatter as I, blue-faced and choking, jerk and spasm. It's like the greatest death scene you've ever seen in a movie, except, unfortunately, I'm not acting.

"Oh my God, Brooks!" Shelby exclaims. "Are you all right?"

"Water. . . ," I wheeze.

Gasping, I snatch a bottle of the bubbly kind and swallow it down. It does me no good. I just spout a stream of fizzy liquid back out. Next I tilt back and try shoving two fingers down my throat. No good either. I flop and flounder like a hooked fish. I'm staring into the Great Abyss. A lifetime of squandered opportunities and unrealized regrets pass in a flurry across my dimming vision. The travels and experiences I will never have. Vacations with the grandkids. Hell, vacations with the kids. Vacations, period. But most galling, the fact that I will never ever bone Shelby.

Good-bye, private dining room. Good-bye, long table. Good-bye, tasseled chairs. Good-bye, people just watching. Good-bye, Fallick smirking happily as I asphyxiate to death. At least I won't be picking up the check. Oh, parting is such, such sweet sorrow. Good-bye, shiny chandelier. Good-bye, plush carpet. Good-bye, Celia Lieberman. Celia Lieberman!

As I crumple, she catches me from behind. Locking her arms around my midsection, she performs a rapid sequence of rib-crunching abdominal thrusts on me. The pain's excruciating but somehow reassuring. The good ol' Heimlich maneuver. A doctor's kid, of course she knows it. The maneuver never fails. But it does on me.

While the brutal display of violence does what it's designed to do, namely compress my lungs thereby exerting tremendous pressure on the meat plugging my trachea, I don't expel it. Not that I don't try my darndest. I hack. I gag. I slobber.

Then Celia Lieberman folds me in half like a wooden puppet and slams me with the heel of her hand on the back in the tender spot between my shoulder blades. Hard. A bunch of times. My eyes bug out and tear up from the repeated impact, but I remain plugged.

"Allow me!" Fallick bellows, rolling up his sleeves.

One sledgehammer blow would do the trick, but Fallick uses three, pounding me with all his mighty might with both interlaced fists. The offending obstruction ejects from my windpipe, out my mouth, and splats against a red velvet wall where it sticks, a glistening glob of goo.

Yes, brothers and sisters, existence, miserable as it is, has been prolonged by Fallick. Oh, the ignominy.

Gulping for air, grimacing from the multiple fractures I've most likely sustained, I nattily readjust my tie and lapels, mustering the shards of what's left of my pride. Everybody's gawking. Fallick, Shelby, Celia Lieberman, Cassie, Trent, and—look, there's Franklin, dippy in black sneakers and black T-shirt stenciled stupidly like a tuxedo. I've put on quite the show.

And then fortune fortuitously intercedes.

The snippy maître d' pops his shellacked head in, attracted by the furor.

"Everything satisfactory?" he inquires warily.

I draw myself up, puffed with indignation.

"No, everything is not satisfactory!" I announce, pointing at the gob on the wall. "You call this Chateaubriand?"

Collective snickers. Superior smiles. Nothing like putting the hired help in place to restore equilibrium.

— — —

How does that line in that book go? *It was the best of times, it was the worst of times.* Or something like that. Well, that's exactly how I'm feeling.

The Best of Times because it's the Prom of all Proms, the Grand Soiree of Grand Soirees. We're talking the Main Ballroom at the Four Seasons. A live major minor band, the kind with two or three megahits now pretty much forgotten. Tables heaped with delicacies of every persuasion. Fields of sushi, a suckling pig, mountains of tropical fruits. Absolute, unbridled, pointless, glittering Excess.

And I'm taking the Queen of it. I should be King of the World.

And I am. Only I'm not.

The Worst of Times because I'm ready for the shoe to drop and squash me any second. All survival instincts are whispering for me to inch my way to the door and hightail it out of Dodge while the getting's still good. However, all primal ones are screaming at me to just fucking go for it.

Shelby shakes her ultra-tight bod to the wild, tribal rhythms, brushing against me, pulling back, brushing again, teasing. I corral her by her slender waist, lead her by the hand, and twirl her. She's supple, responsive to my touch. We move as one. Graceful. Sinuous. Sensuous. Perfectly matched.

"Did you book the room?" she huskily breathes.

"The Hilton," I smile confidently, envisioning Shelby and me in the bubble bath, our wet naked bodies bathed in the flicker of six artfully arranged scented candles and a blizzard of falling dried rose petals.

"The Hilton?" Her smoldering expression slightly cools.

"The Four Seasons was sold out," I lie. "Hey, it's within walking distance."

"Sure, if you want to hike a mile along a turnpike," she all-too-accurately notes.

I smile less confidently. Then my gaze falls on Celia Lieberman and Franklin clumsily box-stepping past. And I must say, now that I've regained a full supply of oxygen and most bodily functions, I can't help registering that Celia Lieberman has jumped well into the Cute Zone. She fills out an old vintage flapper dress she's had altered and must have picked up in the Village quite, quite nicely. She's even showing a little cleavage, not to mention significant portions of leg. Her hair, cut short—at my recommendation, I might add again—is finally under partial control. I mean, I don't want to get carried away here, a flapper dress is kind of a rather interesting—okay, dorky—choice. But still a mega-mega stride forward.

"Ouch!" I hear her squeal. "Franklin, quit stepping on my feet!"

"Quit stepping on mine!" he returns in kind.

I smile despite myself, feeling for poor Franklin. The guy's clearly got no clue what he's gotten himself into. Shelby goes rigid in my arms.

"Having second thoughts?" she says darkly.

"Celia never could dance for shit," I explain lamely.

Shelby angrily jerks away from me. She really has a complex about Celia Lieberman. Go figure.

"Hey, the girl did just save my ass."

"I have to pee!" Shelby announces, stomping off. Huh, I think. Abruptly and ignominiously stranded, I thread my way through the crush to the punch bowl, which has been heavily spiked, and dip myself a brimming fine crystal cup of much needed fortitude when I hear:

"You still haven't told her?" accuses Celia Lieberman, grabbing my drink like I poured it just for her, wincing down the noxious brew.

Great, just what I need right now, an extra conscience. Like my puny one's not pestering me enough. Deftly, I deflect the subject.

"Listen, thanks for rescuing me back there," I say. "For a second, I thought I was a goner."

"Anytime," she shrugs nonchalantly, handing me back my own libation. Up close, I can observe that she's wearing mascara, rouge, lipstick, the whole works, imperfectly applied, but effective all the same.

"Killer dress," I blurt out, to my surprise.

"Thanks, I picked it out myself," she says proudly,

twirling around like a model, returning to me, beaming. "I did it, Brooks, I did it!"

"With Franklin?" I croak, alarmingly alarmed.

"No, my parents," she announces. "I did it. I finally stood up for myself."

And then Celia Lieberman lays out the whole story of her great personal triumph on me. It happened yesterday when Celia Lieberman was just getting back from pre-Prom mani-pedi . . .

"Celia, cupcake, is that you?" trills Gayle, stopping Celia Lieberman short in the doorway, making Celia Lieberman cringe to the very marrow of her bones.

"No, it's Beatrice, your imaginary lesbian lover," retorts Celia Lieberman, thinking what does the woman have, sonar for hearing?

Then, wouldn't you know, Gayle breezes in from the den, holding the latest hideous, poufy monstrosity up to her ample chest.

"Don't you just love it?"

"What is it?" asks Celia Lieberman, although she fully knows what it is.

"Your Prom dress for tomorrow night!"

Gayle giddily whirls around. It's like she's the one who's going to Prom, not Celia Lieberman, according to Celia Lieberman.

"I happened to be at the mall yesterday and I just couldn't resist!"

"You happened to be at the mall?" Celia Lieberman

replies. "You have a PhD in Clinical Psychology from the University of Chicago. You hate the mall. And, for your information, I have my own Prom dress."

Well, it kind of escalates from there. By the time Harvey putters up in the Prius, home after another day on the cutting edge of modern medicine, the usual insanity is echoing from the Lieberman abode, shattering the otherwise peaceful night for miles around.

"YOU ARE NOT LEAVING THIS HOUSE IN THAT RAG! I ABSOLUTELY FORBID IT!"

"I'M ALMOST EIGHTEEN! I CAN MAKE MY OWN GODDAMN DECISIONS!"

"CELIA, I DON'T CARE IF IT IS AGE APPROPRIATE, YOU CANNOT SPEAK TO ME THAT WAY! I AM STILL YOUR MOTHER!"

"THEN TRY ACTING LIKE ONE! JUST LISTEN TO ME FOR ONCE!"

Harvey starts to tiptoe back to make a clean, quiet, electric getaway when the front door swings open, casting an ominous shadow over him. Celia Lieberman looms, hands on her hips, meaning business.

"Not so fast, Dr. Lieberman, this concerns you too!" she commands.

Harvey meekly joins Gayle in the living room. I shudder at the vivid image of the three of them among all those deeply disturbing fertility statues. Then Celia Lieberman, again according to Celia Lieberman, addresses them both somewhat calmly.

"Mother, Daddy, I realize you've come perilously close to destroying my life with the best of intentions," Celia Lieberman tells me she told them. "That you've pushed, prodded and meddled because you don't want me to miss out like you did."

And guess what? They don't interrupt. They just listen for once.

"Well, thanks to you, I haven't missed out," Celia Lieberman reports. "During the last six months, I've been to every social event of the school year. I've been to restricted country clubs, overpriced and overrated restaurants, and a vast array of equally asinine after-parties. I've danced. I've gotten drunk. I've vomited."

"But, honey, isn't that what you . . . ," cuts in Gayle.

"For pity sake, Gayle, shut up for once and let her finish!"

This is a first for Harvey. And, for that matter, Gayle too. She shuts up for once. Harvey motions to Celia Lieberman, relinquishing the floor back.

"And now that I've done the scene, I know it's definitely not for me," resumes Celia Lieberman. "Which should be cool with you because, frankly, and I mean this in the nicest way possible, you're two of the most uncool people I've ever met. I mean, hello, the apple doesn't fall far from the tree."

Gayle nods tearfully. Celia Lieberman hugs her. She hugs them both.

"Please, I beg of you," Celia Lieberman says from the bottom of her soul. "Let me make my own mistakes."

Celia Lieberman glows at me. I am proud. I am proud of Celia Lieberman. And vindicated. Didn't I tell her what she had to do? Knowing Harvey and Gayle as little as I fortunately do, I know what it took for Celia Lieberman to finally stand up for herself.

"Wow," I say sincerely.

Reaching the end of the first set, the band launches into a signature slow tune designed to leave the audience on just the right warm and fuzzy high note. I recognize it. "Love for All Time" or "Eternal Love" or some such mush; I'm not really big on Top Forty. But, like, one of their two giant hits. I mean, once upon a time it was all over the radio. Celia Lieberman and me, we just stand there awkwardly.

"Better get back to Franklin," I finally say.

"No worries," says Celia Lieberman, looking up at me through her new glasses. They really do complement her. "Franklin's decided to sit the rest of the night out."

Across the shimmering dance floor, fairy-tale couples intertwine, becoming one. The guys, tall and jaunty in black tuxes, the girls, lithe and lustrous in silky gowns. Onstage, ablaze in a pool of light above the roiling darkness, the sexy lead singer pours out how her heart's been broken by some thoughtless, insensitive, unable-to-commit, lying scumbag. The same-old-same-old. I glance at Celia Lieberman. She sways to the song, syrupy though it is. Before I can think better of it, I bow formally before her, befitting the majesty of the occasion.

"Madame, would you do me the supreme honor?"

Yes, I'm asking Celia Lieberman to trip the light fantastic of my own free will. Yes, I want to. I can tell she's surprised. And pleased. But shy and hesitant.

"Oh, come on," I coax. "We've never actually danced. For real, I mean."

I extend a waiting hand. She takes it. I guide us into the thick of the steamy action. I loosely encircle her. She drapes her arms tentatively over my shoulders.

The lead singer's emoting up a tsunami, at the part where despite all the terrible shit she's suffered she still can't stop herself from loving the thoughtless, insensitive, unable-to-commit, lying scumbag. Women, I tell ya. But as Celia Lieberman and I press together, shifting ever so slightly back and forth, even I have to concede the cheap potency of the formulaic melody.

"It's too late to tell Shelby," I say out of the blue. "I've already blown it."

"If she really likes you, it's never too late," Celia Lieberman says softly.

"You're pretty smart, you know that?" I smile.

"That's what they tell me," she says, resting her head against my chest. I hold her ever nearer.

"It's weird, but since this whole thing began, you're the only person I can actually be myself with," I note, almost as much to me as to her. "I mean, you're the only person who knows how the whole Brooks Rattigan machine works, how all the moving parts actually fit together."

"Yay me," I hear her muffled voice say. She tightens against me. I tighten almost imperceptibly back.

"Franklin Riggs is one lucky guy," I say, meaning it, wishing her only the best.

Onstage, the emaciated bass player sidles over to the microphone and starts singing along too. I'd forgotten all about this section. And, for a strung-out string bean, the dude can really boom. He's sorry, he tells the sexy singer who's letting it all hang out, quivering, beside herself at being so wronged by him. Just give me another chance, baby, scumbag begs, I'll do better. Yeah, right. Then she, of course, forgives him and they scream into each other's faces at the tops of their respective vocal ranges, declaring undying devotion. And I've got to admit, it really kind of gets to me.

Celia Lieberman and I silently shuffle, caught up in the cheesiness.

"I finished your dad's book," she says.

It's the last thing I expect her to say. But you'd think I'd know by now that with Celia Lieberman you can never predict anything.

"It's really good, Brooks. Really, really good." She looks at me, eyes round and solemn behind her lenses. "He's had it pretty rough. I mean, if even a fraction of it is true, it's amazing he's still in one piece."

"Barely," I say bitingly, the mention of Charlie putting a damper on what could have and should have been a beautiful moment.

"Maybe you shouldn't be so hard on him," Celia Lieberman has the nerve to suggest, like it's any of her business.

"Maybe you should butt out," I counter, but gently, not wanting to tangle with her, especially not here, not now.

Thankfully, the song tapers off into silence, putting an end to our one and only slow dance and my short but way too eventful acquaintance with Celia Lieberman. I unpeel from our now very unwelcome clinch. What was I thinking? How could I ever have let my guard down? Things can never just be with Celia Lieberman. No, you can always count on Celia Lieberman to point out something at the exact point you most don't want it to be pointed out. It's like she can't stop herself. This is Celia Lieberman we're talking about here.

"I'm just saying . . . ," says Celia Lieberman.

"Don't."

"Oh, you're the only one who gets to dispense free advice?" she presses. "That's how it goes with you?"

Suddenly, Shelby lurches into view like the creature from the Black Lagoon, teetering and tottering precariously on her stilt-like shoes, cheeks wet with copious tears.

"I give up," she slurs her words at me.

"She's drunk," Celia Lieberman observes clinically, like it takes one to know one.

"No shit, Einstein!" laughs Shelby, turning to Celia Lieberman, suddenly merry and gay. "I'm fucked up, Celia! Plastered! But it doesn't take a brainiac to know that!"

"Shelby, stop," says Cassie, rushing up to steady her. "You're wrecking your makeup."

Shifting back from comedy into tragedy, Shelby seesaws close toward me, jabbing a sharp painted nail hard in my gut. "What's Celia Lieberman got that I haven't got? Huh? *Huh*?"

"Zits," Cassie soothes, balancing Shelby upright while dabbing her streaked but still spectacular face with crumpled wads of toilet paper. "Bad hair days."

Onlookers quickly swarm around us. Generally, as a rule, on average there's one huge alcohol- and/or drug-induced emotional public breakdown at every major high school social event. Well, apparently I've just been elected this evening's entertainment.

"What's wrong with me, Cassie?" Shelby blubbers. She's a mess. It's jarring to me, to everyone, because it's her. Oh, how the mighty have fallen.

I know I should say something, but I don't know what to say. This night, for no reason I can readily ascertain, is rapidly turning into a nightmare. Worse, I've got the sinking feeling that Shelby and yours truly won't be consummating anything, great or otherwise, anytime soon.

Then Fallick and this Vicuna chick push to the front of the pack.

"Wait, I remember now!" she crows to one and all. "It just hit me when I saw the two of them dancing!"

Did I say nightmare? Try catastrophe, try cataclysm. I'm the *Titanic* and I'm going down with all hands on deck.

"You took Gravity Dross to the Spring Fling at my school in Westport!" this Vicuna chick proclaims, jabbing a prosecutorial finger at me.

I glance at Celia Lieberman. She's gone white as a sheet. But other than her, no one else reacts to this Vicuna chick's triumphant revelation. Why would they? So I was at a Prom in Westport. So what? Probably just coincidence.

"He did?" Fallick's glazed, wasted eyes fight to focus, to think.

"Yeah, everybody was amazed Gravity Dross even had a date," this Vicuna chick explains. "Especially a certifiable cutie like him."

"Why's that?" Fallick persists, curse him.

I shrivel up inside, fearing what's coming. So does Celia Lieberman, only she's gone rigid, reverting back to pre-me petrified state. Shelby tilts her head sideways, suddenly cogent again, her interest piqued by this new tidbit of information.

"Gravity Dross is, like, retarded," this Vicuna chick says.

"Take that back!" I snap, too outraged to revert into customary total-denial mode. I mean, if this Vicuna chick weren't a chick, I'd deck her.

"Okay, okay," this Vicuna chick allows. "Mentally impaired. Whatever."

Everyone's looking at me. My outburst's incriminating. But what, precisely, is my crime? Nobody knows. That is, except Celia Lieberman and me, and we both are quaking. The Moment of Reckoning is at last at hand.

"I don't get it," Fallick says, the cogs laboriously turning. "Why would a guy willingly take out two different losers to two different schools in two different states in the tri-state area? It just doesn't figure."

Celia Lieberman's trembling. I bristle at the insult to her, although this is clearly my cue to take off for the hills.

"You're the only loser around here, Fallick," I say with feeble conviction. I can easily think of another.

"What's your deal, Rattigan?" Fallick demands, crowding me, getting right in my face. "Somebody paying you off?"

Bingo!

Shelby looks at me in dawning horror. Strap in, folks, it's going to get real ugly real soon.

"You're the stand-in?" she asks quizzically, too shocked to be pissed—*yet*.

"Shelby, it's not what you think," I protest, though it totally is.

"I am such an idiot!" Shelby shrieks, anger at last kicking in. "I thought you had so much depth and character! But the whole time you were just being paid to be different!"

Across the vast ballroom, all activity comes to a crashing, screeching halt.

"You were hired to be Celia Lieberman's date!" Shelby discloses to the entire planet. "You did it for the money! Why else would the two of you be together?"

All eyes fall accusingly upon me and Celia Lieberman

as everyone begins to get it. And one by one, Green Meadow's elite of the elite start to laugh uproariously.

"I knew it had to be something!" Cassie crows.

"Figures she had to pay for it!" Trent snickers. He shivers exaggeratedly, howling: "NOT ME, NOT FOR A MILLION DOLLARS!!"

The grand chamber rings with incredulity, ridicule, and scorn in a cruel crescendo.

"You're both pathetic," Shelby says witheringly to me and Celia Lieberman.

Then Celia Lieberman takes off like an unguided missile. Clawing through the howling mob, she flees the scene of the massacre, leaving me to my gory fate. She's been exposed to eternal scorn, forever ruined. And it's all my doing. Because everything was fine, only I had to push it.

"Celia!" I call out, though it serves no purpose.

Shelby quivers with self-righteousness. Her face twists into something scary and unrecognizable.

"This should be one of the best nights of my life and you've turned it into the worst!"

Those emerald eyes brim with hot, injured tears. There's no defense for what I've done. I've really hurt her. Like Celia Lieberman once said, I suck.

"Shelby . . ."

"She said to leave her alone, Rattigan!" Fallick erupts, grabbing me by the shoulder, swinging me around.

"Can it, Penis—I mean, Fallick!"

Then the bastard sucker-punches me in the jaw. I mean, he really crushes me one. Instantly I'm seeing exploding stars and crazy patterns. I go smashing to the parquet where I lie there, stunned. I taste molten metal. My lower lip's shredded. Everything's a red curtain.

Fuzzy teenage faces sneer down at me. Cassie's cackling. Trent's chortling. Fallick's cursing. Shelby's crying. But I can't hear what they're saying because both ears are ringing. I stagger woozily to my feet and then plop back down on my butt. I'm pouring blood. There's more than a good chance I need medical attention.

But no one extends me a helping hand. No one.

I'm in a daze, but not too much of a daze not to remember to be flooded with shame and humiliation. I stumble away to a rising tide of hilarity.

Through the plush, glittering lobby, past more blurry contorted faces, only the respectable, responsible grown-up variety. Even though I'm a terrible sight—bloody, swollen, wobbly-legged—no one comes to my assistance or offers the slightest aid. No captain of industry, no high society matron, no five-star-plus hotel staff.

Not a soul.

I rush out into the shelter and relative anonymity of night. The crisp inky air both revives and assaults me. My lip's an open gash, my head's a deep fog, I can't see or think straight. All I know is I've got to get out of this place, this place that won't have me, that disdains me and my kind. I take off sprinting down the center of the grand, curving driveway, which is ablaze in a constellation of artificial light. Luxury craft squawk and swerve around me.

"Brooks!" I hear. "Are you all right?"

It's Celia Lieberman, curled up on the curb beside what must be Franklin's dippy oblong VW Bug at the farthest reaches of the self-park lot. Prom Night and Mr. Poetry-and-Roses couldn't spring for the valet. That Franklin's all class. Clutching her knees, Celia Lieberman rocks back and forth, traumatized, wracked with mortification.

"Oh my God, what happened?" she gasps through her own pain at my grievous physical condition.

"Finally got what was coming to me," I say grimly.

She sniffles, choking back fountains of tears. Was it really just moments ago that Celia Lieberman was gazing up at me, her face so soft, so lovely? Now it's a battlefield, streaked with her first hopeful efforts at self-beautification. I did this to Celia Lieberman. Me.

"Celia, I'm so sorry," I mumble.

"No, it's not you," she says in a faint, small voice. "It's Them. They've always been like this to me. Since we were together in preschool."

I can't imagine what it must be like. To be the punch line just for existing, for just being you. Unaffluent and unconnected as I am, this is way beyond me, way beyond anything I've experienced in Pritchard. Or maybe I just haven't been looking.

"They have it all," she says, staring down. "Why do they have to be so mean?"

"You got me." And she does. She really does. Why do the strong always have to prey upon the weak? I've never been able to figure it out. "Maybe just because they can."

Then a new voice intrudes into the thoroughly depressing conversation.

"Celia, I just got your text!" says Franklin, sauntering up, chill as can be. "What's wrong?"

"Nothing," says Celia Lieberman, standing. "Just everything!"

"Jesus!" exclaims Franklin, taking in bleeding-and-battered me.

"Where were you?" she demands.

"In the game room. Figured they'd have the new *Walking Dead*. Thing's totally bitchin'," reports Franklin, then he reacts as he gets a better view of me. "Jesus, you really should have that looked at."

Franklin, being Franklin, has missed the whole extravaganza and, as usual, has no clue what's going on with the rest of planet Earth. What Celia Lieberman sees in the doofus defies me.

"Want me to take you home?" Franklin asks, finally registering that she's crying.

To my surprise, Celia Lieberman shakes her head.

"They expect me to just eat shit and die like always," she says, swallowing back tears. "Well, not this time, not tonight. It's my Prom and I'm going to enjoy it even if it kills me!"

Then Celia Lieberman yanks Franklin by the T-shirt and starts madly making out with him.

I don't know why, but it's like another body blow. I back away into the darkness. I turn. I run. Past block after block of baronial splendor. One mile, two—I don't know—but a long way. I run like I'm on the run, like I'm being hunted. I run in my tux and good shoes down the sparkling sidewalks, past the glinting shops, through a gauntlet of guarded expressions that see right through me. Up I stagger all ten flights of stairs in the Hilton garage. To the refuge of the Beast hidden in the corner at the very top.

My hands are shaking so much it takes four fumbling attempts to fit the key in the lock and three for the ignition. Gunning the engine, I floor the gas, zooming back, smashing my rear bumper into solid wall, shearing it half off. Rusted steel scrapes against concrete as I scream off in a spray of sparks down the ramp.

Hurtling southbound in the fast lane on the New York State Thruway, I beep frantically for people to let me by. I'm hyperventilating like a dying man, just gulping air out and in. When I catch my reflection in the rearview mirror, I'm more multi-hued than my most vivid apprehensions. All sweaty, puffy, and purple, I'm the guy who's been beaten to a pulp by the hero at the climax of a third-rate boxing movie. You know, the bad guy.

Which, let's not kid ourselves, is exactly what I am. I'm the villain of my own tawdry tale. It'd be one thing if I had something to show for my self-serving, craven deeds, but I have nothing. No Columbia. No Shelby. And now, no pride. Not a grain, not a particle.

I got what was coming to me.

I'm beneath my own contempt.

As the distance rapidly mounts from Green Meadow, so do the self-recriminations. Mute, accusing faces fly at me, dissolving into mist as they hit the windshield. The Murf, my oldest and bestest pal, who never did me a single bad turn. And how do I repay him? By stabbing him in the back, ditching him, almost getting him killed. Shelby. Hot, sexy Shelby. Classy, perfect, sexy Shelby. All she wanted to do was steal me away from Celia Lieberman and screw my brains out, albeit for mistaken reasons and suspect motives. And what do I do in return? I ruin what should have been the best night of her overprivileged, overindulged life. Poor baby. Well, tough shit.

Then, just as self-pity gives way to self-justification and outrage, yet another face confronts me. Celia Lieberman, inexpertly applied makeup splotched and smeared, eyes runny and raw. Celia Lieberman, whom I have most wronged. Celia Lieberman, whom I have abandoned to jeers, Franklin Riggs, and her own clueless devices.

The turnpike forks ahead. The giant road sign beckons: "NEW JERSEY."

Back I speed to safety, to lowered expectations, to the preordained, to my own kind. Back I speed, soon to be an amusing anecdote, a blip on otherwise glorious, trust-funded horizons. Back I speed to the only place I can call home, tail between my legs.

Then suddenly, deep inside, something snaps. At the last possible instant, I slam the brakes, sharply jerk the wheel. The Beast shoots off the highway through a gap in the median strip. Horns wail as I fishtail around, just missing being flattened by a big rig and a bus, and plunge recklessly into the onrushing tide of northbound traffic, back to Green Meadow. Back where I don't belong.

UNCHARTED WATERS

I can feel from more than half a mile away the heavy bass vibrations of the trance music pounding from where I know the after-party is being held. Dragging the now barely attached rear bumper, my dented, rusted-through Electra clanks up the long driveway, which is lined with stretch limousines and the little people who get paid peanuts under the table to drive them. I skid in a cloud of exhaust right in front of the lavish entrance to the main house, all lit up, the size and style of an imperial fortress. A pimply valet, same age as me, darts up to take the key.

"Keep the motor running," I say, vaulting past him. "This won't take long."

My leaking, bashed-in face tells him it's best not to mess with me. As I start up the front stairs, I hear:

"Oh my God, Brooks?"

It's Celia Lieberman, forcibly tugging Franklin behind her. What's she doing here? Making some futile gesture like me, no doubt. In any case, she's just what I don't need as I struggle to maintain the momentum and muster the courage to re-enter the arena.

"Celia, this is Fallick's house," whines Franklin, resisting each step of the way. "We can't go in there!"

Then a mostly naked girl in her bra and thong panties bursts from the bushes and scampers by, giggling naughtily.

"On the other hand," Franklin reconsiders, "perhaps a quick walk-through might be in order . . ." He starts ahead, but Celia Lieberman yanks him back.

"Not this time," she declares through clenched teeth. "You're sticking with me."

But I have no time for such childishness. Bracing myself, I charge into the compound and the Great Unknown. Instantly, I'm immersed in flashing lights, deafening sound, and teenage debauchery on a monumental scale. Kids in various stages of undress, drunk, stoned, totally fucked up. Kids making out, pawing each other. Kids having fancy food fights. Kids swinging from the chandeliers. I mean, literally.

Celia Lieberman shoves up beside me.

"Are you crazy?" she shouts over the racket. "What are you doing here?"

Ignoring her, I plow through the mayhem until I'm outside again in the backyard, where there's a giant tropical lagoon slash swimming pool, complete with artificial jungle vines, gurgling streams, and spouting waterfalls. Boys and girls, more than a few topless, grope, splash, or frolic, some all at once. And there's the man of the mansion himself, Fallick, taking a victory-over-me soak in the bubbling Jacuzzi grotto, basking in Vicuna's fawning, buxom glow. He does a double take as I march past and then frog hops out from the grotto in a bulging red, white, and blue American flag G-string. What's with these water polo guys and their burning need to exhibit their junk?

"HEY!!" he yelps, too astonished by my return to be suitably outraged by it. Gladly I halt and turn back to him.

"Don't get cocky, punk," I warn. "It was a sucker punch."

The party jostles for position around us like vultures to feast on the bloody spectacle of *SLAUGHTER II: The Rematch*. Somebody turns off the sound system. The thunderous music becomes ringing silence. Fallick, barechested, buff, and dripping, fists clenched, swaggers over to me. And in the red corner, the challenger: smaller me, bruised and battered. It's not fair. But Life isn't.

This is an invitation-only party, Rattigan," he snarls. "And you ain't on the list."

"I'll leave as soon as I talk to Shelby," I reply grimly.

I turn to resume my mission. Fallick takes a wild swing at me, but this time I know what's coming and I'm more than ready. I mean, normally I'd never stand a chance with the troglodyte. But he's way wasted and I'm way amped. I duck and deliver a devastating uppercut to his nose. Seventeen-plus years of lower-middle-class resentment, seventeen-plus years of striving for no good purpose, of ceaseless angst and hopeless confusion combine into one lucky, brain-rattling, cartilage-crunching punch. Fallick windmills backwards, crashing on and over a buffet table, crumpling in a soggy, sashimi-covered heap on the other side. I dust my hands. I'm probably facing major legal action.

"That's how we do it in Jersey," I announce to one and all.

I barrel ahead. The cowed pack parts for me like the Red Sea, clearing a ragged path to Cassie and Shelby, both in string bikinis, doing shots and bumps at a round glass table. Smoking a cigarette, Shelby regards me coolly, a party girl again.

"I just want to say one thing," I stammer, lost as always in her exquisiteness. "Celia Lieberman never asked for any of this. It was her parents' doing."

Shelby flicks an ash, mildly interested. "Her parents. And how's that?"

She just doesn't get it. How could she? Despite myself, I grow exasperated.

"For the same reason they all do," I heatedly reply. "Because they love their precious darlings. Because they all want their little princesses to be cool and popular like they once were or weren't. To be able to do all the stupid high school stuff they did or never got to do. But you'll never understand what it's like way out there in orbit. You're always at the center of it all."

"How sweet. Brooks Rattigan, defender of the downtrodden. Oh, please," says Shelby, downing a shot, sucking on a lime.

"And another thing," I press on. "I'm not from Manhattan, I'm from Pritchard!"

Puzzled murmurs and stumped shrugs ripple around the lagoon. Nobody at Green Meadow Country Prep's ever heard of it.

"It's in central Jersey," I add, going all in.

Gasps. Jersey. Now *that* is shocking. Shelby looks at me, incredulous. Jersey. It can't be true.

"More lies," she says dismissively.

"No one lies about being from central Jersey. And actually, the part about my father going to Harvard's true. For a brief second in time, he was a writer, but now he works as a letter carrier in Hoboken . . ."

Another round of gasps. A mailman. In Hoboken. The horror. Could it get any worse?

"Tell her why you're a stand-in!" butts in Celia Lieberman, emerging with Franklin beside us.

It could. And just did.

"Celia, would you please let me handle this?" I hiss under my breath, determined to keep up my brave front.

Exhaling smoke rings our way, Shelby eyes Celia Lieberman and Franklin with detached bemusement.

"Celia, I see you have a date," she says dryly. "Are your parents paying for him too?"

Zing! Bam! Man, that's gotta sting. But Celia Lieberman doesn't flinch.

"Nobody paid me a cent!" protests Franklin, who has a rep, warped though it is, to protect.

"I can definitely believe that," says Cassie, laughing.

"As I was saying," I glare, annoyed at the constant interruptions.

Snickers. Celia Lieberman, ignoring them and me, fixes on Shelby.

"I just want to tell you why Brooks works as a stand-in."

"I've heard quite enough about Brooks Rattigan for one night, thank you."

"Me too!" chimes in Franklin.

"He got into Columbia but doesn't have enough money to go," Celia Lieberman loudly declares.

Jesus! That was the one bean I wasn't planning to spill. I mean, the last thing I want is their pity, not that they're giving that or anything else away, for that matter.

"You should appreciate Brooks for who he is!" continues Celia Lieberman on some kind of deranged roll.

"Oh, and what's that?" Shelby asks derisively.

A decent, hard-working guy who's always had to struggle for everything you, me, and every other spoiled brat at this stupid party take for granted!"

After all I've done, Celia Lieberman is defending me. I'd be touched if I wasn't so appalled. Whose big scene is this anyway?

"If Brooks is so terrific," Shelby asks sarcastically, "why aren't you with him?"

"Because she's with me!" Franklin pipes, indignant.

"Do you *mind*?" I snap at Franklin, then spin back to Shelby. "Uh, where was I?"

I can't remember. I'm derailed, off the tracks. My offensive, such as it was, has been thoroughly blunted.

"It's bad enough you're a stand-in," Shelby jumps in, quietly furious. "But why would you lie about who you are, where you're from?"

"I was afraid if you knew the real me, you'd bail."

And there I am—the person I try my best never to be. Vulnerable. Putting it all out on the line. Exposing myself to universal ridicule and certain rejection.

"That's not true!" she says vehemently.

"Isn't it?" I ask softly. Could it really be? Could I have misjudged her? If I hadn't so completely blown it, could I have really had a sliver of a chance? Somehow that only makes it all the more tragic.

Then she glances away, averting my persistent look. And I have both my crushing answer and dim worldview reconfirmed.

"I never meant to hurt you," I say dumbly, as if intentions matter. "Sorry for wrecking your big night."

In one swift motion, she springs up and slaps me. Hard. Right on my already sore, swollen kisser. The pain's sharp and blinding. More exploding stars, more crazy electric patterns.

"Go to hell, Rattigan."

She gets up and pushes though the crush. I gingerly touch my again-bleeding wound, swivel my now even more throbbing jaw, and straighten my black bow tie. Everybody's quiet, a single super-attractive entity, staring at me.

I have no idea what they're thinking, but then I never have. Not really. What is it that F. Scott guy wrote in AP English? *The rich are different from you and me.*

"Show's over, folks," I announce to my riveted audience. "Have a good life. Don't worry about us peons."

The haves part for the have-not. As I leave, this time for the last time, I overhear Franklin whisper to Celia Lieberman.

"Hate to say it, but that was way cool."

— — —

My chariot awaits me right where I left it, idling in front. I tip the kid a twenty.

It's only money.

— — —

It's not until well after two that I roll into Pritchard. The dark, deserted streets are no longer familiar. The boarded-up windows, the long-shuttered storefronts, the tattered homes have become phantoms of an unrecoverable me. I'm a stranger in my own forlorn land.

I trudge up the three endless flights of stairs and down the dingy walkway to the place I reside, the place where I can at last rest my weary bones. But when I creak open the door, there's not the usual darkness but the flickering glow of the TV replaying the Yanks game.

"Hard night?" Charlie's voice calls out from the couch, all casual-like, breaking what was supposed to be my refuge of silence.

He's sitting up in his clothes, wide awake. I want to cry. After weeks of mutually agreed-upon disengagement, this is when Charlie chooses to ambush me? I can't deal with it, with him, especially now when I'm a mental and physical wreck.

"Where is it you say you work again?" his silhouetted figure says when I don't respond.

"What do you care?" I shield my face as I hurriedly shuffle past him into my room. Before I can kick it shut, he's in the doorway, which surprises me. I've never known the old guy to move so fast. I turn, forgetting too late not to, and Charlie gasps as he takes me in.

"Sweet Jesus, Brooks. What'd you do, walk into a door?"

"No, just a Cold Dose of Reality."

I'm so tired I can't keep putting up a front. I just want to burrow under my blanket, curl up like a fetus, and nod off forever. Only I know Charlie's not going to let me. I flop onto my side on my bed. A heart-to-heart with Charlie, the one we've so far managed never to have. Will this torture never end?

Charlie flips on the overhead lights. I squint in the harsh brightness. He flinches again as he fully witnesses my black and blue glory.

"Brooks, you mind enlightening me on what the hell's going on? And please don't insult what's left of my brain cells by telling me you've saved over ten grand bussing tables at bar mitzvahs."

"I take girls to social functions," I mumble into my pillow, every fiber of me screaming for sleep.

"What kind of functions?" I hear him say.

"Homecomings. A few Sweet Sixteens. Semi-Formals. Formals. I'm very versatile."

Charlie slowly sits on the bed beside my dead form.

"They pay you?" he asks shakily. It's a lot to take in.

"Their parents. Look, I'm beat, so could you please spare me the paternal lecture? You're hardly qualified."

Usually that would be enough to get him to back off, but tonight, after what I've just disclosed, my missiles just deflect harmlessly off his force fields.

"You didn't sleep with them? I mean, you used protection . . ." He trails off, aghast.

Even in my deep torpor, this gets to me. Does he really know me so little? Unlike him, I do have some standards, low as they may be. Fueled by outrage, I scramble past him to the door, motioning him out.

"If you don't mind, I'd appreciate a little privacy," I say hotly.

He doesn't move but just keeps sitting there.

"Brooks, it may not seem like it, but I'm trying my best to understand . . ."

"Well, it's like this, Charlie. Short of robbing a bank or hitting the lottery, it seemed like my best chance at getting the money for Columbia."

Charlie looks up as if seeing me for the very first time.

"Good God, Brooks, you really want it that bad?"

I don't know. I don't know anything anymore. All I know is that I want him to get the hell out of my room, to just stop it already, but he won't.

"It really doesn't matter where you go to school, Brooks. Nobody's out there keeping score. I mean, I went to Harvard. Look what happened to me."

There he goes again. My whole life he's been using himself as a shining example of what not to do and be, and I'm so sick of it. I've had it with his great failed promise, which hangs like a poisonous black mist everywhere.

"What did happen, Charlie?" I blurt. "You had everything. How'd you fuck it up so completely?"

It's the question I've been waiting to ask my whole life. The same question he's spent my whole life avoiding answering. We're both equally stunned that I've actually asked it.

Charlie gets up and leaves. I slam the door after him and lock it, too beat to feel rotten about what I just said, though I know I should.

What a night.

TAKING STOCK

So now you know why a mere week after the Great Blood-bath, I'm in Hackensack on a Saturday night in May with Gabby Dombrowski. Regrouping in the back of a stretch limo at the tail end of what's proven to be a very long, very arduous evening, I again reflect on my litany of misdeeds. And what it comes down to is this. I'm a jerk, basically. What they call a heel, a cad, a total scoundrel. I should be tarred and feathered, run out of town on a rail. And yet there must be some tiny morsel of good in me. Because even in my reduced circumstances, I can't bring myself to stand up somebody who's been stood up for Prom, which Mrs. Dombrowski has confided in me Gabby Dombrowski has been. Twice, in fact. I hope the collective Dombrowskis have a pleasant memory to savor, because I have one more I want to forget. Every nerve ending, joint, and muscle in my already tender carcass is aching after hours of Gabby's over-strenuous exertions.

I mean, the girl's a regular Energizer Bunny. She just goes and goes.

"PARTY!" Gabby shouts out her open window to nobody. "ROCK ON!!"

She whacks me enthusiastically, so hard my teeth jar. How did it all come to this? Where did I go wrong? Or rather, where didn't I? I can't stop thinking about all the bad choices I've made. There are so, so many. The people I've hurt. A lot of them too. But mostly I can't stop thinking about poor little me, alone and friendless in a cold, cruel universe.

"Brooksie, I've got this teammate, Tina, in Teaneck," Gabby prattles. "Heckuva power forward. Her Prom's next week . . ."

I manage to focus through the haze of self-inflicted misery.

"Thanks, Gabby, but after tonight, I'm hanging up the tux for good. You're my final gig."

Gabby's face drops, making me realize how it could sound. "Was I that bad?" she asks timidly, the usual complexes returning.

"No, you've been terrific," I assure her. "Uh, very invigorating . . ."

She smiles, relieved.

"It's me," I say. "I just can't anymore."

— — —

Four days and counting 'til Graduation, and the entire Pritchard senior class has pretty much checked out. By Friday, I'm practically the only person who makes an appearance in homeroom. Seems while I've been off doing the Greater Metropolitan Scene, my own scene's moved on without me. As a result of my prolonged absence, I've turned into a marginal presence, the odd man out, no longer involved, invited, or even registering on the social radar. So, while I'm single-handedly forcing disgruntled teachers to come up with lesson plans, everyone but me's out partying at the beach, getting stupid at Six Flags, or, if of the female persuasion, prepping for Prom.

Prom. If I never hear that word again, it'll be too soon. Just the thought of another night of confining cummerbunds, accessorized females, gratified parents, oily maître d's, fatty food, crushed toes, and mindless excess makes me want to join a monastery and take a vow of eternal silence. I am so Prommed out. Thankfully, there'll be no more Proms after high school. This is it. My last one. And, as the wise man once said, "Include me out."

Cruising in the now-bumperless Beast down Main Street, I can't help noticing the line of customers snaking out the doors to The Gun. Under The Murf's inspired weekend supervision, what was a misconceived, dying enterprise has become the happening spot with regular events like Karaoke, Open Mic, All-You-Can-Eat Spaghetti nights, even Bingo. Next thing you know, they'll be taking reservations. But for me, for months now, The

Gun's been forbidden territory, exiled as I am from the bestest-pal-any-guy-could-ask-for's good opinion. But not anymore, I impulsively decide, nosing into a space across the street.

It takes a full ten minutes to reach the front of the line. Like I said, the joint's unrecognizable since I slaved here. Mood lighting, checkered tablecloths, laminated menus. The Murf, all decked out executorial-like in a natty pin-striped suit and vintage fedora, is performing register duty. He ignores me when my turn comes up.

"May I take your order?" he politely asks the woman in line right after me.

"Hey, what about me?" I squawk in protest.

The Murf taps a printed sign on the wall.

"Sorry, but Management reserves the right to refuse service to anyone."

"On what grounds?" I challenge, indignant.

"On the grounds that you're a total dirtbag!" He registers my still slightly puffy jaw. "And who rearranged your face?"

"Yeah, well, you should see the other guy."

"Yeah, well, I'd still like to shake his hand," The Murf declares. Snapping two fingers to a minion to take over, he rolls a mop and bucket on wheels right at me from around the front counter so quick I have to hop out of the way.

"Remember that superhot chick at the Pixies concert?" I volunteer in his wake.

"Faintly," he says bitingly. "We were never actually introduced."

I follow him into the men's room. And I must confess, I'm way impressed. They say the true test of a fine culinary establishment's not its chicken stock but its men's room. And take it from *moi*, I've been in some pretty iffy johns in some pretty snooty restaurants. You'd be surprised how even the ritziest skimp on the paper towels, one of my pet five-star-dining peeves. I ask you, is there anything worse than wet, soapy hands and nowhere to dry them? But here the towels are plentiful and abundant. And the floors—I could rhapsodize about the floors. They're shiny, virtually spotless, a far cry from the putrid swamp we used to enter at our own risk.

"Drizzle," states The Murf, steering the bucket into a stall. "I hate drizzle."

Standing clear as he mops around the toilet basin, I summon the fortitude to go on. Because what I have to say is going to be painful to all parties.

"The real reason I ditched you at the concert was because I didn't want that superhot chick to know we were friends . . ."

"Oh, that makes me feel much better!" I hear him say sarcastically.

"I was afraid if she met you she'd find out I'm from Jersey." I look down at my feet. My palms are sweaty. This part is the hardest of all. "I was ashamed."

A long, ominous pause. Then The Murf's head pops from the stall, staring at me.

"Ashamed of Jersey?" he asks, the concept inconceivable to him.

I can't look him in the eye. I feel like the spineless worm I am. Because we both know it's not just my home state I've been ashamed of, but him.

"I don't know who I am anymore, Murf." Truer words I have never spoken. Not only who I am, but what I am, what I'm about. I don't know anymore, if I ever did. "It's like I'm a stand-in in my own life."

"That's fucking beautiful, Brooks." To my surprise, The Murf laughs, but harshly, in a way I've never heard him laugh before.

"You think so?" I say, hopefully.

"But you're still a total dirtbag!"

Back in the day, The Murf calling me a dirtbag would have been funny, a witty riposte of sorts, and I would have responded in kind. But that day has come and gone, because The Murf's totally and completely serious. His normally good-natured face is tight and rigid, his jaw set, his expression blank. Like we don't know each other. Like all the history we have together never happened. Like we're strangers, even.

"You don't know the half of it," I mumble feebly.

The Murf marches to the door and swings it open for me to leave. As far as he's concerned, even the crapper's too good for me.

"I may just be the weekend manager of a piddly-ass sub shop, Rattigan," he says with great dignity. "But I wouldn't take your job for all the money in the world."

I don't know what I was expecting, but it wasn't this. I flee, walking faster and faster, until I'm running from The Gun, from The Murf, from yet one more humiliation, but mostly from the awful reality of me. I'm watching a movie of myself scuttling down the sidewalk for cover. I'm like a cockroach.

"GET YOUR SHIT TOGETHER!" The Murf shouts out the entrance after me.

– – –

Get my shit together. If only I could. My shit's so un-together that I don't even know what my shit is anymore. The days pass slowly, the last of high school existence. Slumped in bed, I dejectedly lob another dart at the sheet of paper pinned across the bulletin board mounted on the wall, my mind laboring to excuse the inexcusable. Again I ask you, what was my real transgression? The bottom line: I wanted More. Is that really so terrible? To not just accept the hand that's been dealt, to not just settle for Less? Is it a sin to desire a Shelby Pace, to aspire to a Columbia? So I cut a few corners along the way. Okay, a giant steaming heap of them. But everybody does. Pushing, striving, taking no prisoners. Isn't that what I'm supposed to do? That's the American Way, right?

"Hey, isn't your Prom tonight?"

Charlie stands tall in the doorway. He looks different, more defined-like. Then I realize that he's clean-shaven, his hair neat and cut short, his jeans and collared shirt new, still creased from the package. Most amazing are his eyes. They aren't bloodshot or droopy. Even so, I'm too immersed in the depths of despair to comment on the remarkable transformation.

"I'm not going," I grunt, flinging another dart. The target's my official acceptance letter from Columbia, now riddled with pin holes.

"How come?"

"Couldn't find a date. Poetic justice, don't you think?"

I am being for real. Earlier, I accidentally-on-purpose neglected to mention that, in a brief moment of weakness, I did ask Gina Agostini, but she was already going with—get this—Burdette. The thought of them hooking up—well, it makes my stomach turn. Actually, the thought of Burdette coupling with any living, breathing creature makes my stomach turn. Rising, I yank the darts from the corkboard to begin the masochistic ritual over again.

"Charlie, I'm fine about going to Rutgers," I announce, remarkably calm, almost magically drained of bitterness and anger. Now that it's finally over, I'm strangely resigned to my life's sentence. "It's a great school. I'm lucky I got in."

"That's all true, Brooks, but you're not going to Rutgers."

I halt in mid–dart throw. Wait a minute, this isn't in the script.

"What are you talking about?" I say.

And Charlie, he grins this lopsided grin, which I distantly recognize from another time.

"Sorry, kiddo, but it's too late," he says, offhandedly. "I've already put down your deposit at Columbia and if you think I'm giving that up, you're crazy."

It doesn't register. Because it doesn't add up. The numbers are too daunting.

"But the tuition," I stammer. "We can't afford—"

"I sold the comic book collection."

"You sold your collection?" I can barely get out the words.

His collection? His whole life, his whole reason for being is that collection. For Charlie, it's the ultimate sacrifice, one I'd never ask of him. As incredible, selfless gestures go, it just doesn't get any bigger. And I'm moved to a core I never knew I had.

"Don't get too excited," he cautions, coming into my room. "It's only enough for three semesters. But I figure we'll take it as it goes . . ."

My universe is spinning off its axis, and I have to sit back down.

"Dad . . . ," I rasp.

It's the first time since I can remember that I've called him that. And it feels good to say it. In fact, it feels terrific. It feels right.

He reaches out, squeezes me by the shoulder. His eyes glisten brightly.

"I know I'm not much, Brooks, but damn it, I can do this!"

I stare back at him, dizzy with possibility, awash in expectation.

I will go to Columbia. I mean, let's skip the obligatory bull, shall we? We all know it's worth the extra money and it does make a difference, a super-huge one. But however it goes, it'll all work out. And if it doesn't, that's fine too. Because for the first time there are two of us battling the Forces of Darkness. At last I belong to something bigger than me, part of something solid to lean on and to be leaned on. I'm half of a family. At a loss for words, I suddenly embrace my father, who fiercely returns my grip.

"I just didn't have it, Brooks," he says in hoarse voice. "Only had the one book in me. That's the God's truth of it. But you should have your chance, like I did. Just make sure you go to college for the right reasons. For the best education in becoming a decent human being. Because, in the end, that's all that really matters."

I nod, all choked up. I will take his counsel to heart. And I will read his book. I will try to understand.

As we both blink back tears, wouldn't you know it, the doorbell buzzes.

"Hmm, wonder who that can be?" Dad asks a bit rhetorically, giving me the distinct impression he's in the know. "Better go answer it."

The bell sounds again. I look at him, bewildered. It's almost seven thirty, well past the time for FedEx or UPS, not that they ever visit our door. Probably some idealistic nut job begging for a handout. Well, sorry, Mack, not at this garden apartment.

"Would you answer it?" Dad says, giving me a little push.

Stumbling, reeling from my suddenly unlimited prospects, I unbolt the succession of locks. The bell buzzes once more.

"Cool your jets, I'm coming!" I holler, opening the door.

And there, hand on her hip, posed demurely on the landing, is none other than Celia Lieberman. Hair styled and piled high, in high heels and a slinky cocktail dress that's snug in all the right places. A total babe.

"Word is on the street, you're in need of a stand-in for Prom."

She smiles shyly, uncertain.

"Hi, Mr. Rattigan," she waves demurely behind me.

"Hi, Celia," Dad beams, knowing who she is without being introduced, an obvious co-conspirator in on her secret plot, the dog.

I'm beyond stunned. By the way Celia Lieberman looks but mostly by the fact she's here in Pritchard. I can't believe it. I can't believe Celia Lieberman has ventured from her cloistered fantasyland to where the other 99 percent–plus of us wage to just barely make ends.

And she's here for me. It's mind-blowing.

"Franklin . . . ," I stutter like an imbecile.

"For somebody who's supposed to be a genius, Franklin's kind of an idiot," Celia Lieberman shrugs. "I mean, I think I look tons better than before. And the Backstreet Boys, come on."

"For sure," I agree. "Not that appearances matter . . ."

But they do. And I can't emphasize enough how hot Celia Lieberman is looking.

"Well, get changed. Can't go to Prom like that."

Hot diggity damn. I'm going to Prom! Okay, twist my arm, I admit it—I've wanted to go all along. I mean, it's the last blowout, the end of one road, the start of another. And this one's Mine. The occasion demands to be commemorated. Grinning, I head to my room when I see a sight over Celia Lieberman's bare shoulder that you don't see every day, at least not in Pritchard.

On a street lined with rusted clunkers and unwashed compacts, an elegant black Lincoln Town Car eases up along the curb behind Celia Lieberman's parked Prius. She turns and sees it too. We're both mystified. A chauffeur in a brimmed hat and calf leather gloves hustles out and ceremoniously swings open the gleaming back door.

A shapely tanned leg in a sexy stiletto heel steps out. Attached to an impossibly perfect body and an even more impossibly perfect face. Shelby, in a sheer, racy designer gown. The vision of nubile loveliness. More breathtaking than ever.

"Shelby?" I whisper. What in the world is she doing here? I look at Dad, who shrugs, this time as mystified as me. Spying me, Shelby waves up, supremely comfortable in her flawless skin. I watch, transfixed, paralyzed. I look at Celia Lieberman, then back at Shelby, then back at Celia Lieberman again. I don't know what to do. I'm telling you, I can't take any more of these sudden reversals of fortune.

I don't move. I can't. The three of us just stand there.

"Brooks!" Shelby calls, standing her exquisite ground at the curb. She's gone as far as she's willing to go. She's not coming up and won't leave until I do something.

"Go ahead," Celia Lieberman says softly. "It's your night."

"I'll be right back," I promise. Then I'm off like a shot. Drums are pounding, heavy metal guitars are thrashing. I windmill around landings, leap down stairwells in a single bound.

Suddenly, there she is right ahead of me. Her long silky tresses and sparkly wisp of a gown flutter in the gentle night breeze. The gray drabness of Pritchard melts around her, her golden aura of privilege prevailing wherever she goes. Before I can get out a syllable, she pounces like a tigress and kisses me. I struggle to resist. Her hips grind against mine. I can feel there's not much, if anything, under there, which isn't helping matters. Finally, we both come up for air.

"Shelby, what are you doing here?" I wheeze, almost doubling over. "How did you know . . . ?"

"Cassie overheard Celia tell that Franklin dip they were history because she was going to Prom with you," Shelby explains, reapplying gloss. "Then we Googled your school, saw when Prom was, and did a search for your address. It was easy."

Shelby's here because she knows Celia Lieberman is here. Would Shelby be here if Celia Lieberman wasn't here? Should I care? Because Shelby's impossibly here, mine for the asking. And this time without false pretenses.

"You really live here?" Shelby surveys my graffiti-marred complex with tangible repugnance. "Do you own or do you rent?"

I look at her. To own or not to own? That is the age-old question. Whether it's nobler to be a lofty landlord or suffer the slings and arrows of lowly tenancy. I ask you, seriously, who gives a flying crap? It doesn't matter, especially in Pritchard because, let's face it, the whole town's a shithole. But somehow it will always matter for Shelby. There will always be divisions, subtle gradations of status, the insatiable need to feel superior. And this, I abruptly realize, is her imperfection. And as imperfections go, it's a whopper. I mean, it must be exhausting to always have to be devising new and better ways to look down on other people.

Shelby leans toward me, parts her shimmering lips, and shuts those emerald eyes for another go-round. Mine are wide open, for the very first time.

Beauty. Grace. Sophistication. Shelby possesses all these qualities and many more. But she's no Celia Lieberman. It would never occur to Celia Lieberman to ask the question. Celia Lieberman has too much class—real class, the kind that can't be bought or sold. Celia Lieberman's the Genuine Article. And no slouch in the looks, sophistication, and smarts departments either, although I'd never put the word "grace" and Celia Lieberman together in the same sentence. Celia Lieberman's a total klutz, but hey, that's part of her charm. And that's when I realize something truly earth-shattering.

I've fallen for Celia Lieberman.

– – –

I've fallen for Celia Lieberman? How can this be? I've fallen for Celia Lieberman. Hard. Head-over-heels hard. Celia Lieberman! How could I have fallen for Celia Lieberman?

Yet I have.

Holy shit, I think, as I sprint back the way I just sprinted, I'm looney tunes for Celia Lieberman! I'm deep in the throes, besotted, down-for-the-count, hung up on Celia Lieberman! Holy shit, my mind races as my body struggles to keep up, what if I'm too late? My heart's jackhammering to break out of my rib cage as I catapult five stairs at a clip. Holy shit, what if Celia Lieberman's gone?

Careening around the second landing, I almost run right past her. She's sitting on the bottom step, her face cradled against her knees. Thank God! Bent over, gasping, I attempt to play it casual-like.

"Ready to go?" I ask nonchalantly.

Celia Lieberman looks up at me. Her makeup's all runny, her hair's gone frizzy. She's crying. I want to lick away the tears, drop by adorable drop.

"I said I'd be back," I gently remind her.

"But Shelby?" she asks, uncomprehending.

"I told her I couldn't go to Prom with her because I was madly, hopelessly in love with Celia Lieberman," I report. And that, word for word, is what I did tell Shelby. I guess maybe she was right about me and Celia Lieberman all along.

Celia Lieberman rises, furiously brushing the wetness from her cheeks. I'm such a stupid dick. I've hurt her. Badly. Really badly. Most likely too badly. But all that counts for now is that she's here.

"You ignore me, take me for granted, treat me like second best . . . ," she blubbers, the droplets, now hot, angry ones, returning.

"Yes."

And then I'm tearing up and blubbering too. Afraid I've blown it. Terrified I've lost her. I don't know what I'll do if I've lost her. We stand in the grungy stairwell so close together yet so far apart. We stand there, streaming tears, two of a kind, a pair of complete and total emotional wrecks.

"And now you expect me to just forget it?" she says in a choked voice. "To just forgive you?"

"If you could, I'd greatly appreciate it," I whisper. "Yes, please."

And man, somewhere along the line I must've done something right despite myself, because miraculously, she's in my arms. We kiss our first of—I fervently hope—many kisses. Because we're talking fireworks, my friends, sweet symphonic music. Major, major, major wood.

– – –

The ballroom at the Radisson's packed tight with sweating adolescence. We move hypnotically, one great churning mass, to Nas throwing beats on the fuzzy sound system. It's dark, a little rank even. No fancy light shows here, no glitz or glamour. And no prescribed dance steps. Here, it's strictly freestyle. My peeps. We take our lumps, we pay our dues.

Tomorrow we go our separate ways to wherever Fate takes us. Well, fuck Tomorrow. It's Prom. Tonight, all that matters is Today.

"WHOSE WORLD IS THIS?" Nas riffs. *"WHOSE WORLD IS THIS?"*

"IT'S MINE! IT'S MINE! IT'S MINE!!" we all thunder in refrain.

The name's Rattigan. Brooks Rattigan. 3.83 Overall GPA. 4.14 Weighted. 720 Verbal. 760 Math. 680 Writing—but everyone knows that section's bullshit. National Merit Letter of Commendation Winner. Tri-State Liar. All-Around Jerk. I've been them all in my time. From here on in, I'll settle for just being me. It's a tough enough gig as it is.

In the crush, a hand gives me a friendly shove. The Murf, resplendent in a fluorescent purple tux, grins wide, flashing an emphatic thumbs-up of approval at my date. Then I catch a load—and I mean load—of his. Julie Hickey. Spilling out, hanging all over him. The Murf shoots me a wink. Mission accomplished.

I laugh. The Murf, my main man. The mother did it. Celia looks at me questioningly, as she always has and always will. Smiling, I draw her near.

Success. Noun. Being cool with who you are.

ACKNOWLEDGMENTS

First and foremost, I'd like to thank my amazing, steadfast manager, John Tomko, who's stuck with me through thin and thinner, even when he probably shouldn't have. Thanks for having the patience and keeping the faith, man.

To my self-appointed guru, Julianna Baggott, whose beauty, work ethic, and talent are surpassed only by her generosity of spirit. It's been my great pleasure and distinct privilege to be gently guided by her.

Old pals Bob Rodat, George Rush and John Spiegel. Thanks for the read, wise counsel and/or moral support, guys. New pals John Katzenbach and David Wolpe, likewise.

To Heather Whitaker, who showed me the errors of my characters' ways.

Alix Reid, editor extraordinaire, of course, for trusting her instincts and having the courage of her convictions and not just settling for the tried and untrue. I won't mention her boundless good cheer and infuriatingly well-taken notes.

Beth Davey, my agent, imperturbable and *indefatigable*—adjective, tireless, tenacious. Thanks for fighting my battles for my own good.

Finally, mountain ranges of appreciation and love always to Jennifer, for reading, re-reading, and re-re-reading the never-ending drafts, listening to all the rants, and just plain putting up with me.

A working screenwriter for TV and movies for over 30 years, Steve Bloom attended Brown University and the graduate film production program at University of Southern California School of Cinematic Arts. Among his produced credits are the films "The Sure Thing," "James and the Giant Peach" and "Tall Tale." *The Stand-In* is his first novel. The idea came to him when a friend asked if Bloom's daughter might know someone who could escort his daughter to a dance when her date suddenly canceled. Steve lives in western Massachusetts with his wife, Jennifer, and their French bulldog, Ricky.